THE LIGHTHOUSE KEEPERS

In *The Lighthouse Trilogy*:

The Lighthouse Land

The Lighthouse War

The Lighthouse Keepers

THE LIGHTHOUSE KEEPERS

THE LIGHTHOUSE TRILOGY
◆ BOOK III ◆

ADRIAN McKINTY

AMULET BOOKS

New York

Library of Congress Cataloging-in-Publication Data

McKinty, Adrian.
The lighthouse keepers / by Adrian McKinty.
p. cm. — (Lighthouse trilogy ; bk. 3)

Summary: After teenage friends Jamie and Ramsay travel back to Altair to save the last citizens of that dying planet, Jamie learns about the origins of the wormhole-creating Salmon of Knowledge and is faced with a terrible choice.

ISBN 978-0-8109-7070-0 (Harry N. Abrams : alk. paper)
[1. Space and time—Fiction. 2. Magic—Fiction. 3. Ireland—Fiction. 4. Science fiction.] I. Title.
PZ7.M4786915Lh 2008
[Fic]—dc22

Printed and bound in U.S.A.
10 9 8 7 6 5 4 3 2 1

Amulet Books are available at special discounts when purchased in quantity for premiums and promotions as well as fundraising or educational use. Special editions can also be created to specification. For details, contact specialmarkets@hnabooks.com or the address below.

HNA ▪▪▪▪▪
harry n. abrams, inc.
a subsidiary of La Martinière Groupe

115 West 18th Street
New York, NY 10011
www.hnabooks.com

For Diane, Lorna, Roderick, and Gareth. And for Leah.

CONTENTS

THUS THE GREAT CIVILIZER SENDS OUT ITS EMISSARIES, SOONER OR LATER, TO EVERY SANDY CAPE AND LIGHT-HOUSE OF THE NEW WORLD . . .
—Henry David Thoreau, *Cape Cod* (1865)

Chapter I
THE SEARCHERS

A MAN ON A HORSE in the Sangre de Cristo Mountains north of Taos, New Mexico. Stars vanishing from the western sky. A hesitant golden light creeping from the Texas hills.

The land was parched, and the scent of piñon and jasmine percolated in the high, dry air. The man had come all the way from the valley floor, and in the space of an hour the landscape had changed from desert to burned brush to semi-alpine forest.

He was tracking something. *Something.* The horse knew what it was and it was nervous. The man thought he knew what it was and that was why he was carrying a rifle.

In the breaks between the trees he could see nearly all the way to Arizona and there was still a dusting of snow on Mount Wheeler.

The horse snorted. The man tensed.

He was no cowboy and he'd be the first to admit that he had no right to be out here on a strange horse at his age.

But what other choice was there?

None, he said to himself.

He was on his own. When he moved here it was with the idea that it would be an "assisted living" ranch. Apart from his octogenarian sister in Georgia, he had no family; the plan was that Alejandro and his two boys would stay on the property all year round and take care of the fundamentals. All *he* had to do was enjoy the countryside and occasionally go for a ride or a hike in the surrounding woods and hills.

It would be perfect. He could spend his golden years away from the city in the peace and quiet of the mountains and maybe write those memoirs he'd been contemplating.

The horse paused, and he let the dust settle on the path.

The sun appeared over a hill. It was now the *hora en limpio*. The golden hour when everything became imbued with a sharpness and loveliness that took the breath away. He swallowed water from his canteen. Yes, he was alone. The boy who came to exercise the dogs was off today, and since Thursday Alejandro had been down in Juárez with his kids, visiting his ailing mother.

He wondered if the mountain lion had sensed that. Had it been aware that the ranch was more vulnerable than usual? He shook his head. Nah, the timing was just bad luck. He jangled the stirrups and his mount moved forward. He'd been on a horse about half a dozen times since he'd moved out here, but before that his previous equine experience had been finding quality oats for George Patton's mare when he'd been a member of the general's Third Army, liberating Europe in 1944 and 1945.

Thaddeus smiled to himself. That was a long time ago.

A long time, and when his next birthday came around he was going to be eighty-five years old.

The tracks bent around a cholla cactus. He yawned and wondered why he hadn't taken a moment to make some coffee. It would be nice about now.

The day was coming to life. Hummingbirds were hovering over bees' hives, and way above him huge voleries of honking geese were flying north from their winter watering grounds in the Sea of Cortez.

The horse again seemed skittish. It had the beginnings of a cold muck sweat cooling on its neck. Alejandro would no doubt have said something reassuring in Spanish.

He thought for a moment.

"*Buenos días* . . . um . . . *por favor*," he attempted in a soothing whisper.

The horse, though, was not convinced. Thaddeus didn't even know its name. The Big Black Scary One was what he generally called it. He nudged it but it wouldn't move. It was his fault, not the horse's.

"Old fool. What in the name of all that's holy are you, a city boy, doing in New Mexico?" he murmured rhetorically.

But he knew the answer.

As in the rest of Manhattan, real estate prices in Harlem had gone through the roof, and someone had offered him a million dollars for his large pre-war duplex near City College. He had refused. He had refused when they upped the offer to a million and a quarter. And still said no when it had been raised to a million and a half. Finally, though, when they said, "Mr. Harper, we are prepared to offer you two million dollars for your apartment and your parking space," Thaddeus gave in.

Everyone, he reflected ruefully, had their price.

With the money, he reckoned, he could buy a little place in the country. Actually, with the money he could buy a twenty-two-acre ranch in the Sangre de Cristos and pay a man to live there and look after the horses.

And yes. Horses. He'd always wanted to have horses. In his grandfather's time a black man would have been lynched for riding a horse in Georgia. But when he'd told people his plans they had been skeptical.

"Out there in the West they have snakes and black widow spiders and wolves and stuff like that," one friend had protested. "You'll get snake-bit, Thaddeus, and at your age, it'll kill ya."

He'd laughed at that. *Well, the joke's on me now,* he thought. *Here I am tracking some wild animal from the mountains. Nobody with me, anything could happen.*

But he had to do it. Two nights ago something had gotten into the corral and attacked one of the ponies. At first he'd thought it was a coyote, but when he looked closer, the prints were those of a cat. A mountain lion. He'd seen a few of them before up on a redoubt. He'd left them alone, and until now they had kept their distance from him. But this one had come right up to the house. He hadn't seen it but he'd let off fireworks, shot his gun in the air. And it had come again last night. Around three in the morning he'd heard a commotion in the stable. By the time he'd gotten out there, it was gone, but one of the horses must have kicked it because when he hit the floodlights, there was a bloody trail that led off into the wilderness that you didn't exactly need to be Kit Carson to follow.

A mountain lion attacking horses was rare enough, but this one had to be desperate to come so close to man's territory. It was rabid maybe, or injured somehow. In either case, now he was ready with his rifle to send it to a better place.

The air grew thinner as the way turned up into the

southern extension of the Sangre de Cristo Mountains. There were few insects. A hawk in the air. The sky free of clouds and vapor trails. Heat-caked blue. He took another swig of water.

The horse lost its footing on a narrow part of the path, but still the tracks continued to climb, the back paw prints barely distinguishable but the dried line of blood from a wound on the creature as good as a homing beacon. Bound to be after six. He looked at his wrist but the watch was back on the nightstand. He stared at the sky and the rising sun. Yeah, it could be close to seven. Maybe he should give up this hunt and head back. He still had to pack his suitcases for the trip to Ireland the next day. And he would need all his strength to get through the twelve-hour flight from San Francisco, never mind the prospect of watching Jamie and the mysterious adoptee, Wishaway, for an entire week.

He took off his Yankees cap and wiped the sweat from his brow. He had a think about it. "I'll track for five more minutes and then we'll go back," he explained to the horse. Alejandro claimed that horses could understand about two-thirds of what you told them, and the Big Black Scary One shook its bridle as if in agreement.

The cougar couldn't be that far ahead now anyway. It had lost a lot of blood and as the day came it would want to find somewhere to hole up. He mopped his forehead with a shirt sleeve. Suddenly the horse began to shiver, whinny, and back-step, and Thaddeus had to pull hard on the reins to calm it down. Perhaps they were getting close.

The birds stopped chirping.

The hairs stood up on the back of Thaddeus's neck.

He unhooked the rifle from his shoulder. He held the reins tight in his left hand and kept the rifle in his right. Alejandro's gun was an old Remington bolt action, so he'd need both hands free to shoot it, but that was OK: He could drop the reins fast, keep the horse steady with his feet and knees, and shoot.

"Easy now, girl, I think we're close," he whispered.

He passed a rock that had an ancient handprint on it, then a dead tree and more rocks. The horse edged gingerly around a bend in the path. The tracks went into a small brambly wood, and the Big Black Scary One was very reluctant to go farther. He had to reason with it and encourage it with more words of comfort. He had pretty much exhausted his Spanish, so he dragged up a line from grammar school: "*Lente currite noctis equi.* You got that? Easy now, easy. Steady, easy now. Five more minutes and we go back."

He nudged it gently with his boot.

"That's a girl. OK, that's it."

They turned a blind corner and suddenly they were at the rock with the handprint again.

The cat had circled around on him.

Oh no.

A growl. A blur of movement. The cat jumped. The horse reared, threw him. He landed heavily in the dirt, sending the rifle sailing through the air. He looked up to see the horse scrambling away through the thorn trees. His shoulder had taken a nasty knock. Dislocated. Maybe a rib broke too.

He got to his knees, slowly.

And then he saw it.

The cat.

Except that he was completely wrong. A competent tracker would have spotted it immediately. This was no mountain lion, no hundred-pound glorified kitty cat. This was a three-hundred-pound, top-of-the-food-chain, man-killing carnivore. Long and sleek with black and yellow markings, a huge head, a large and powerful jaw. A jaguar. Twice the size of any cougar. Three times as powerful, ten times as deadly.

Massive, poised, angry—its furious eyes cold and fixed upon him.

If he'd been a scientist, perhaps he would have been excited. A jaguar in these parts, probably up from Mexico, was an extremely rare phenomenon, especially with the border patrol putting up new fences all over the desert. Thaddeus was not excited. Terrified, yes. Excited, no.

A jaguar could bring down a four-hundred-pound stag or tapir. A human was easy meat. Thaddeus knew it could kill him just by jumping him. It wouldn't need its razor-sharp claws. The blow alone would snap his old man's spine.

But, more likely it would stalk him, pounce, rake him until he lost consciousness from blood loss, and then apply a suffocating choke-bite to his throat.

He looked for the rifle and spotted it on the other side of the clearing, between him and it. The jaguar examined him for what seemed like a long time but was probably a few seconds.

It watched him and did nothing. *Perhaps it will wait me out all day and attack at dusk,* he thought. The beast yawned, lay down, and began to lick its wounded paw. He wondered if this might be a sign that it wanted to let him go. He got to his feet and began slowly backing away into the brush. The jaguar responded instantly, letting out a small growl, standing, arching its back.

"Oh God," he whispered.

He got down into a nonthreatening crouch, and man and cat went back to looking at each other. A vulture landed on a nearby tree limb and examined the little diorama unfolding on the mountaintop. At a zoo you forgot about the otherness of a wild creature. Not here. Thaddeus suddenly remembered reading something about staring at a grizzly. Either you're supposed to make eye contact or you're not supposed to—he couldn't remember which.

The jaguar's growl subsided to a throaty rasp. And then it got up and came closer.

Well, this is it, Thaddeus said to himself. *My only chance is to somehow get in a lucky punch in the eye, and even then . . .*

The big predator angled its way closer until it was only a few feet away, moving with grace and economy. He could see the wound on its back leg, the muscles shimmering beneath its skin. He could practically feel its breath.

The vulture was joined by another. His heart was pounding. Now the inner voice was saying, *Are you ready? Are you ready for death?* And the weird thing was, he was not ready. He had been in situations where whether he lived or died seemed a matter of little concern. Existence teetering on a knife's edge. But now he didn't want to die. He had things to do. *I want to live,* he thought. He looked for a weapon.

A stick, a stone, anything. But there was nothing. Sand and gravel. He grabbed a handful. *I'll throw it in its eyes before it leaps.* The cat padded closer. Its jaw open.

The battered teeth. The black, unfathomable eyes. Its mouth already reeking of blood. It leaned on its hind legs, coiled for a jump.

Breeep, breep, breeep.

The jaguar froze.

Breeep, breep, breeep.

A sharp, ungodly sound.

Thaddeus's cell phone.

Breeep, breep, breeep.

After nine harsh rings, the phone started playing "So What" from *Kind of Blue* by Miles Davis. The jaguar was completely spooked.

Miles Davis continued to toot, the melody becoming more discordant and interesting by the moment.

The jaguar hissed at the old man and then, discombobulated and terrified, it turned sharply and ran, its tail disappearing into the brush so quickly and quietly that in a moment it was almost as if it had never been there at all.

Thaddeus struggled to his feet, hunted for the rifle, found it, grabbed it, cocked it, and then when he knew he was safe, he hit Talk on the cell phone.

"Hello?"

"Thaddeus? Hi, it's Jamie."

Thaddeus caught his breath.

"Hello? Thaddeus?" Jamie said.

"Yeah."

"What are you doing? Where are you?"

"Um, I don't really know," Thaddeus said.

"What do you mean you don't know? What are you doing? You're at your new house, right? Sheesh, you can barely talk. You weren't out for a run at your age?"

"I went after a cat."

"A cat? Are you climbing a tree? Thaddeus, wait till I tell my mom."

Thaddeus breathed deeply for a few more moments.

"Is there something wrong?" Jamie asked.

"Nothing's wrong. Everything's fine."

"Are you sure? You're not having a heart attack?"

"Of course not," Thaddeus said, irritated. "And I'll mind you not to be impertinent, boy."

"Sorry, Thaddeus. You don't sound so good, though," Jamie said.

"I'm OK. I got thrown off my horse."

"Are you kidding? Are you all right?" Jamie's voice was flooded with concern.

"I'm OK. Nothing's broken."

"Are you far from the house?"

"I'm OK. I'll call the Hendersons in the subdivision next to the ranch," Thaddeus said. Then, thinking aloud, "One of them has a quad bike."

He shook the dust off himself.

"Are you sure you're all right?" Jamie asked again.

"I'm fine. I saw a jaguar."

Jamie sighed. "Did you have a bad dream or something? Did you hit your head?"

"No," Thaddeus said firmly.

"There are no jaguars in the United States, Thaddeus."

"Well, I saw one. I tracked it."

"Are you in the mountains? How will they find you? Are you sure you're OK?"

"What did you want?" Thaddeus asked, starting to get annoyed.

"I just wanted to make sure you got your passport," Jamie said. "I've missed you. I'm looking forward to seeing you."

I've missed you too, Thaddeus thought.

"Yup, passport came through last week," he said.

He began walking back down the trail. It was about five miles to the house. It would be slow going, even though he now realized nothing was actually broken.

"I better head, Jamie," he said.

"You'll be OK?"

"I'll be fine. I'll call the Hendersons."

"But how are they going to find you?"

"I don't know. I'll climb a tree. Wave to them."

"Don't climb a tree, Thaddeus, for goodness' sake. Your phone has a GPS feature, just dial 911."

Thaddeus sighed. Maybe the boy was right.

"OK," he said heavily.

"OK, Thaddeus, I'll see you the day after tomorrow. Take care of yourself. Remember, we'll meet you at Dublin Airport. Don't leave the airport, we'll meet you at the baggage claim."

"Yes, yes, I know. I ain't hog stupid just yet."

"OK. Bye, Thaddeus."

As irritating as Jamie could be sometimes, he couldn't let the boy hang up just yet.

"Wait. One more thing," Thaddeus said.

"What?"

"Um, uh . . ."

"What?"

"Um, thank you, Jamie," Thaddeus said quietly.

"Thanks for what?"

Thanks for not letting me have the horrific death of my homo sapiens ancestors on the African savannah.

"Oh, um, just for you being you," he said cheerily. He could almost feel Jamie smiling.

"OK, man. Bye, Thaddeus," Jamie said, and hung up.

Thaddeus began dialing the Hendersons.

"Well, world, you haven't killed me yet. I'll live to fight another day. Good news for me. Good news for thee," he muttered with a chuckle, and a truer thing was never said that day in the whole of New Mexico.

Ramsay looked with disdain at the movie Netflix had sent him. It was called *Bananas in Your Pajamas,* and starred Ellen Page in what was "a hilarious and wonderfully delightful romp from start to finish," according to Mike Lamplighter, who worked for the Fox radio affiliate WZQP in Akron, Ohio. It was about a teenage girl in California who has the remarkable ability to stop time but who apparently uses that gift solely to put overripe bananas in her enemies' trousers.

If he had the ability to stop time, Ramsay reckoned, he would become the world's greatest magician, burglar, or darts player. He wouldn't waste time making people think they'd had a bathroom accident.

He picked up the DVD packet. Despite Mike Lamplighter's ringing endorsement, the reviews hadn't been kind and Ellen's career and street cred had been put in jeopardy. He would send it back to Netflix unviewed.

Still, the thought of rotten tropical fruit had clearly had some kind of effect on his psyche, and now he felt a little hungry.

He went downstairs and decided to take a stab at the remains of the dinner Brian had made last night. It was an enormous shepherd's pie that looked as if it might contain the whole shepherd. He shoved a plateful of the stuff into the microwave and watched it revolve. It dinged, he took it out, put HP sauce over the whole thing, and gobbled it down in a few minutes.

Brian wasn't a bad cook and Ramsay wasn't choosy anyway. He appreciated Brian staying here and living with him. Ramsay's parents were undergoing a "trial separation." His mother had gotten an apartment in Dublin and his father's job as a rep for Hasbro took him away most of the time. Had it not been for Brian, the house would have been very lonely indeed.

Ramsay sighed. The trial separation had been going on for three months now. It was obvious that his mother wasn't coming back. Maybe if she saw his prizewinning story entry in the *Irish Independent* . . .

He shook his head, washed the dishes, and went to the CD player. He rummaged around for something upbeat.

"Let me see," he said to himself. "Cheerful, but not seventies Paul McCartney cheerful." He put on Cat Stevens's song about his dog and then, with a growing sense of happiness, he carefully took the letter out of his jeans pocket.

He'd reread it about fifteen times since yesterday and he'd shown it to his big brother three times. Now he wanted to show it to his best friend, Jamie. But it was so important to him that he wanted Jamie to read it, not just hear about it. It had been hard to keep the news to himself and he'd nearly spoiled the surprise by phoning Jamie last night—he'd also barely stopped himself from sending a text, BlackBerry, e-mail, or Morse code message with his living room lights.

"Are you reading your letter again?" Brian yelled from the downstairs bedroom.

"No," Ramsay said, and hastily put the thing back in his pocket.

The letter said that Ramsay had gotten one hundred euros and third place in the *Irish Independent*'s annual Children's Short Story Contest. His tale was about a girl who finds the Ark of the Covenant in her back garden, and uses its holy power to propel her school chess club from victory to victory. Not unlike *Bananas in Your Pajamas*, there was a stern moral lesson in the end involving hubris and abuse of power.

Still, it was a hundred euros and the story would get published in a future Sunday *Irish Independent*.

Outside, the car honked.

"That's Anna," Brian said, coming out of the bedroom.

Ramsay looked at him.

He was wearing a tweed suit, waistcoat, and red tie, and it looked suspiciously as if he had combed his hair.

Now that he was teaching at Queen's University Belfast, he had to look a little bit respectable, but this was going overboard, especially for a Sunday.

They were all going to a matinee in Belfast—a last little treat before Brian and Anna went off to London on holiday. Anna would be driving, and Brian, with the longest legs of them all, would no doubt be in the shotgun seat.

Perhaps that was the reason for his sartorial efforts.

"Did you comb your hair?" Ramsay asked.

"So what if I did," Brian said defensively.

The car honked again.

"You don't need to try so hard. You've already made a good impression, you know. She wouldn't have agreed to go on holiday with you if you hadn't."

"You don't know what you're talking about," Brian snapped, amazed at his brother's perspicacity.

"Hmmm," Ramsay said.

They ran out to the car. Brian got in the front, Ramsay sat next to Wishaway and Jamie in the back. Jamie was squished in the middle but he didn't mind.

"Hello," Ramsay said.

"Hi," the others replied, except for Jamie, who merely nodded.

"What's the matter, gloomy guts? The old *weltschmerz* getting you down again?" Ramsay asked.

"My *weltschmerz* is fine, thanks for asking," Jamie said.

Ramsay grinned like a Pentecostalist in a snake pit. "Glad to hear it, mate, glad to hear it. Well, I have to tell you things are pretty rosy on the mainland too," he said.

"How come you're so bloomin' cheerful?" Wishaway attempted.

Ramsay sighed. "Don't try to use gangland argot or cockney slang without clearing it with me first, Wishaway. 'Blooming' went out with singing chimney sweeps and London fog."

"This from the guy who's opening sentence contains *weltschmerz*. Sounds like a nasty skin disease," Jamie said, leaping to her defense.

"Knew you didn't understand it. Anyway, getting me sidetracked. I've got news. Big news. Earth-shattering news."

Brian groaned from the front seat.

"Here, take a look at this," Ramsay said, and handed Jamie the letter.

Jamie read it and passed it to Wishaway.

"Congratulations, Ramsay, I can't believe you won with that crazy, crazy story," Jamie said, delighted, shaking his friend's hand.

"Well, I didn't win, but I did place," Ramsay replied modestly.

"You must let me see your tale," Wishaway said, also quite surprised that anyone would find Ramsay's bizarre narratives readable, never mind publishable.

"What do you win?" Anna asked, only now paying attention.

Ramsay explained.

"And it looks like they're going to print it in the newspaper and everything," Jamie said.

"My little brother, the real talent of the family," Brian said, which made Ramsay beam happily.

Jamie shook the big Irish boy's hand again and then Wishaway reached across Jamie and did it too.

Both were peculiar experiences for Ramsay.

When he'd first met Jamie, Jamie had only had one arm, and now he had two. Shaking Jamie's left hand was a very odd feeling. Wishaway, the girl from the planet Altair, gave him a delicate four-fingered hand clasp that was also weird, as well as unmistakably alien.

An arm mysteriously regrown and an alien girl, Ramsay mused. But Ramsay's problems were nothing compared to Anna's. To say that Anna had had a lot of explaining to do in the year since they had crashed in the Irish Sea would be an understatement.

Obviously the truth was out of the question, but she'd improvised a lie that seemed to satisfy most people. Where had they been for the two weeks before their alleged plane crash? Answer: Iceland, where Jamie had undergone experimental transplant surgery and where they had adopted an orphan girl called Wishaway.

Wishaway did look Nordic, and after minor plastic surgery at a discreet Dublin clinic where they had rounded out her ears and nostrils, she could pass for a striking-looking human girl—perhaps the daughter of a Scandinavian fashion model. What couldn't be ignored, though, was the fact that she had two four-fingered hands instead of the more fashionable five-fingered. But that was explained by hinting at a tragic accident involving a trawler/polar bear/killer whale (depending on who was telling the story).

She had an odd accent, blond hair, glacial blue eyes, and after Jamie sewed a couple of Björk, Sugarcubes, and Sigur Rós patches to her backpack, that seemed to satisfy most people regarding her nationality.

After a week or two no one discussed it much further. In Ireland it was considered bad manners to probe deeply into someone's personal life—indeed, even people who have known each other for fifty years seldom venture beyond the conversational staples of the weather, horse racing, and the sad decline of morals in the kids today.

Of course there were those in Portmuck and Islandmagee who did not believe the Iceland story. These were the same individuals who knew that funny things had been going on for centuries on Muck Island and that all those legends about the Tuatha Dé Daanan,

Tír na nÓg, and the faerie folk were not merely legends. But fortunately these were also the people who knew that it wasn't wise to talk about such things. Foolish was the man who messed with the magic of the wee people and their human allies.

Anna had adopted the "orphaned" Wishaway, and she lived with Jamie in the Lighthouse House on Muck Island.

For Jamie this had good and bad consequences. Good that Wishaway was just down the corridor, bad that in the eyes of society she was technically his sister. In the year she'd been living with them, they had wisely decided to steer clear of each other romantically.

"Seat belts tight?" Anna asked.

"Yes," everyone said.

Anna put on the radio, and a dense Brahms piano concerto wafted through the speakers.

"What the heck is this?" Ramsay asked.

"Mom takes her responsibilities seriously. She's attempting to give Wishaway a firm grounding in Earth culture, so she plays classical music all the time. But when Mom's not around I've been steering Wishaway toward Zeppelin, the Stones, Duffy, and Franz Ferdinand," Jamie said.

Indeed Wishaway had caught up pretty well with the last four centuries of Earth music and even, digitally challenged, she had managed to master most of the sheet music for Jamie's guitar, except for songs that required the tricky F-minor chord.

"Brian, change the station," Ramsay said from the backseat.

"I like it," Brian lied with a little smile at Anna.

"Ramsay, I talked to your father yesterday," Anna said.

"You did? I thought he was in America," Ramsay replied with surprise.

"They do have telephones in America," Jamie said. "We invented the phone."

"Yeah, the phone, atomic weapons, carpet bombing," Ramsay said, irritated. Anna had heard the boys fight over much less, so she quickly continued: "Your father says it's OK if you want to stay at the Lighthouse House while Brian and I are away. Thaddeus won't mind watching an extra body."

Ramsay considered it.

One of the reasons Thaddeus was coming to Ireland was to watch Jamie and Wishaway while Anna went with Brian to London for a week. Since Ramsay's dad wasn't due back from Rhode Island until Thursday, and his mother was unlikely to drive up from Dublin, he'd be by himself at the cottage in Portmuck.

"What do you say, big boy? Are you going to stay with us?" Jamie cried, poking his friend provocatively in the ribs.

"I don't know if I want to spend the week with you and Wishaway and a grumpy old man on that damp island," Ramsay said with what he hoped was haughty disdain.

Anna shook her head. Essentially Jamie and Ramsay liked each other, but that didn't stop them arguing about something nearly every day. She knew the two boys were going to take a while to sort this one out; she smiled at Brian and turned the volume up on the radio. Brian noted the smile and congratulated himself on his hair-brushing skills.

"Thaddeus isn't grumpy. He's cool. He goes horse riding and he saw a jaguar this morning," Jamie said loudly.

Ramsay looked at him skeptically. "I thought there weren't any jaguars in America. I thought the farthest north they got was Mexico," he said.

"Apparently not," Jamie replied.

"Did he get a picture of it?" Ramsay asked.

"No, how could he take a picture?" Jamie asked.

"There's a camera on his phone. Remember, I picked it out for you so you could send it to him for Christmas."

"Oh, he can't work that thing," Jamie muttered.

"How convenient," Ramsay said ironically.

"Listen, Thaddeus wouldn't make something like that up. If he says he saw a jaguar, he saw a jaguar."

The jaguar debate lasted all the way to Belfast. When they got to the city, depressingly, rain clouds were lashing the place all the way from Cave Hill to Black Mountain.

They got soaked in the brief run from the car park to the cinema.

The movie was terrible. It starred Hayden Christensen, who had the ability to teleport from place to place and look moody while doing it.

Only Wishaway seemed to enjoy it, as she did every single Earth movie she had ever seen.

Ramsay kept pointing out plot flaws and Jamie had to shush him continually.

"Be quiet. We'll get barred from the cinema," Jamie said, shaking his head in annoyance.

"Stop worrying," Ramsay whispered loudly.

"I'm not worrying," Jamie said.

But he should have been.

What Jamie O'Neill didn't know was, at the precise moment he was bickering with his best friend in rainy Northern Ireland, three thousand miles away in a basement in Langley, Virginia, his name was about to come up as a potential target for research, surveillance, and possibly kidnapping. And the people who were gunning for him were capable of doing much, much worse than banning him for talking in a cinema in Belfast.

Darkness. Terrible dreams. Fire from the ocean to the sky. The boiling of the oceans. The burning of the air. Things from the End of Days. For weeks now. Make them stop. Make them stop. Make them . . .

"I know it's difficult but everyone concentrate, please," Victor said.

The dark.

Half light through the shade over the window ledge.

Silence.

Breaths.

Silence.

Breaths again.

Finally, in the stillness, a material feeling of harmony and syndicate. A union of wills. A molded togetherness.

Six hearts, six mouths. Six pairs of lungs that moved together.

Six minds.

Folded into the breathing of one.

A rhythmic cycle of directed respiration. A relaxed Zen state of inner tranquility. A sense of openness that began in the pit of the stomach and moved outward in concentric circles, touching arms and skin and flowing out like electricity from the tips of fingers.

"Be aware of everything. But not aware."

The tree through the window. The scent of ash and honeysuckle.

Leaves.

"Control," he told them. "Focus." His voice an ebb of gentle persuasion. Guidance.

A place within the murk. A glow. A tiny light. In the center of the illumination, a candle burning, sending a musky incense into the cool, gelatinous air. The candle resting on a tripod and the tripod resting on a cloth on which a pentagram had been stitched.

There was water in the tripod and its metal base had, in a previous incarnation, been part of a church font in Syria, and, before that, part of the altar of a temple of Baal. The walls too had been kitted out in symbols. The magic numbers. The arcana. The witching words. The ninety-nine names of God. The one true name of God. The menorah. The crucifix. The shaman pole. The crescent moon. The trail of the Great Spirit. The beatific Buddha. The elephant god. The gypsy god. King sea. Osiris. The horned god. The sum of the Kabbalah. The perfection of the spheres . . . and on and on. Hundreds of totems from all over the world.

But he knew that all of that was completely meaningless.

It was only atmosphere.

It meant—nothing.

What was important were these minds.

These receptive brains. These very, very few with genuine abilities.

"How are we doing?" Alan asked.

"Sssshhh," Victor said, noting that Fiona had slipped deeper into her trance. Her eyes were fluttering and sweat was beading on her upper lip.

Fiona was probably the most gifted of them all.

"I was only asking," Alan whined.

"Quiet," Sonia said in her singsong accent. "I'm getting something."

Until she had been recruited by the CIA, Sonia had been a shaman for her tribe of Inuit in the Northwest Territories. After Fiona, Sonia was the most gifted.

"Sorry. Patience, *sursum corda*," Alan said.

Time passed.

Everyone was waiting.

Concentrating. And finally a chink of awareness. Something growing. A seed of information. A channel. A tiny moment of expectancy. "Does anyone else feel this?" he asked.

"Yes, there's something," came a hissed reply. Fiona. Her face drenched in sweat now. He liked Fiona. She was a large lady, second-generation Latina. They'd found her in a fortune-telling booth in Coney Island. She'd been good. Too good. Her predictions had begun to attract attention. That kind of notoriety would have spoiled her.

"Excellent," Victor said. "Let the strongest be the conduit."

"Me. I see it, a place," said Fiona. "The room, the bed."

"And on it?" Victor asked, his eyes tightly closed.

"A man, sleeping," Alan muttered.

"The same man?" Victor asked.

They'd been seeing the *man*, if he was a man, for weeks now.

"There's something about him, though, something odd," Fiona added.

"He's like the Tarot. The Drowned Man. Dead but not dead. A coma perhaps," Sonia said.

"The man will lead us to the *boy*. The man knows the boy," John said. John was an older character, who had come to them from Las Vegas, where'd he made a living betting small sums on other people's turns at roulette. He almost never spoke, but when he did it was usually worth listening to.

"The man knows the boy?" Victor asked.

But John was silent now.

Minutes passed, perhaps a quarter of an hour. Then, suddenly, a face appeared in their minds' eye. It was *him*. Alison, the youngest, began to whimper at the far end of the table. Yes, it was him. The boy. A fifteen-year-old with pale skin and blue-green eyes. He was sitting by a window, in a house on an island next to a lighthouse.

Victor could feel the tension in the room double. He knew he had to say something reassuring.

"Everyone just relax. It's OK. We're here sooner than usual, but it's fine," Victor said, trying to keep the fear out of his voice.

He knew their eyes were open and they were all looking at him.

The boy made everyone nervous.

No, more than nervous. The boy terrified them. The circle of hands tightened.

Alan nearly jumped out of his skin as the ancient stone tripod suddenly moved on the table. "He sees us!" Alan cried.

"It's only the vibration of the delivery truck outside," Victor said calmly, secretly hoping that was the case.

"Yes, it's just the Poland Spring truck," Alan agreed with a nervous laugh.

"That's it. Relax, everyone. Remember, he can't see us. We're looking into the future, he can't see us," Victor said.

After a few moments, they all began breathing together again.

The boy's face became clear and then around him there was a strange and terrible darkness.

"Evildoer," someone muttered.

"Murderer," someone else said.

There was a gasp of pain as the boy faded. They were going deeper now. They were close to getting something new.

"Are you all still with me?" Victor asked.

They nodded.

Fiona's eyes were fluttering. Sonia was breathing hard.

Victor knew that they didn't have much time.

"OK, everyone hold it. Hold it. Now synthesize it. Bring it together," he said gently.

"I see it, a world on fire," Fiona said, on the verge of tears. "A world burning. And it's him. It's him. It's the boy that does it. It's all him. He's the one that brings the great, great . . ."

"What?" Victor insisted.

"The great dying," Fiona said.

"What does he do?" Victor demanded.

Fiona opened her eyes and looked at him from deep within her trance.

"He's the one that brings the end of the world," she said coldly.

"Are you sure? Him?" Victor asked.

"Yes," Fiona said.

"His name?" Victor demanded quickly.

"J . . . something," Fiona said.

"Jim?" Alison suggested.

"Jack?" John wondered.

"No, Jamie!" Sonia exclaimed.

"Jamie," they all said together.

"Jamie," Victor repeated, for now that they had it, he didn't want to lose it.

The vision of the man in the coma had been bringing them to the boy. The boy they now knew was called Jamie.

"Yes."

"The Chinese diviners have seen him too," Fiona said.

"Don't worry, we'll find him," Victor said.

"Will we?" Fiona asked.

"We'll get him first," Victor assured her.

"Kill him first," Fiona said, angrily, as if the boy had already destroyed the world.

Victor nodded. They had discussed this. They would not allow the boy to fulfill his evil destiny.

"Yes, we'll kill him first," Victor agreed.

"Yes," Fiona said.

"Yes," they said together in a moment of catharsis.

Fiona let go of the hands on either side of her. She fell back in her seat utterly exhausted. The circle was broken.

They were done for the day.

"Thank you, everyone," Victor said.

And with that, he stood, opened the blinds, and went to tell his immediate superior in the Central Intelligence Agency that they finally had a name.

Chapter 11
THE PATIENT

THE BIG, SOLITARY MOON was drooping its long tail down into the sea. Lights were winking off along the western shore of Scotland and dissolving into the dark background of the sky. The girl on the bluff sat patiently with a sketchbook and a pencil, eagerly awaiting the dawn. She smoothed down her skirt and did up a button on her coat.

Sunrise was the best time to see the many species of birds that inhabited the rocky cliffs of Muck Island.

And Wishaway loved birds.

Of all the wonders of the Earth, it was birds that amazed and enchanted her above all things.

Yes, television and cinema were marvels, and yes, it was extraordinary to drive in Anna's car—a vehicle that moved faster than any *draya* or galloping *kalahar*—but for some reason she got used to those wonders very quickly. Television was confusing and the car was often stuffy and hot. But birds . . .Wishaway knew she would never tire of them. How could anyone not be delighted by the little multicolored hopping things that were so good as to come down from the sky into every garden and onto rooftop and wall?

Because there'd been no dinosaurs on Altair, there was no such life-form as a bird, but an evolutionary niche like the air could not remain unexploited. There were creatures on Altair that could fly, but apart from insects, Altair's only large denizens of the sky were the ugly, lizardlike, black-winged *rantas* that perhaps no one save a naturalist (or maybe a teenage goth) could love. Birds were superior in their beauty, their diversity, and their music.

Ireland was on the migration route for many arctic species and also it had coastal raptors, songbirds, and at least a dozen types of gull. Muck Island's isolation meant that it was one of the few places in all of the British Isles where rare species such as sea eagles mated and nested. Wishaway had twice seen and sketched a long-winged male eagle bringing a fish into his nest. And that wasn't the half of it by any means. In the last few mornings she had observed terns, guillemots, hawks, and even an albatross that had somehow got seriously lost. In less than a year, from this very spot on the north shore of Muck Island, she'd already filled three sketchbooks with a host of different migratory and native species.

An unkindness of ravens. An exaltation of larks. A murder of crows. A siege of herons. If you didn't mind the cold, this was a birder's paradise.

A typical Scotch mist had risen over the Ayrshire coast but there was now enough light to begin sketching, so carefully she opened up her pad, folded back the waterproof cover, sharpened her soft pencil, and began.

She looked through the binoculars at the nearby puffin colony, found a bird that wasn't doing much of anything, and began drawing him. He was a cheerful fellow with an odd upright posture. She drew his outline and began charcoaling in his body. She sketched the puffin's feet, and couldn't help but give his head a slightly anthropomorphic jauntiness. Just then a razorbill hopped inquisitively along the shore toward her and she almost stopped drawing the puffin, but when the razorbill realized that she wasn't going to throw food or do anything remotely interesting, it squawked snootily and flew away.

Wishaway laughed at that. It began to rain but she hardly noticed, and she didn't see Jamie coming until he was almost at her back.

He regarded her for some time.

Despite her oddness, her alien features, her spectral blue eyes, her damp hair, and her muddy jeans, she was, without a doubt, extraordinarily beautiful.

She had been here with him on Earth for fourteen months now and Jamie, of course, had had his arm back for the same amount of time.

He was whole again and he was actually living with the girl whom he almost certainly loved.

Yup.

He had everything he wanted.

He frowned.

Why then was he so unhappy?

He pulled the hood on his sweatshirt off his head and let the rain drip down onto his face. It was cold, almost freezing.

Perhaps it was because now that she was living in his house, she was more like his sister than his girlfriend. In fact, in the eyes of society (because Anna had adopted her), she *was* his sister.

Wishaway and Jamie knew that they could never have a relationship, and because of this she was often shy and circumspect around him.

And the arm too, yes it was amazing to have his arm back, but it didn't mean that he didn't have other problems. He was doing well in school, but he didn't have many friends. He didn't play sports. (He'd been a pretty good shortstop before the cancer but no one played baseball in Ireland.) And the band he had been in with Ramsay had at last self-destructed, with everyone going their separate ways.

In fact he saw less and less of Ramsay. The big Irish boy was obsessed with writing stories or doing well in his exams (things called GCSEs that apparently would determine whether he would be able to get into Oxford or Harvard one day).

Jamie didn't care about what university he would get into or even if he was going to go to university at all.

He stepped back from the spot where Wishaway sat and walked through the drizzle to the edge of the cliff.

"Maybe I'm just an ungrateful wretch," he muttered. "I'm lucky to be alive, I'm lucky to be whole again. Lucky, lucky, lucky."

Wishaway turned at the sound of his low baritone.

Her hair was plastered against her face.

"Hello, Jamie," she said. Now she always called him Jamie. No one on Earth called him Lord Ui Neill or the Laird of Muck, and Wishaway had a horror of appearing eccentric or different.

"Hi," he said sotto voce.

"What's going on?"

"Ramsay was right, the old *weltschmerz* unfortunately *is* getting me down again," Jamie very nearly said. But he didn't. Wishaway was the last person on Earth he would reveal something like that to. "Mom sent me to get you. We're going to have to leave early. It's snowing in Dublin and there might be traffic problems on the way to the airport."

Wishaway looked at the sky.

Ireland was a small island. It didn't seem likely that it could be snowing in Dublin but drizzling up here. Could Jamie have invented the story so that he could follow her out here, to talk to her, to tell her what had been on his mind for the last few months?

Wishaway put the waterproof cover back on her sketchpad and waited for the other shoe to drop.

But Jamie just stood there without saying anything.

He offered her a hand to help her up.

She got to her feet without his assistance and they walked back to the house.

"So, um, what did you see this morning?" he asked, trying to sound interested.

"Nothing new, but I think I have confirmed the albatross. An albatross! I know it sounds impossible but I'm pretty sure. I will ask to borrow your mother's camera tomorrow. If I'm going to send it to the *Twitcher Times*, they will want proof positive."

Jamie knew he should ask why it was impossible that she could have seen an albatross, but he just couldn't fake the enthusiasm this early in the day.

When they got inside the Lighthouse House, Wishaway carefully put the sketchpad in her binder and put the binder in her rucksack.

She changed out of her coat and put on her school blazer.

Now, alas, she was fully dressed in the ridiculous costume they made young humans wear for school in this country. A short pleated skirt, white socks, a white shirt, a striped tie, and a blue blazer. It was a most impractical ensemble that did little to keep out the wind or rain—two things the Irish coast had in abundance. The boys were allowed to wear trousers but not the girls. It made no sense. Still, a lot of things made no sense on this planet. She would, she realized, come to understand them all in time. Understand, but not accept, she told herself determinedly.

She took the tie off and put it in her skirt pocket. That choking device did not need to be around her neck for a few hours at least. Although it was a school day, they weren't going in until lunchtime because they were picking up Jamie's friend Thaddeus at the airport.

She knew Jamie was worried about the old man. Last night she had heard him pacing the landing and repeatedly going downstairs to check flight times on his computer. Thaddeus was eighty-four years old and, as Jamie said, anything could happen to the old geezer.

"Come on, you two, Thaddeus has been flying all night and he's going to be exhausted. I don't want to be late," Anna said, dangling the car keys in a threatening manner.

Jamie looked at his watch. "We don't have to go this

early. He's not supposed to get in for another four hours. I doubt he's even over the Atlantic yet," he protested.

"Get in the car. It's snowing in Dublin and the weather people on all the channels seemed pretty excited about it," Anna said.

They followed Anna outside and without another word got in the backseat of the big Volvo Estate.

The smell of fish-and-chips came wafting out of the exhaust as the engine growled into life.

Doing her bit to end the energy crisis, Anna had had her car converted to run on used cooking oil. It was an ideal fuel source. There were as many chippies in Ireland as gas stations, and most stayed up till midnight. Ubiquity, convenience, and price were a plus. A slightly unpleasant aroma was the only side effect. And as Ramsay said, for most Irish people it wasn't unpleasant at all. He claimed that the only stink more warming to the Irish senses than a chip shop was a sweaty horse or the hoppy stench that wafted down the Liffey from the Guinness brewery.

"Are we all set back there?" Anna asked.

Jamie nodded.

Wishaway smiled pleasantly.

"OK then, let's go," Anna said.

They drove across the Muck Island causeway and through the village of Portmuck. They had almost reached the hill out of town when Anna saw Ramsay waving at her from the side of the road.

She pulled on the hand brake with a squeal of tires and then she put the car in reverse.

"What are you doing, Ramsay? We're in a rush here," Jamie said through the window.

"Tried to call. Cell phone died. I want to come. Haven't been to Dublin in ages," Ramsay said.

"We're not going to Dublin. We're just going to the airport," Anna said. "But if you want to come you're very welcome."

"Don't mind if I do," Ramsay said, getting in the front.

"You'll have to switch to the back for the ride home," Anna explained.

"Oh, no problem," Ramsay said with a grin.

"And you're still going to have to go to school today," Anna insisted.

"Fine by me," Ramsay replied cheerfully.

Unlike Jamie and Wishaway, Ramsay liked school.

They drove through Belfast without incident but, to everyone's surprise, when they got to the Mourne Mountains of County Down it was indeed snowing.

Irish snow was softer than the snows of New York. There was a lightness to it—a hushed transparency in the big puffy flakes that were tumbling from the black sky. You couldn't deny its loveliness. Along the doublelaned road to the border it had made concrete shapes of the oaks and chestnut trees and wrapped cottages and farm buildings in a deeper solitude than they had already assumed this early in the day.

Everyone in the car shivered. But not from the cold. It wasn't cold. Not really. On this island the moderating breath of the Gulf Stream warmed even the bitterest of days, and the old Volvo's heating system worked pretty well.

And besides, Anna thought, *cold is standing on the raised platform of the 125th Street IRT stop in February with a northerly gale taking the windchill down to the minus thirties.*

No, everyone shivered because the last time any of them had seen snow was on that dreadful journey across the Gag Macak glacier on Altair over a year ago.

Anna put on the radio. After a bit of static she found the news.

The reporters were excited. Three inches of snow had brought Ireland to a standstill. Buses weren't running, factories were closing, people were being advised to stay indoors, and the streets were being kept clear for ambulances or expectant mothers on their way to the hospital. It amused Anna and Jamie. Back home they didn't even think about stopping the buses or closing schools unless there were a couple of feet of the stuff outside.

But apart from witnessing one accident and getting

stuck behind a slew of terrified drivers crossing the Boyne Bridge, they made it to Dublin Airport with plenty of time to spare.

Jamie manufactured a sign from a piece of cardboard that said WELCOME TO IRELAND, THADDEUS and they stood behind the barrier waiting for the old man to come through.

Thaddeus, flush with cash from his killing in the Manhattan real estate market, had flown business class. He had slept part of the way and watched *The Lord of the Rings* on his personal viewing screen. He hadn't enjoyed it. He didn't like films or books in which magic played a part. Magic made everything a bit too easy, too deus ex machina.

Dublin Airport didn't impress him either. It looked like every other airport in the world. There were no Irish touches—whatever they might be.

However, they didn't lose his bags and Customs treated his age and hand-tailored suit with respect; after only a few impertinent questions about whether he had visited any farms or was carrying any meat products, he was detained no longer and he was in fact the very first passenger through the Green channel.

"Over here!" Jamie cried.

Anna kissed him, Jamie hugged him, and Ramsay shook his hand.

Wishaway observed the deference that the others paid the old man. As a sign of her own respect, she bowed deeply and would have touched her forehead on the ground in front of him had not Jamie grabbed her arm and pulled her up.

Several people in the airport stopped playing with their cell phones for a moment to observe this strange little scene.

"That's what they, er, do in Iceland," Anna said loudly to Thaddeus and anyone else in earshot.

"They did an amazing job on your arm, Jamie," Thaddeus noted.

"Yes," Jamie said absently.

"They can do wonders nowadays," Anna said, lying boldly. "Only the third successful arm transplant in the world."

"I'm surprised I didn't read about it in the papers," Thaddeus said.

"We didn't want the publicity . . . OK now, folks, we all better hurry up," Anna said.

"Ah yes, we need to make the famous tide," Thaddeus said happily, for it was really quite exciting to be heading to a place that was cut off from the mainland twice a day. He had lived in Manhattan most of his life, but with dozens of bridges and tunnels to the rest of North America and to Long Island it hardly seemed like an island at all. The Isle of Muck, how-ever, was the real deal.

"It's not the tide. The radio said that this 'blizzard' of three inches of snow is causing traffic problems all over Ireland. Who knows what it could be like on the way back," Anna explained.

"Oh," Thaddeus said, disappointed.

They walked outside to the car park.

Thaddeus patted Jamie on the back. "Well, Jamie, it's really great to see you, and I'm so proud that you were brave enough to have that surgery," Thaddeus said guile-lessly.

Jamie nodded and slunk behind them so Thaddeus couldn't see his cheeks burning. It had been easier to lie to the old man about their adventures on the planet Altair when he was just doing it through e-mail. But now, in the flesh, it made him feel awful.

When they got in the car, Ramsay transferred to the backseat and Thaddeus sat in front. They loaded his two neat suitcases into the trunk.

They all had to admit that Thaddeus was looking a lot better than they'd been expecting. He wasn't pale, he wasn't sickly, and he didn't seem that tired.

He could pass for sixty-five, Jamie thought, and this cheered him up some.

"Good flight?" Anna asked as she eased out of the car park and through the north Dublin traffic.

"Very," Thaddeus replied. "Hadn't flown Aer Lingus before but they were most kind and accommodating."

As well they might be. Thaddeus bore more than a passing resemblance to Morgan Freeman and the rumor had gotten around that he was in fact the famous actor traveling under a pseudonym. He had gotten excellent service and gamely fielded the whispered question "What's Brad Pitt like in person?" with the answer "Never heard of him"—a reply that delighted the flight attendants. "Mr. Freeman's quite a wit," they all agreed, and they later sold his unused socks and peanuts for a small fortune on eBay.

"You came San Francisco to Dublin, right?" Ramsay asked.

"Albuquerque to San Francisco, San Fran to Shannon, Shannon to Dublin," Thaddeus said.

"Wow, they made you go through Shannon, that sucks," Ramsay said.

"It did rather," Thaddeus agreed.

"What movie did you see?" Jamie asked.

"I watched the entire *Lord of the Rings*," Thaddeus said, as proudly as if he had just done an Ironman triathlon.

"Cool," Ramsay and Jamie said simultaneously.

"Perhaps you could explain to me why the eagles at the end didn't just fly the ring to Mount Doom in the first place?" Thaddeus asked.

Jamie looked at Ramsay but Ramsay did not reply.

"It seemed illogical to me," Thaddeus sniffed.

"Yeah, the eagles could have just dropped the ring in the fire, end of problem," Jamie said.

Ramsay looked shocked. *Et tu, Jamie?* he wondered. He wouldn't hear a word against *LOTR* or Saint Peter Jackson, even if the Kiwi director had left out the Scouring of the Shire, the best bit in the book. But since Thaddeus was an old man who had just gotten off a twelve-hour flight, he decided to hold his fire.

They drove north out of Dublin, passed the Hill of Tara, the many wonders of County Meath, and the Boyne Valley, and didn't have any traffic problems until the Mournes again, where the snow was heavier.

A van had slid off the road and into a ditch and several cars had slowed to gawk.

"I didn't think it snowed in Ireland. It's quite lovely," Thaddeus said.

"Yes, it is," Anna said. "Only the second time since we got here."

"Must remind you of home," Thaddeus said, arching an eyebrow at Wishaway in the rearview mirror.

"Yes," Wishaway squeaked.

"So, um, Ramsay, what are you going to do while your father and Brian are away? Are you going to stay at the Lighthouse House or are you going to suffer by yourself in your cold, lonely cottage?" Anna asked, to change the subject.

"Gibbon said that society improves the understanding, but solitude is the school of genius," Ramsay reflected.

"Oh, this is the monkey? The talking monkey from *Tarzan of the Apes*?" Wishaway asked, remembering a bizarre film Jamie had shown her over the weekend.

Jamie winced. Wishaway was still doing her best to digest the last few hundred years of Earth history and the last century of pop culture. Sometimes she got things mixed up.

"A gibbon is a type of monkey, yes," Jamie explained patiently. "Tarzan's friend was a chimpanzee, called Cheetah, which is a very fast type of cat, um . . . I'm just confusing you more . . . Gibbon, I think, was a very boring writer who wrote a long tedious book that Ramsay keeps on his bookshelf and pretends to have read."

"I have read it, actually, or at least the abridged version. Where do you think I got the idea for the Greek Fire that sank the iceships off Aldan City?" Ramsay said indignantly.

Jamie coughed.

"Aldan what? Iceships? Oh, you mean when we were playing Dungeons and Dragons," Jamie said.

"Uh, yeah. Dungeons and Dragons, or maybe it was from Warcraft, um, yeah, something like that," Ramsay agreed, looking shifty. A blind man on a galloping horse would have noticed Ramsay's attempts to be subtle.

"So, Ramsay, are you going to stay on Muck Island or not?" Anna said, putting him on the spot.

"Stay in your house? Well, I don't see why not, I suppose," Ramsay replied.

"Oh, we'd love to have ya, if it's not too much trouble," Jamie said with sarcasm.

"Solitude is tempting, though. I am trying to become an artist. Obviously music wasn't my medium, but perhaps prose will be," Ramsay said dreamily. Netflix had just sent Ramsay *32 Short Films About Glenn Gould* and he'd been very impressed by Gould's need to go off into the forest by himself when he'd been around people too long.

It started snowing a little heavier, and the conversation ebbed as Anna turned her full attention to driving.

Thaddeus took the opportunity to examine Wishaway. He was struck by the snowflakes that were coming in the window and resting like diamonds in her golden hair. She was poised, intelligent-looking, and there was certainly something about those eyes. An unusual girl by any stretch of the imagination. They had obviously not told him the truth about where she had come from. Her name sounded more Polynesian than Icelandic. He had no idea why they would dissemble, but perhaps they had their reasons.

The drive continued, and despite his best efforts, Thaddeus began to reminisce. He had been to Ireland twice, sixty-five years ago. He'd been a sergeant attached to the staff of General Patton when the general had visited Sunnylands Camp near Carrickfergus. At Sunnylands, the U.S. Army was raising a new division to be called the Rangers. The Rangers had been promised only the most dangerous assignments in the coming invasion of Europe, but the young soldiers couldn't have been happier about it. They wanted danger and they got it. Half the people Thaddeus had met at Sunnylands had died in Normandy.

He sighed and peered through the windshield.

The snow had turned to rain.

"Fifteen minutes and we'll be home," Anna said, breaking his reverie. "I'll leave you off at the Lighthouse House and then drop the kids at school."

Thaddeus smiled but he hardly heard her.

They were now on a small country road called the Tongue Loanen.

That was the problem with overseas. Instead of I-95 or the Jersey Turnpike, they had roads called the Tongue Loanen.

Behind stone walls and barbed-wire fences, wet cows and sheep were staring at the car with wonderment as if they had never seen such a device before.

I like cows, Thaddeus thought.

Everyone in the car was suddenly looking at him.

"I didn't say that out loud, did I?" Thaddeus asked Jamie.

Jamie leaned forward and patted the old man on the arm. "Let's see how you feel after you're stuck behind herds of them blocking the road every morning and night."

"Yeah, in this part of the country no matter where you turn, you're continually stepping in sheep, bull, or cow shi-i . . ." Ramsay began before catching Thaddeus's steely eye, whereupon his voice trailed off into a curious, embarrassed, hushing sound.

Cow excrement was the least colorful of the many pejorative epithets that Dan Connolly, the acting deputy director of the CIA's Special Projects Division, could have used upon reading the latest memo from Victor Astatin in Section 22.

Dan was new on the job, not only in Special Projects, but actually in the CIA itself. He was an outsider who had previously worked for the FBI. He had no loyalties to anyone in the CIA and no preconceived notions. The president had appointed him with the mandate to be a new broom who would sweep away some of the old guard.

The first thing on his agenda was Section 22.

Dan was a chubby, skeptical, streetwise man, the son of a New York City beat cop and a schoolteacher. He'd done well in the FBI and got the reputation as a hard-headed reformer.

On the first day in his new job he'd been briefed about Section 22.

He had tried hard to contain his amazement behind a coughing fit and then a supposed need to go to the bathroom.

Section 22 was a revival of a discontinued Cold War CIA plan to hire psychics.

Psychics.

Dear oh dear, thought Dan in a stall in a bathroom of an anonymous-looking gray building in Langley, Virginia.

Still, he'd taken the job.

Two weeks in now, and he had thoroughly digested the entire compendium of Victor Astatin's monthly reports.

They were not pretty reading.

Apparently in the entire five-year history of Section 22, Victor's team hadn't turned up one single piece of worthwhile intelligence. But then how could they? They were obviously charlatans and con men, the lot of them. They couldn't know the future. No one could know the future. Section 22 was a sad chapter in many recent sad chapters of a once-great agency.

Now only a few days away from his confirmation hearings in front of the Senate Intelligence Committee, Dan had called a meeting with Victor Astatin to tell him that he and everyone who worked for him in Section 22 was going to be fired.

"Mr. Astatin to see you," his secretary, Mandy, said through the intercom.

"Let him wait," Dan replied.

Perhaps Section 22 had seemed like a good idea at the time, his predecessor's attempt to think outside the box in preventing another terrorist attack on the United States. But the psychics were an obvious failure, and he had to get rid of the lot of them before it got known to the press. If this came to light, the *Times*, Leno, and Letterman would all have a field day. Back in the 1980s, when it had been discovered that First Lady Nancy Reagan employed an astrologer to arrange her husband's schedule, the late-night talk show hosts were in clover for months.

Dan leaned back in the chair of his ground-floor office and watched planes making the final turn for Dulles.

He reached in a drawer of his polished mahogany desk and removed a pipe. His father's pipe. It helped him think. Of course smoking was banned not only in every CIA building in Langley but up to fifty feet from the entrance too. You had to walk halfway into the parking lot if you wanted to light up.

"Mr. Astatin is still waiting," Mandy said in an insistent tone.

Dan put the pipe back in the drawer and closed it.

"Send him in," he said.

Victor came in.

"Take a seat," Dan said.

Victor sat.

He was a wiry, trim man in his fifties with dyed hair and a Botoxy, fading-movie-star face. Dan resisted the urge to feel sorry for him. Victor's vanity and delusions of grandeur were things to scorn, not to pity. Victor was a native New Yorker who had become famous briefly in the 1970s, bending spoons and fixing people's watches using "telepathy." Victor claimed to have psychic and telekinetic abilities, but they obviously didn't extend that far into the future since after defrauding the IRS for years, he had finally been arrested, bankrupted, and sentenced to eighteen months in prison. The calamities mounted after that. His model wife divorced him and he was exposed (in a bestselling book) as a cheap fraud by his ex-manager. The book revealed in detail how he had pre-bent the spoons and switched keys from real ones to bent ones by sleight of hand. His ex-manager even revealed how he did his famous picture trick that had so impressed Johnny Carson. Before the show Carson had drawn a picture, sealed it in an envelope, and then Victor had read Johnny's brain waves and replicated the picture for the TV cameras. There was nothing psychic about it. In fact Victor's ex-manager had simply distracted *The Tonight Show*'s producers and looked in the envelope and then told Victor what Carson had drawn—nothing could have been simpler.

For Victor there had then been a long wilderness period when he'd worked for prospecting oil companies, a Vegas casino, and finally as a fortune-teller in Atlantic City.

There he'd been found by CIA scouts and brought to Langley, where he was recruited by Dan's immediate predecessor and given orders to assemble a team of psychics and precogs—people who supposedly had the ability to see into the future.

It was obvious to Dan that it hadn't worked. They had produced five years of absolute garbage. This meeting would be the very last time Dan would ever have to look at Victor's perma-tanned, unctuous face.

Or it probably *would be,* Dan thought uneasily.

Probably, because only this morning he had had an

incredible briefing from one of the CIA's moles in British intelligence. Most of it was uninteresting stuff. But one thing had made him take notice.

The Brits were holding a most unusual patient at a minimum-security hospital in Belfast, Northern Ireland. The man was in a coma, and why he was unusual no one seemed to quite know. But apparently he looked very strange, and the Brits had been pretty excited about their mystery patient for some time.

Victor coughed.

Dan looked up from his own reflection in the mahogany desk.

"Did you get my memo?" Victor asked anxiously.

Dan nodded. "Yes, I got it. I read it," Dan said with only a trace of contempt.

"We have the first name of the boy, the Evil One," Victor said excitedly.

"The, um, the boy that causes the end of the world," Dan said, deadpan.

"That's right. The Chosen One. Death Bringer. *An Fadras*. Evil incarnate . . . He's called Jamie. We know his name!" Victor said, pounding his fist into his hand.

Dan nodded. On any other day he wouldn't have been able to take much more of this. He looked past Victor's head to the window outside. The sun was sinking over Virginia, silhouetting the cigarette smokers in the car park and the players on the CIA soccer pitch.

He pushed the chair back from the table, opened the drawer, looked wistfully at his pipe for a moment, and then removed a can of Fresca from the mini fridge he kept on the floor.

"Fresca?" he asked Victor.

"No," Victor said impatiently.

Dan popped the can and took a sip.

"You have to take this to the president," Victor said.

Dan looked at Victor square in the face. Of course he remembered watching Victor when he was a kid. He'd been a wonderful performer. What a pity it was all a lie.

Dan shook his head. "Look, Victor, I like you personally, but I'll be honest with you. I'm afraid I just don't buy it. I don't see how it's possible to look into the future. And furthermore, I don't believe that some innocent little kid called Jamie does some crazy thing that leads to the end of the world."

Victor frowned. "Well, in the memo I suggest—" he began, but Dan interrupted.

"I mean, how do you suppose he does that, exactly?" Dan asked.

"I haven't a clue, I—"

"He builds a neutron bomb with his chemistry set? Invents a new killer virus? Come on. You're an intelligent man, surely you can see that the whole thing is quite pre-posterous."

Victor spread his hands on the table.

He had encountered skeptics before. And the skeptics were only encouraged by all the fakers. Newspaper astrologers. Water diviners. Crystal-ball gazers. Palm readers. He had gone down that road himself for a while. Indeed, of the many, many people he had met in his life claiming supernatural abilities, perhaps four or five had had the genuine gift. And all of those he had corralled into his own team.

Their presence and dedication had given him his own gift back.

"Mr. Connolly, I know what you must think. Yes, it's preposterous, but all of my team has seen it. Before last month I hadn't had a vision for twenty years and now even I've seen it."

"Seen what?"

"Terrible things. Fire from the ocean to the sky. Something very, very bad is going to happen and this boy Jamie starts it somehow. Look, there's an Arab historian called Cide Hamete Benengeli who talks about the Chosen One who brings the end of the world, and Nostradamus himself—"

Dan raised his hand. "This isn't the Carson show, Victor, this isn't Coney Island. Explain to me in a simple sentence how you are supposed to be able to see into the future."

Victor was ready for this one. He had thought long and hard about how anyone could see things that had not yet come to pass, and after much reading he'd come up with an answer.

"Have you heard of quantum physics?"

Dan nodded.

"OK. Quantum physicists have been troubled for years by what Einstein called *Spukhafte Fernwirkung*—spooky action at a distance. How two quantum events can happen simultaneously on opposite sides of the universe. This violates the theory of relativity. Nothing can travel faster than light so nothing can happen simultaneously, see?"

"No, not rea—"

"Ah, but the equations work if the light cone from those events taking place at the quantum level extends backward as well as forward along time's arrow. If a quantum event happens in the future and the signal gets sent back in time, then relativity isn't violated."

"Say that again more slow—"

"So, according to this theory, hints of the future, very small hints, sometimes leak into the present. And sometimes, if you're attuned and very, very sensitive, you get a hint. Especially if that event is going to be a catastrophe."

Dan looked intrigued.

"Really?" he said.

Victor nodded. He had him on the hook, now he had to reel him in.

"Pick a number between one and ten," Victor said.

"Oh, I don't think—"

"Go on, pick one, go on . . ."

"Four."

Victor reached into his inside jacket pocket, removed a sealed envelope, and placed it on the desk in front of Dan.

Dan opened it.

Inside the envelope was a note that read: "The number you are going to pick is four."

Dan got up from his desk, walked around it, reached in the side pockets of Victor's jacket, and took out several more envelopes. He ripped them open, revealing the messages: "The number you are going to pick is five," "The number you are going to pick is three," et cetera.

"You're an old fraud, Victor," Dan said.

He returned to his chair and sat down. He took another sip of Fresca.

"Then why aren't you kicking me out of your office?" Victor asked.

Dan looked at him.

"Now that is the smartest thing you've said all day. Why am I not kicking you of my office? There's a reason. Tell me about the man in the coma."

"The man in the coma?"

"According to your reports, you've been seeing a man in a coma, yes?"

"Yes. We have. I don't know who he is or what his connection is to the boy, but we've been seeing him for weeks now. Somehow the two are linked. We believe that the man in the coma will lead us to the boy."

"Have you seen his face in your . . . in your whatever you call them."

"Visions. Yes, we've seen his face. Hints of his face, yes."

Dan nodded. "And the man in the coma does what? Helps the boy destroy the world?"

"The man in the coma leads us to the boy," Victor said. "Or so we believe."

"What do you think we should do when we find this boy?" Dan wondered out loud.

"The consensus of the group is that we should, uh, get rid of him."

"And you?"

"I think we should get rid of him too. The signs are very clear."

Dan was glad that he wasn't taping this conversation or keeping notes. Plotting the murder of a teenage boy called Jamie probably wouldn't get him much praise in the *New York Times*.

He examined Victor. The tan, the fake smile. A pathetic con man or someone who really could see things that others couldn't?

"I'll be honest with you, Victor. I usually pay no attention to your memos, and I was on the verge of recommending the suspension or termination of your section, but, you see, something's come up."

Victor's eyebrows raised. "Yes?"

"How would you like to go into the field?" Dan asked.

"The field?"

"The field. We have a mole in British intelligence—well, several actually, but this one is particularly reliable . . . Anyway, I was reading a briefing from him this morning that, to be frank, gave me the willies."

"Go on."

"There's a hospital in Belfast, Northern Ireland, where for the last year or so they've had a most unusual patient."

"Yes?"

"I can't tell you any more than that except that he's in a coma and he seems to resemble the man that you've all been talking about for the last month."

"Aha!" Victor said triumphantly.

Dan smiled.

"You're going to have to go take a look at him."

"Me?"

"You."

"Go to Ireland?"

"Yes."

"When?"

"Today."

"Are you kidding? I don't think I even have a passport, I—"

"Your group believes that the man in the coma will lead you to this boy that you all want to get rid of to save the world, right?"

"Yes."

"OK then, this is your big chance. You're going to have to go to Ireland and get a look at this patient that British intelligence seems so excited about."

"But I've never done fieldwork before," Victor protested, the color draining from his face.

"Oh, there's nothing to worry about. The patient is in a private sanatorium just outside Belfast. Not a prison. No armed guards, it won't be dangerous. I'll have someone brief you further on all our procedures."

"But, I-I—" Victor stammered.

"No buts, Victor. You want to save your job? You want to save the world? Well, let's see if your story holds water. Can I count on you?"

Victor gulped and said nothing.

"Well?"

"Yes."

"Good. Take a look at this mysterious man, see if it's your guy, and if it is, question him about anyone called Jamie."

"How can I question a man in a coma?"

Dan grinned, crumpled his empty Fresca can into a ball, and threw it into the wastepaper basket.

"You wake him up, Victor, you wake him up."

Victor moved from his hiding place behind the apple tree and approached the neo-Gothic archway to the hospital.

He had never been to Ireland before and he'd actually been expecting rain, not snow.

He was wearing a leather jacket, jeans, a thin shirt, and Converse sneakers.

He was underdressed, jet-lagged, and cold.

The flight from D.C. to Dublin had been fine, if you didn't mind screaming babies, horrible food, and the dimensions of an economy seat. (In his heyday Victor had flown only first class, and that was back when first class really meant something.)

He examined his watch. It was three in the morning. According to his briefing notes, the hospital security guard went home at midnight and didn't come back on again until nine. There was, therefore, a nine-hour window to get into the hospital without having to resort to force.

Not that Victor could have resorted to force if the need arose. He'd insisted to Dan Connolly that his was strictly a mental ability.

Still, if he followed Dan's plan and all went well, he wouldn't actually have to see or encounter anyone. The patient was kept in D wing. The night nurses were all in A wing, and there should be no janitors, porters, orderlies, or anyone else in that part of the building from three until six, when the doctors began their morning rounds. Interestingly, when the mysterious patient had first been transferred here, he had come with a couple of soldiers who had taken turns guarding the door outside his room, but as the months had worn on and the patient had shown no signs at all of waking up, the soldiers had been withdrawn.

Now it would be as safe as houses.

Or at least so the CIA claimed.

Victor sniffed the air skeptically.

It smelled of peat smoke and boggy fields.

He was in the southern suburbs of Belfast, where housing was less dense and a bit of the countryside was creeping in. It was quiet, the only sound the gurgling of the River Lagan behind the hospital, and in the distance the muffled sound of a church bell.

The bell stopped ringing.

Stillness descended upon the courtyard.

He picked up his backpack and slung it over his shoulders.

There was nothing else for it.

With trepidation, he removed himself from his hiding place and walked across the car park.

He approached the entrance and took a piece of paper from his pocket.

There was a keypad next to the glass-fronted door. Dan claimed that the code to get into the hospital was 1271690, the date of some famous battle in Irish history.

He entered the digits, and much to his surprise, the door opened. Well, well, well, so his masters weren't complete idiots.

OK, what now? Oh yes, first left, all the way to the end of the corridor, Victor said to himself.

He turned left, walked along a short passageway, and then stopped at another door. There was another keypad.

This time the code was supposedly 000000, which wasn't very imaginative at all.

Victor pressed in the digits and the door opened.

"So far, so good."

It was a small ward with only three patients, all in comas or persistent vegetative states. All hooked up to heart monitors and saline drips.

The first patient was a bearded man whom Victor didn't recognize; the second was a slight, bald man covered in bandages who had obviously been in some kind of terrible accident. But after a close inspection, Victor saw that he too was not his target.

The third man was in the bed nearest the window.

Victor approached cautiously.

He gasped. *It's him,* he said to himself.

The room was dimly lit but there was enough ambient light for Victor to know with absolute certainty that the patient in the third bed of D wing in the South Belfast Hospital for Long-Term Care was the person that he and the others in Section 22 had been having visions about for the last few weeks.

Somehow this man helped cause the end of the world.

Victor came a little closer.

When he was only a few inches from the bed, he realized why British intelligence had kept this patient away from the general public and why everyone who worked in this private hospital had had to sign the Official Secrets Act.

A chill coursed along Victor's spine all way down to his retro sneakers.

He felt faint and had to put his hand over his mouth to stop himself from crying out.

The patient in the bed, although similar to a human being, wasn't in fact a human being at all.

He had pointed ears, a freakishly small nose, and four fingers on each hand.

Victor took a step backward and looked at the case notes on the clipboard hanging from the end of the patient's bed.

**NB: ALL PERSONS VIEWING
THIS PATIENT OR THIS CHART
MUST FIRST CONTACT DR. MARLEY
AND MUST SIGN THE
OFFICIAL SECRETS ACT.**

Auth. John Aubrey Div. Sec. Officer MOD ref no. RVH #1412

PATIENT: NAME UNKNOWN
AVO: COMA
NEEDS: NO SPECIAL NEEDS
HISTORY: UNCHANGED
INCIDENTS: NONE
DNR: DO NOT ATTEMPT
      TO RESUSCITATE THIS PATIENT

NOTES: This patient was brought to us from the Royal Victoria Hospital. Picked up by the Royal National Lifeboat Institution from a wrecked vessel in the Irish Sea, he has been in a coma for at least the last year as a result of trauma to the head and severe exposure due to immersion in the ocean. The patient exhibits many unusual features, not the least are his absence of thumbs, an almost nonexistent nasal cavity, blood of no known type, no DNA or RNA detectable in his body, and possibly an unusual internal structure (this may be confirmed on autopsy). Dr. Marley's survey team would welcome any suggestions regarding this patient or notes from anyone with previous knowledge or experience with such a case.

Victor put back the clipboard and forced himself to calm down.

He knew.

The Irish didn't know but he knew.

This wasn't some mutant or some victim of a government experiment, this was an alien who was working with the boy, Jamie, in a conspiracy against Earth. The Irish might not know what to do with him, but he did.

He had seen the fire, he had seen the boiling oceans, he seen terrible death, and he was going to stop it.

He would go down in history not as some loser who'd enjoyed a brief period of fame in the 1970s. No, he would go down as the man who saw the future, the man who saved the world.

Yes. Victor smiled and found that he was no longer afraid.

He set his backpack on the bed, unzipped it, and removed a bottle of clear liquid that was marked ADRENALINE. He found the leather wallet containing the needles.

He loaded up a syringe, found a spot on the patient's arm, and injected a mighty dose of adrenaline into his body.

Victor knew nothing about medicine and in his excitement he had overloaded the syringe, doubling the amount that Dan had told him to use. The dose was too big and, in fact, if it had been a human lying on the bed, Victor would certainly have killed him.

But of course it wasn't a human.

The hormone adrenaline was completely unknown to the patient. Its effects could not be predicted.

Kill or cure? Victor would get his answer in less than a minute.

The man began to shake and convulse.

Froth appeared on his lips. His back arched. His legs thrashed. He kicked the sheets from his lower torso and ripped the saline drip from his arm.

He cried out and for a moment Victor was sure that

the man was going to die. The man, the *thing*, thrashed wildly on the narrow bed, clawing at his skin, moaning.

But eventually the fit began to abate.

The man muttered something in a foreign language and his breathing became regular. He seemed to fall back into a kind of doze.

Then, quite abruptly he sat up, stretched, and finally, after what had seemed like the sleep of a thousand years, the alien from the planet Altair opened his eyes.

Chapter III
THE GENERAL

JAMIE WOKE WITH A START. He rubbed his face, swung his legs over the edge of his bed, and pulled the curtain away from the window. It was still several hours before dawn. The clouds were black and low and blotting out the stars, giving the sky a terrible aspect of loneliness and negation. As if the souls on this poor world were cut off from the heavens. Doomed. "Oh boy," he said, and smiled at the melodrama of this idea.

But something had woken him.

Something *was* wrong.

A nightmare perhaps? He tried to remember his dreams but all he got was a vague feeling of foreboding, as if a ghost from the past had slipped its way into his consciousness. Was everyone in the house OK? Maybe Thaddeus had had a fall or something.

His heart pounding, Jamie tiptoed out of his room and ran lightly down the hall of the Lighthouse House.

He creaked opened the door of Thaddeus's room and peered inside.

The old man was snoring soundly.

"Hmmm," Jamie mumbled.

Perhaps someone other than Thaddeus was in trouble. Maybe his mom? He walked back along the hall and pushed on her door.

Her reading lamp was still lit and a copy of *The Bridges of Madison County* was lying on the floor.

But she was snoring soundly too. Not that surprising. Between the two of them, Thaddeus and Anna had polished off a bottle of red, a bottle of white, and a third of a bottle of cognac Thaddeus had gotten from duty-free.

Jamie gently closed the door.

Maybe Wishaway was up? Should he check? He'd have to be careful with her door because she was such a light sleeper.

He tiptoed to her room and nudged open the door, but there she was, sleeping on the Ikea foldaway with the moonlight on her face, a faint frown on her red lips.

Everyone was in slumberland but him.

Jamie closed Wishaway's door. He padded down the hall and went back to his own room. He flipped on his light.

"What time is it?" he wondered out loud.

At some point in the night there had been another brief power outage, so his electric alarm clock was flashing 12:00, revealing nothing.

Have to get batteries for that thing, he said to himself.

He opened the window. The sea air wafted into his nostrils. It was chilly. Too chilly. Perhaps they were going to get a snow day. The teachers said if it ever snowed two days in a row in Ireland, all the schools would close.

He closed the window again. The blast of icy air had been like a mild electric shock. "Well, now I definitely won't get to sleep again."

He climbed under the sheets and picked up a dog-eared copy of one of Ramsay's *Hazel Weatherfield, Girl Detective* novels. But even that couldn't hold his interest for long. He looked at the author photograph—an elegant woman sitting on the stoop of a New York brownstone. He tried to figure out where it was. Manhattan probably, if she was a successful novelist. Looked a bit like the West Seventies.

He sighed and put down the book. He missed New York sometimes.

He hadn't had a decent slice of pizza in two years.

"Or a good tamale," he muttered.

He put his hands behind his head and stared at the ceiling. Finally he got out of bed and walked downstairs.

The living room had a big old-fashioned fireplace and there were a few logs still smoldering in the grate. He warmed himself by the hearth, sitting down on the thick carpet and letting the hot air wash over him like a blanket.

He listened to the night sounds.

A dog was barking on the mainland and another hound was giving it an answer. Above him the roof timbers were creaking in the breeze and far off over the water there was a plane on the Trans-At. He closed his eyes to hear it all better. The wind dropped. In Portmuck there was a small whirring sound like that of an electric vehicle. Milk arriving, or the mail, or the paper. He shook his head.

"What's the matter, Jamie?" he whispered to himself.

But he couldn't think of an answer. He leaned closer to the fire and stirred the embers. There wasn't much heat but it was better than nothing. A coal glowed for a moment, casting a red presence out into the room.

"Damn it!" he said.

He rubbed his forehead, stood, and attempted to gather his wits about him. He didn't feel at all sleepy but he was on edge. He wondered if maybe there was any trace left of last night's caffeine floating around in his system. They'd had a big welcome meal for Thaddeus and of course, in American fashion, they'd finished it off with coffee.

"Kids and coffee don't mix," his mother had said, but he'd wanted a mug to prove to Thaddeus that he wasn't a child anymore.

"I suppose she was right after all," he said.

He walked to the window and put his hand on the glass. He shivered. There was condensation on the sill and a dewy layer of frost on the pieces of Waterford crystal next to the door. Cold air was coming down the chimney.

"House is freezing," he said to himself.

He went to the kitchen and found a packet of HobNobs biscuits. He poured himself a glass of milk and dipped a cookie in the glass.

He dripped a little milk on the kitchen table and made the shapes of islands with his finger. The islands of Altair.

He finished his cookie and flipped open his laptop. It woke from its sleep and began searching for the wireless network.

The home page was CNN.com. He clicked down to sports and checked how the Yankees and Mets had done. Both lost. Typical.

He clicked the inbox on his Hotmail account.

Several e-mails from Ramsay.

The first was about Ramsay's MySpace page, where he had posted some of their jointly composed music without asking Jamie's permission first.

Jamie groaned loudly.

The second e-mail was a long, rambling explanation of why he wasn't going to stay in the Lighthouse House while Brian and Anna were in London. Jamie skimmed to the conclusion: If Ramsay spent the week alone in Portmuck, cooking for himself and doing his own laundry, it would prepare him better for when he had to go away to college. Jamie shook his head.

The third Ramsay e-mail was an impassioned defense of *The Lord of the Rings.*

Jamie deleted this one unread.

Jamie heard a sound and looked at the stairs.

A pair of feet in Hello Kitty slippers appeared, followed by Wishaway in a long nightgown.

"Are you up?" she asked, looking at him.

"Yeah," he replied.

"Me too," she said.

"Couldn't sleep?" he wondered.

"No, I actually was asleep but something woke me. I thought I heard a howling noise," she said.

"A howling?" Jamie asked.

"Perhaps a wolf," she said, a look of fleeting terror passing over her pretty face.

Jamie fought back a sneer. This was an opportunity to mock, but he would go easy on her. It wasn't a simple thing to digest all the information about Earth's millions of animal species.

"There aren't any wolves in Ireland," he said simply.

"But I saw them in the museum in Belfast."

"Extinct."

Wishaway nodded and sat opposite him at the kitchen table. It was one of the curiosities of human beings that they would allow another animal species to go "extinct." That concept didn't exist on Altair and there was not a word for it in any of the Altairian languages that she knew.

"It was probably me groaning," Jamie said. "Ramsay's put some of our songs on his MySpace page. They're my lyrics so he should have asked. And they're mostly about Altair so it's not very discreet either."

"Altair," Wishaway said sadly.

"You ever get homesick?" Jamie asked.

She nodded. "From time to time."

"Sorry," Jamie said.

"What woke *you* up?" she asked, to change the subject.

Jamie shrugged. "I don't know, I had this strange feeling. I was having a dream. I think it might have been about Altair too, I don't know."

"We'll never go back there, will we?" Wishaway said.

Jamie looked guiltily at his Wallace and Gromit slippers.

"I don't think so," Jamie replied.

They sat in silence for a moment or two.

He looked into her eyes. Sometimes in the silence

between words they said more than he and Wishaway ever communicated aloud.

"Are you hungry?" Wishaway asked, breaking the gaze and going to the fridge.

"No, no, but help yourself."

Wishaway took out some crusty bread and her favorite: thick, golden-yellow Irish butter.

"You want some bread and butter? It is delicious," Wishaway said.

"Yeah, Brian says beer from the Trappist monasteries in Belgium and Fenway Park hot dogs and Irish buttered scones are the greatest man-made foods on Earth."

"You have had this beer?" Wishaway asked.

Jamie shook his head. "No, my dad let me have some Bud once during a Super Bowl, but nothing since. It wasn't anything to write home about."

"And the dogs?"

"No, never been to Fenway. My dad took me to Shea and Thaddeus took me to Yankee Stadium, but that's it."

"You are glad Thaddeus is here?" Wishaway asked.

"Yeah, I'm glad he got in safe."

"You like him?" she said.

"Yeah, he's cool for an old guy. Bowie cool. David Byrne cool."

She nodded and Jamie watched her eat her bread and butter, sitting by the fire and looking out to sea. It could have been a scene from the Ireland of a hundred or even a thousand years ago.

"You seemed troubled, Jamie," Wishaway said when she was done, surprising him.

"Me? I'm fine," Jamie denied.

"Is everything OK between you and Ramsay?" Wishaway asked.

"Are you kidding? Everything's great. He doesn't want to do the band anymore but I can respect that. He's trying to make it solo. Fine by me."

Wishaway pursed her lips.

"I want you to always remain friends," she said seriously. Wishaway had noticed a coolness between the boys. There hadn't been an incident, no big blowup, just a certain dip in the level of their friendship. She didn't like to see it. Ramsay played on the school rugby team, he had a lot of other friends and outside interests. Jamie did not. Ramsay was Jamie's main interlocutor at school. Even Wishaway had more friends than Jamie did.

"Ramsay and I are still as tight as ever, don't worry about that," Jamie said with a grin.

Wishaway nodded. A wave crashed on the rocks outside.

"The polar ice caps are melting. I worry about that," Wishaway said. "We saw that movie."

Wishaway had an understandable tendency to take movies a little too literally. She understood that they were only stories, but it took her a long time to shake the visual and visceral impact.

"Don't worry about that either. Fill a glass full of ice cubes and water, measure the level, and measure it again when the ice has melted. You'll see it's not a problem."

"What happens?"

"When the ice melts the water level falls. Frozen water displaces a greater volume of water than H_2O in its liquid form. Don't worry about the poles melting."

"What about the Greenland glacier?"

"It'll take five hundred years to melt."

"And the oil?"

"The oil?"

"What will we do when the oil runs out?"

"You shouldn't have watched that Thom Yorke interview. There's enough oil for fifty years, there's enough oil sands and oil shale for another hundred years, and enough coal for another two hundred. That'll give us plenty of time to crack nuclear fusion . . ."

He could tell Wishaway had stopped listening and she didn't object when his sentence trailed off into silence.

She walked to the toaster and put in two slices of thick batch bread. She came back to the table again.

"What do you want, Jamie?" she said after a pause.

"What do I want? In life, you mean?"

"Yes."

"Why is it girls always ask the big questions? Boys never do. Boys talk about *South Park* and *Star Wars*."

But Wishaway was not to be put off. "What do you want to do with your life, Jamie? What do you want to be? Do you want to be rich?"

"Rich, sure, who wouldn't?"

"An ascetic."

"A what?"

"A monk," Wishaway explained.

She had memorized the whole dictionary. If she were in America, doubtless Anna would have entered her in a spelling bee.

"An ascetic," Jamie repeated. "I like that."

Wishaway looked at him with a strange expression that he thought was either admiration or mock admiration. It was hard to tell.

She picked up the glass of milk on the table.

He tensed. For a second he thought she was going to do something crazy with it, like smash it on the ground or pour it over him. She took a sip and then set the glass gently back down.

Milk made a ring of white around the bottom of the glass, coating the sides in V shapes. Then Wishaway smiled at him. It was an incredible, broad gesture that seemed to light up the whole room. It made her look older. Caring.

Her hand reached across the table and rested itself on top of his. He was surprised at the tenderness of it.

"It must be hard, sometimes," she said, as if she knew all about it.

What was she doing? Why was she comforting him? She was the poor alien girl, ninety-six light-years from her planet, destined never to see her father, her hometown, or her friends again. She needed the comfort, not him.

But despite himself, he said "yes" in a tiny whisper.

"It's the pressure," she said, her voice dropping a register so it became all the more soothing and considerate.

"The pressure. Yes."

She squeezed his fingers harder and behind her the toast popped up.

"Oh," she said, startled, and then quickly she grinned again. Her eyes were a dark blue. She knew they were arresting.

She blushed.

They looked at each other for a moment longer and then reluctantly he let go of her grip. Leaving the cool soldering of her touch in fragile increments of loss. Finger by tiny ache of finger.

The alien sat up, looked at Victor, and touched him with his odd four-fingered hand. He opened his mouth to speak, but it was dry and his vocal cords were rusty after a year of inactivity.

His body, though, was in excellent condition.

He had been drip-fed with vitamins, proteins, and sugars, and the Earth food was rich and wholesome. He felt lean and strong, and the adrenaline, no doubt, helped too.

His mind was clear and strangely alert. A TV or a radio had been on somewhere in the background for twelve solid months, and although he had been in a coma, at some level his brain had been taking things in.

He got off the bed, and after a moment's shakiness he stretched his arms and breathed deeply.

The air was moist and smoky. Thick and warm.

Victor regarded the creature for a horrified moment, and then began to back away.

He had been tasked to inquire if this patient was somehow connected to the boy, Jamie, but now that he had revived the thing, he wasn't at all sure he wanted to be within a thousand miles of it, never mind sitting it down for a chat about who it was and what it knew. You didn't wake up Frankenstein's monster and then sit around for small talk afterward.

He began making his way slowly to the exit.

"*Kaaarak!*" the creature said, and Victor froze in his tracks.

It walked toward him. Under the light, Victor could see its face more clearly. It was not unattractive, but it seemed to have been burned on the left side. Its skin was very pale and its eyes were an odd bluish black. A thick beard covered much of its lower jaw, and if it hadn't been for the pointed ears, it could have passed as a Russian mountain climber or weather-beaten trawler captain.

"*Kava uul, soma?*" it asked.

Victor shook his head.

"*Kava uul tava?*" it demanded, examining his face.

"I-I don't understand you," Victor said.

"*Ka?* . . . Earth?" the creature wondered.

"Earth, yes."

The creature's eyes widened with excitement.

"We are yet on Earth?" it inquired in English.

"Yes. Earth," Victor said.

The creature nodded.

"I thought perhaps that this was the *sheol*, the underworld. Earth? I am alive then," it said almost to itself.

Victor's confidence was coming back. It didn't seem hostile. And it should at least be grateful to him for bringing it out of its coma. Maybe he could give it a drink of water and then ask it a couple of easy questions.

"You should sit," Victor suggested. "You've been in that bed for a long time."

The creature sat on the edge of the bed and tugged at the thin hospital nightgown that had been draped about it.

"How long?" it asked.

"A year," Victor said.

The creature's eyes closed.

"A year," it said. "A year on Earth."

"W-where are you from, um, originally, if you, if you don't mind me asking?" Victor asked hesitantly.

"Altair," the creature replied.

"I assume that's another planet. Yes?"

"Yes."

"OK. And how did you get here?" Victor inquired.

"I came in a ship that flew in the air. The Ui Neill flew it. We did not know that it was a vessel for journeying among the stars. We in our ignorance called it the Tomb of the Ice Gods," the creature said in a monotone.

"You landed in a spaceship?" Victor said.

"We crashed into the ocean."

"Yeah, that's right. You were picked up by the British coast guard floating in the sea. They've kept you prisoner in this hospital ever since. You probably would have stayed here forever, but, you see, I saved you, I woke you up," Victor said, his confidence now fully returned.

"You woke me?"

"Yes," Victor said, patting the thing on the shoulder.

The alien examined him for a moment. Its first reaction was gratitude, but its next seemed to be suspicion.

"Why?" the creature asked.

"I helped you, and you can help me," Victor said.

"Yes?" the creature said.

"I'm looking for a boy called Jamie. You see, we believe that he causes the end of the—"

The creature bolted to its feet and grabbed Victor about the throat.

"Jamie of the Ui Neill. Where is he?" it asked, snarling with hatred.

Victor tried to break the alien's terrible grip, but he wasn't nearly strong enough.

"I don't know, I had hoped that—" Victor began, but the creature slapped him brutally around the head.

"I will not ask thee again. Where is the Ui Neill?"

"I, I don't know, I—"

The creature squeezed hard on Victor's throat until his eyes were bulging from his sockets.

"I don't know," Victor managed.

The creature examined the needle lying on the bed

and the knapsack full of strange equipment that the human had brought. It all seemed to become clear.

"Yes, doubtless the Ui Neill sent you to kill me," the alien snarled in Victor's ear.

"No, no, you've got it all wrong. I woke you up, I—"

"Lies! Lies! You overstep. You shall not kill me, human. The Ui Neill will not triumph. Twice I have been cast into the fire. Let it be thrice or a thousand times, he will not triumph. I will best him and his confederates."

Victor could feel the life being squeezed out of his throat.

He knew the creature was going to murder him. His hands reached out desperately for something to grab.

They touched the clipboard.

He clasped it in his right hand, lifted it off the edge of the bed, and brought it down as hard as he could on the alien's head.

The alien released its grip on Victor's throat, staggered backward, tripped on a nightstand, and fell heavily to the floor.

"*Sammka, lass,*" it snarled and began getting up again.

Victor ran to the door and pressed the code, but he must have pressed something besides an 0 because it didn't open.

Behind him the thing was on its feet.

In a few seconds it would be on top of him.

He pushed the code again, but the lock was frozen now. The glass door was single-glazed, one thick opaque sheet.

"*Vaaama val,*" the alien said, lurching for him.

There was only one thing for it.

Victor ran at the door and shoulder-charged it.

It gave instantly.

Fragments of glass exploding everywhere. Cuts on his hands and face.

He tumbled to the floor.

He gasped for breath and pulled a chunk of glass out of his cheek.

"Come back," the creature said, but now some of the arrogance had ebbed from that voice.

Victor got to his feet. Blood in his mouth, cold sweat pouring down his face. He had to get out here.

Halfway down the long hall there was a fire exit that led outside into the hospital gardens. That would do.

He scrambled to the door and pushed on the bar of the emergency exit. An alarm went off—a loud ringing Klaxon that would wake up the whole hospital.

The night nurses would be over here in a jiffy and they would definitely call the police.

Thank God.

But no point lingering anyway.

Victor ran into the gardens, slipped on an icy patch of stone, fell, got the breath knocked out of him, and got up again. He looked back. The alien was coming out of the fire exit. It seemed distressed. The loud fire alarm was obviously upsetting it.

The game's up now, pal, Victor said to himself, hardly able to contain his glee.

And whoever or whatever this thing was, it was going to have a lot of explaining to do when the law showed up.

Victor leaned against an oak tree.

"The cops are coming. You better run for it!" Victor shouted to the alien.

The creature looked at him for a second, and then smashed the flashing fire alarm with a closed fist.

The Klaxons stopped immediately.

"Damn," Victor muttered, but surely the nurses, the police, the fire department would still come?

The alien laughed and began walking toward him.

It was sleeting now and the grass was covered with a slippery film of icy water.

"What do you want from me?" Victor yelled in a voice trembling with fear. Was this creature the agent of the boy, Jamie? Could he and it really destroy the world?

One thing was for sure, it would destroy *him* if it got another chance.

Victor turned and ran across the hospital grounds all the way to the edge of the River Lagan.

He turned left at an embankment and darted up the steps of a small wooden veranda that surrounded some kind of boathouse. A sign said: QUEEN'S UNIVERSITY BELFAST BOAT CLUB.

And sure enough a series of rowboats and punts were pulled up on the other side of the veranda next to the shore.

Yes, Victor said to himself.

He ran down the steps to the riverbank. There were dozens more punts stacked together on a pontoon and there were even some in the water.

He grabbed one of the many large barge poles lying on the ground, jumped into the nearest punt, and tried to push himself off the bank and into the current.

It wouldn't move.

He pushed harder but then he saw that the punts were fixed together with a heavy chain that was connected to a massive iron ring on the boathouse itself.

"For God's sake," he muttered.

He tried ripping one of the punts away from the chain but it just wouldn't come.

He picked up the barge pole and smacked twice at the chain, but that didn't do anything.

"Come on!" he yelled, dropping the pole and pulling frantically at the chain.

He looked up and saw the alien step onto the veranda.

Victor knew there was nothing else for it.

He leaped into the River Lagan.

Icy water shocked him like a Taser. He gasped and swallowed and scrambled to the surface. The river only went up to his waist, but it was so cold, it was like being in a chokehold from an underwater wrestler. He waded in until he reached midstream and then attempted to swim for the far bank.

On that side there were trees and a wild meadow. He knew if he could make it there he could disappear into the long uncut grass.

But Victor hadn't been swimming since his childhood, and that had been in a heated pool in Brooklyn. Nothing had prepared him for this thick, slimy Irish river.

Fortunately the Lagan was not a wide stream. It was only a few strokes to the bank. He took a quick look back to see the alien walk to the water's edge.

"Come here," the creature said.

"No chance," Victor muttered.

He kept swimming through the slippery, frigid water. Nearly there. Two more strokes.

He felt the bottom under his feet and began wading

to the shore. He didn't look behind him to see what the alien was doing. Standing there fuming or wading in after him—it didn't matter, he had to keep going.

Yes, the Lagan was narrow but it was fast flowing, and he was exhausted by the time he made it completely out of the water. He struggled halfway up the muddy far bank and collapsed.

He was shivering convulsively.

Paralyzed.

He couldn't move.

"Get up, Victor," he told himself.

He began crawling for the safety of the meadow, but it was difficult and he felt weak. He slipped on the mud and almost fell back into the river.

He grabbed at a tree branch and saved himself.

And then he did look back.

With incredible strength the alien had ripped a punt from its protective chain and was pushing it across the water with one of the long barge poles.

"Oh God," Victor said.

He watched, paralyzed with horror as the punt crossed the Lagan and touched the far shore only a few yards upstream from where he was lying in the mud.

On the verge of total panic, he heaved himself up the embankment into the long grass. He began to run. He got about ten yards before he was tackled to the ground.

The creature's long, sinewy arms and terrible, strong fingers were around his legs. He kicked at it but the alien swatted away the blows and rolled him on his back. Victor flailed at the creature's face and punched it on the top of its head.

The alien sprung to its feet and kicked Victor in the stomach. The pain rocked him into the fetal position and he threw up.

The alien kicked him again in the kidneys.

"You don't have to do this," Victor said desperately.

The alien sat on Victor's stomach. It put Victor's arms under his knees. Across the rooftops of Belfast a church bell sounded the half hour.

Victor's legs were numb but he tried kicking anyway.

The alien pushed down with all his weight, pinning him harder.

No, Victor thought. *No! I came here to find the boy Jamie so that our agents could kill him and save the world. This isn't how it's supposed to be This is all wrong, all wrong.* With an almighty kick Victor shoved the alien off him. Before it could react he scrambled to his feet and began running blindly.

Unfortunately he was running in the wrong direction.

He tumbled down the embankment and fell into the river again.

"Oh please—" he managed as he felt hands violently

grip his shoulders. Before he could say anything more he was being plunged beneath the water and held there.

He fought against it. The powerful creature's arms dragged him to the surface.

Victor stopped gasped for air. His head was spinning. His world was turning inside out.

"Jamie dies, not me," Victor said in dazed indignation.

The creature said nothing.

But Victor knew that it was going to kill him. The first death of the many, many deaths to come.

The alien's hands went around Victor's throat.

It plunged him under again.

The murky water.

The black sky.

Who was this thing that was killing him? What was it? A dybbuk? A specter? The devil himself?

He looked at it through the water. It had the shape of a scarecrow. The clouds ate it up. And now he was falling. Falling into the earth itself. Down, down, through the river bottom, past the bones of mammoths, the remains of dinosaurs.

The creature pulled him to the surface again. "Who—who are you?" Victor gurgled as the last of his strength ebbed from his body.

But it was too late. Too late . . .

He let go.

The fate of the world was no longer his concern. It would be up to others now.

"Where is Jamie of the Ui Neill?" the alien demanded.

Victor's eyes closed for the final time. Blackness came down from the sky. A splinter of the Dark enveloping him in its terrible shroud.

It was done.

The alien let the limp body drift a little into the current.

He had been too rough on the puny human. An Altairian would have withstood more punishment, even one of those effete Aldanese.

He would know better next time.

But the human's question hung in the air unanswered.

The alien looked at his reflection fluttering in the river water.

"Who am I? Who am I?" the alien said aloud, seeming to ponder the inquiry for a long time before his full title came flooding back from the basement rooms of his memory. "I will tell you who I am, human. I am Ksar, of the Ninth House of Alkhav, General of the Armies, Lord Protector of the Alkhavan People."

Ksar stepped out of the water and climbed the embankment, dragging the dead man after him.

He looked at the river and the hospital and the city lights beyond.

"Aye, I am Ksar, come to seek my place on Earth," he proclaimed. "And when the Ui Neill and his retainers are dead like ye, human, all will know my name and tremble at its very utterance." He knelt and began stripping Victor of his clothes.

Chapter IV
THE ASSASSIN

THE AIR IN BEIJING was as clear and lovely as the Yangtze River. In other words, it was yellow, thick, filled with chemicals, pollutants, and dead things.

Michael Lee placed the shutter back against the window and let the phone continue to ring.

"Another horrible day," he said to Nadia, the stray cat he had adopted and cared for these last few months.

The cat said nothing.

The phone went into message mode, and then after the caller refused to leave a message, whoever it was immediately began calling again.

Lee sighed.

It was important, then.

He picked it up.

"Yes?" he said irritably.

"Lee, it's Dan Connolly. I want you to head into the office for a briefing. Go now and don't get followed."

"I'm in the middle of something," Lee said.

"Whatever you're working on isn't as important as this. Now hang up, get dressed, and get into the office," Dan said.

"I won't be able to leave the building until the security police change their shifts," Lee said.

"When will that be?" Dan asked.

"About an hour," Lee said.

"Well, get a move on when you can. This is an emergency," Dan said irritably.

"You want to tell me what this is about?" Lee asked.

"Not on this connection, just get into the office," Dan said.

The line went dead. Lee rubbed at the stubble on his long, angular chin. He was a good-looking if somewhat skinny character with gray eyes and a penetrating, intelligent face. He was from San Francisco and his name was Lee, so maybe that's why Dan Connolly, whom he'd never met, had sent him to Beijing. Everyone thought he was Chinese American, but in fact, he was a typical German-Irish mix.

"I better go. Whatever they're cooking up isn't going to be pretty," he said to the cat.

Why's that? the cat seemed to wonder with its cocked head and quizzical expression.

He picked it up and stroked its neck.

"You'll see," he said.

He waited until his watch said exactly eleven A.M. before he opened the ground-floor window and slipped out into the filthy blackness of the *hutong*. The sweep had cleared the garbage from the courtyard itself but the walls were thick with soot from two-stroke engines, coal dust from the city's power plants, and the thin red sand that had blown in all the way from Mongolia.

Lee walked along the alley and noted another thin stray cat. He reached into his pocket, unfolded a piece of tinfoil, and gave it a piece of dumpling, which it ate with relish. Still, he knew the wretched thing wouldn't last long in these streets. It would be better to strangle the poor creature.

He stood and shivered and kept his Italian shoes out of the reeking potholes as he walked along the alley. *Hutongs* were becoming rarer and rarer in Beijing as the authorities demolished entire neighborhoods to make way for high-rise apartment buildings and shopping complexes. The Summer Olympics had only accelerated this process.

Old Hang nodded to him at the gate. Hang was a kind of security guard for the residents who lived off Xo Hutong in the center of the city. Hang knew everyone by name, knew what they did, knew what their families did.

He was always there, he never seemed to sleep, and there was no other way around him. Hang knew or suspected that Lee was a spy working for the Americans.

"Morning, Mr. Lee," Hang said in a fast Beijing ghetto dialect.

Lee smiled and approached the heavy iron gate that led into the street beyond.

"Am I too early, Mr. Hang?" Lee asked.

"No," Hang replied, and sat back in his dirty glass booth, which was stocked with cigarettes, American candy bars, and the day's newspapers. There was an electric heater and a small black-and-white TV tuned to a channel playing pop songs. Even at this cold, unholy hour, Hang seemed alert and watchful. Hang handed him the book he'd borrowed—an English title with Chinese characters. *The Grasshopper Lies Heavy.*

"Like it?" Lee asked.

Hang shrugged.

"Tell me, Mr. Hang, what's happening in the wide world today?" Lee asked.

Hang looked at him warily.

"The usual," he said.

Lee opened the door to Hang's booth and passed him a crisp ten-dollar bill. Without any subtlety at all, Mr. Hang held it up to the light and examined it carefully, checking that it wasn't one of the forgeries from North Korea.

"You didn't see me today, Mr. Hang," Lee suggested with the slightest of winks.

Hang took the money in his old-man's hand and put it in the pocket of his jerkin.

"Yesterday I noticed that you had a cold. You must

have decided to spend the whole day today in bed," Hang said, grinning toothlessly.

"Very good," Lee replied.

Without another word, Mr. Hang opened the big iron gate and let Lee out into the street. Lee looked at his watch.

It read 11:06. He had nine minutes.

He slunk into the shadows, being careful not to be seen or to step on anything significant.

He looked for the black Mercedes but it wasn't there.

He smiled to himself.

The secret police had a scary reputation but they were still bureaucrats—well-paid civil servants, and Lee knew how to use that to his advantage. From careful observation he knew that at precisely 11:00 the night crew watching the entrance to his street left their position to go home to bed. The day watchers were supposed to take over at 11:01, but they didn't usually arrive until 11:15 because they stopped at a famous noodle stand just around the corner to get the very first lunch soup of the day.

That gave Lee a fifteen-minute window to leave his house without anyone ever knowing about it.

He hurried across the broad avenue and hid behind a cypress tree until he saw the Mercedes pull up on the far side of the street.

Perfect.

He ducked down Red Victory Street, and within fifteen minutes he was at the back gate of the embassy annex off Tiananmen Square.

Tiananmen Square of course was packed with secret police watching for Om Shinry Kuo protesters or foreigners trying to pass out Bibles or student protestors, or anything really. So they paid no attention to him.

He nodded to the giant portrait of Mao, muttered "Horrible old gangster" under his breath, and went into the embassy annex.

No one had managed to follow him. It had all worked out well, but now he was a little sorry he'd given Hang the ten dollars. Five would have been sufficient to keep his mouth shut. Ten would only inflate future transactions of this type and might be enough to get him very curious. Still, there was nothing he could do about it.

He opened the heavy steel gate with a key and crossed a garden filled with dead leaves. He paused at a massive, ornate, rusting metal fountain and gave it a kick. Water began squirting from the blowhole of a Yellow River dolphin.

He walked to a wooden door, took out another key, and entered the building.

It was too early even for the cleaning staff, but of course Genghis was there at the reception desk playing chess on one half of his computer screen and reading the BBC headlines on the other.

Genghis was from Fo Pok in Inner Mongolia—a passive, gentle character with thick glasses and a pathetic attempt at a beard on his cheeks. The nickname, of course, was ironic.

Next to him there was a Stars and Stripes that hadn't been dusted in months.

"Morning, Genghis. Is the old man in?"

"He's in. What kept you?"

"I had to avoid the watchers."

Genghis laughed. "Big deal," he said.

Lee ignored this slight. "Are you winning?"

"Easily. It's a college professor in Michigan. He thinks he's good but I can see right through him."

Lee nodded. "Shall we go in?"

"You go first, I want to finish the game, two minutes."

"How do you get the BBC?" Lee asked.

The BBC was banned in China, and it was impossible to get it even in the embassy.

"I have my ways," Genghis said mysteriously. Lee frowned. If a low-grade employee like Genghis could do it, it couldn't be that complicated.

Lee nodded and went into the room.

Incense was burning in one corner.

Xi was sitting in the center of a circle he had drawn

around himself in gold-colored chalk. Yarrow stalks were scattered over the floor in front of him and the *I Ching* was open on his lap.

Xi picked up the yarrow stalks in his bony hands and cast them in the air. He looked up a page in the *I Ching*.

"Oh, my people. I cry for you in this time. In my palms are my tears. Look. See. Do I lie?" he muttered to himself.

Lee ducked back outside the room.

"The old man's gone nuts," he said to Genghis.

Genghis shrugged. "Yeah, he's been like that since the phone call."

"What's going on?" Lee wondered.

"Above my pay grade," Genghis said.

"Helpful," Lee said and went back into the room.

Xi was easily eighty years old, probably much older. He was a former official in the pre-Communist government and had been working for the Americans since Chiang Kai-Shek fled to Taiwan. He was a withered, yellowy-brown, gray-haired, and stooped old man but somehow he still managed to carry himself with a tremendous dignity.

For fear of arrest, Xi seldom left the embassy these days. He would probably die here. But that was OK. He could still walk in the garden, he could order food from the best of restaurants, and although he had no official standing, most of the diplomats were afraid of him.

Lee was a little afraid himself this morning because of this weird display.

Xi picked up the yarrow stalks and threw them again.

The muttering recommenced not long after. "You speak of things of which you have no understanding. No. On the black coast there is no walker and no voice. A long finger against the Earth and the breakers. He lives in the west where men in silk sip from liquid boiled in the commerce of leaves and air . . ."

Lee kneeled on the cushions that were scattered willy-nilly over the mahogany floor.

Xi became aware of his presence.

"Good morning," Xi said in perfect, slightly British-accented English.

"Good morning, sir," Lee replied.

"You have been to Ireland before?" Xi asked.

Lee was taken aback by the question. Xi seldom asked about personal histories or families. He made it a policy not to get too attached to his agents in case they wound up in a Chinese gulag or, more likely, dead.

"No, never been to Ireland," Lee said.

Xi's old-man face wrinkled so intensely that Lee couldn't help but be reminded of Yoda.

"I spent a year in London, though," Lee offered.

"That was not my question," Xi remarked.

Xi looked at the yarrow stalks on the floor, concealed the copy of the *I Ching* he'd been consulting in a sleeve of his hand-tailored silk peasant jerkin, and leaned back on the cushions.

There was a long period of silence. Lee was used to this.

"You are from San Francisco, is that not so?" Xi asked.

Lee nodded.

Xi sighed.

"Well, there are sages even in San Francisco," Xi said sadly.

Finally Lee could take no more of this nonsense. "What's got into you today, Mr. Xi?" Lee asked.

Xi smiled.

"I spoke to Dan Connolly in Langley, Virginia," Xi said.

"Yeah, he called me too. Told me to come see you," Lee said.

Xi nodded.

"We are sending you to Ireland, Michael. We want you to find a boy called Jamie, and when you find him, we want you to terminate him," Xi said.

Lee took a second to digest this information.

"A kid? Don't think I've ever terminated a child before," Lee said.

Xi shook his head. "He or his accomplices have already killed a man called Victor Astatin, a precog working for Dan Connolly. The boy is dangerous," Xi said seriously.

But Lee wasn't having any of it. "A kid? Come on."

"The boy will bring great destruction to this world," Xi insisted.

"Oh yeah?"

"Let me ask you a question. Would you have killed Hitler if you'd had the chance when he was a teenager?"

"If I was a time traveler?"

"Yes."

Lee nodded reluctantly. "I suppose so," he said.

"That is the case with this child. It is the belief of those at Langley that he will cause the destruction of our entire planet."

Lee scoffed. "How can anyone know a thing like that?" he said.

"The CIA employs a team of psychics who have been working for them since September 11. They have been using various methods to gaze into the future . . . Just as we in China have been using the *I Ching* for generations."

Lee nodded. So that explained the yarrow stalks on the floor and Mr. Xi's crazy rambling. He expected this sort of thing from an octogenarian Chinese man but not from the CIA, which was obviously wasting good tax-payer money on this madness.

"I can see the skepticism on your face, Lee. It is important that you believe me. Please allow me to explain how it works in Western terms," Xi said calmly but firmly.

"Go ahead," Lee said.

"According to your physicists, every single event in the universe, big and small, creates a probability wave that extends into the past as well as into the future. The bigger the event, the more likely we are to know about it. The more likely that hints about it will leak backward," Xi said.

"OK," Lee said.

"For some time the psychics working for Victor Astatin have been receiving hints about a very big event. An event that is caused by a boy in Ireland. A boy called Jamie."

"All right, you've hooked me, go on," Lee said.

"The team kept seeing an image of a man in a coma in a hospital in Belfast, Northern Ireland. Victor went out to Ireland to question this man, but the man or the boy called Jamie killed Victor, drowning him in the River Lagan."

"The man woke from his coma?" Lee asked.

"Apparently Victor attempted to wake him, to question him."

"Whose idea was that?"

"Dan Connolly's."

"Hmmm," Lee said. Typical CIA stunt.

"So, Dan and I would like you to go to Ireland to find the man in the coma or the boy and if necessary terminate both of them," Xi said.

"Because of what a bunch of psychics say?" Lee said with an ironic grin.

Xi became angry.

"This is not a matter for levity. You will go to Ireland and you will obey your orders."

Lee nodded, somewhat taken aback.

"I've never disobeyed an order yet," he said. "Just a little wary about killing some kid on the word of a bunch of frea—uh, people who claim to see the future."

"The hints are becoming stronger. Even I, who have no gift, have seen them in the *I Ching*," Xi said, pointing again at the yarrow stalks on the floor.

There followed a long period of silence that Lee broke with a cough.

"What troubles you?" Mr. Xi asked.

"I don't know, sir, I don't know. Everything. The CIA has hundreds of agents, dozens of—" Lee began, but he couldn't bring himself to say "hit men," or even worse, "assassins."

"Continue," Mr. Xi said.

"Well, there are a lot of people who do what I do for the agency, so why me? Why a man who is on the other side of the world? I'm sure they have people, good people, in England or Ireland right now, who could do this job."

Xi's lips thinned.

"I will tell you the truth, Lee. Dan Connolly called me and requested you because he knew that I would believe him. He knows of my interests in the Holy Oracle. He knows that I approve of the work of Section 22. Most of the other field officers do not. Dan was skeptical himself until Victor was killed, but like the famous convert on the road to Damascus, he is now an ardent advocate."

"So this hit on the boy has not been approved by the CIA director or by the president?" Lee asked.

"That I cannot tell you, but Dan has given me an official order and I have passed it on to you," Xi said.

Lee frowned. "I'll want that order in writing," he said.

"You shall have it," Xi assured him. "Now, are you done questioning the wisdom of your superiors or is there more to come?"

"I'm done," Lee said.

"Good."

Xi reached into the pocket of his jerkin and passed across a paper wallet containing air tickets.

Lee looked at them. Beijing to London, London to Belfast, the first of these flights leaving in one hour.

"You're not giving me much time, are you?" Lee said.

"No. You must leave immediately. Time is of the essence. Immediately after the man in the coma murdered Victor Astatin, a member of his team back in Washington, a precog called Fiona Arroyo, began having visions."

Lee tried to keep the sarcastic look off his face. "Visions," he said.

"Yes. She was the first one to see the man in the coma, then she came up with the name of the boy. Now she has seen visions of a certain day in the future. A date. We have been given a date," Xi explained.

"What date?"

"December 21, 2012," Xi said.

"OK, I'll bite, what's supposed to happen on that particular date?" Lee said.

Xi looked very serious for a moment.

"That, my friend, is the date of the end of the world," he said.

At the honking of a car horn, Thaddeus put down his copy of the newspaper and looked out the window. He had been reading an article about the Mayan civilization, the only culture on Earth whose view of "deep time" was close to the actual age of the universe. The Mayans actually predicted the world was going to end in a few years, but the big problem with the Mayans (as Thaddeus had once told Jamie) was how could you believe anything from a people who hadn't even invented the wheel?

The car honked again.

"The taxi's here," Thaddeus called out, and gamely attempted to quash the dread that had been on his face all morning.

He caught his reflection in the window.

It was still there. A look that was worse than that which appears on the faces of those poor souls who realize that they'll have to go to the post office on a Friday afternoon, worse than that of the man who discovers that the person next to him on a long-haul flight is a salesman, and perhaps worse even than the dread that comes upon all of us when we realize that the only place left that the TV remote can possibly be is between the cushions at the back of the moldering brown sofa.

Thaddeus's horror was more lingering and more intense. He had volunteered to look after two teenagers for an entire week.

Anna came rushing down the stairs with two suitcases, a backpack, and a shoulder bag.

"How long are you going to London for?" Thaddeus asked, a little satirically.

Anna grinned.

"I know, I know, we are only going to be away for eight days, but you never know what the weather is going to be like," she said with a touch of chagrin.

Brian appeared from the living room.

"I'm only bringing this," he said, lifting up a small backpack.

The taxi driver honked again. Brian grabbed Anna's bags and went outside.

"Kids, get down here!" Anna yelled upstairs.

Jamie and Wishaway came down from their rooms.

Anna hugged and kissed them.

"OK, you two, do everything Thaddeus tells you, and behave yourselves. I'll be back in a week."

"OK," Jamie and Wishaway said together.

"Come on, Anna!" Brian called from outside. "The driver's freaked out about getting back across the causeway."

"OK, bye, guys," she said, and then paused for a moment. Her expression became very somber. "And no going in the lighthouse until I get back, OK?"

"OK," Jamie said diffidently. He hardly ever went in there nowadays anyway.

Anna kissed them both again and went outside.

Thaddeus got up from his chair, and all three of them waved as Anna and Brian were driven back over the causeway to the mainland.

When they were inside again, Jamie immediately slinked off to the kitchen to indulge in the forbidden foods that his mother kept him from scarfing down. Wishaway slipped back upstairs. *No doubt*, Jamie thought, *to watch the Jerry Springer show while pretending to read* The Iliad. Thaddeus retired to his armchair and picked up the paper again.

Jamie opened the fridge.

"Ben and Jerry's Chubby Hubby, five greatest words in the language," he said to himself.

Upstairs, Wishaway was neither watching Springer nor reading *The Iliad.* Instead she was observing the taxi drive off the causeway into the village of Portmuck and having a good long think about things. She was wondering how Jamie would be without his mother for the next week, wondering how difficult it was going to be faking Icelandic characteristics for Thaddeus, and, not for the first time, wondering if everything was all right back on the planet Altair. Was her father still the Council president? Did the Alkhavans dare menace Aldan again? How were her old friends?

Generally she didn't worry too much about Altair, but perhaps Anna's departure had reminded her that she hadn't seen her own father for over a year and would never see him again.

She felt tears form in the corners of her eyes but

before they began dripping down her pale cheeks, she pulled herself together and got off the bed.

"Must do something," she said softly.

She had a small portable television, but in the mornings there was nothing on TV but "talk shows" that always seemed to feature men with pillowcases over their heads called Klansmen fighting with other men who were not wearing pillowcases.

She picked one of the books from the bookshelf. Anna had been very kind. She had bought her lots of nice clothes, CDs, and a whole bookcase full of books—though most of them had come from a jumble sale in Ballycarry where Anna had bought someone's complete collection of the Great Books in Literature series. There were 104 great books in the set, and Wishaway had now read most of them.

She began reading *Lord Jim,* one of the few she hadn't tackled.

It was, apparently, a sea story, and just like Jamie, the lord of the title seemed to get no respect from anyone.

In fact that was one of the things that surprised her most about Earth. Jamie, a great peer, the Laird of Muck, Guardian of the Passage, was actually considered quite *uncool* by most of her contemporaries at Carrickfergus Grammar School. Smallish, not very studious, shy, Jamie rarely attracted any interest. Whereas

Ramsay—tall, athletic, and clever—was considered among her friends to be the better catch . . . if Ramsay had ever had the nerve to ask any of the girls out.

Poor Jamie, Wishaway thought, wondering how it was she had started out feeling sorry for herself and once again ended up feeling sorry for him.

For some reason she remembered something Ramsay had said back on Altair. Humans and Altairians could never have children together because of a thing called DNA.

She put *Lord Jim* back on the shelf and flipped open her laptop.

She brought it to the window so the wireless would work, and looked up DNA on Wikipedia. It turned out to stand for deoxy-something. There was a picture of the molecule—it resembled a flight of stairs with basketballs at the ends of each step. It wasn't very interesting.

She closed the computer and looked out the window. Someone was cycling over the causeway. Probably the postman—not that there were ever any letters for her. How could there be?

She sighed and examined the Great Books set.

Whoever had owned these books had obviously been very religious or had had a child who they wanted to protect from the iniquities of the evil world. Many of the texts had been censored with a black felt-tip pen. *Moby-*

Dick was a mass of black ink and *Absalom, Absalom!* had had the last few chapters torn out. Earth novels were all like that: beautiful and fun, but also dark and terrifying. It was a planet (like all worlds, she supposed) that was full of contradictions.

She gazed out the window and was surprised to see that the cyclist pedaling madly over the causeway was Ramsay.

"Ramsay's coming!" Wishaway yelled downstairs.

Downstairs Thaddeus shook his head grumpily. "Another child," he muttered. He put down his newspaper. Didn't matter anyway. The *Belfast Telegraph*'s coverage of the New York Yankees left a lot to be desired, whereas they had three full pages on some outlandish game called hurling.

Jamie returned from his trip to the kitchen with chocolate biscuits and something in a brightly colored bag that smelled vile.

"Pork scratchings?" Jamie asked Thaddeus.

"What?"

"Pork scratchings?" Jamie asked again, offering a bag of this delicacy to the old man.

"Pork scratchings? I have never heard of such a thing. What barbarities have human beings sunk to now? How do they get it off the pig? Do they do it while it's alive? Periodically?"

Jamie had no idea.

"They kill the pig. It's very humane," he said.

Thaddeus shook his head. "I'm afraid I happen to agree with Dr. Johnson that pigs are very often unjustly treated. Of all the farm animals they are most intelligent and loyal. The opposite of sheep, even though I like sheep. Also recall what Winston Churchill said: 'Dogs look up to us. Cats look down on us. Pigs treat us as equals.'"

"This stuff is great," Jamie said, scarfing a big handful of the delicious Irish treat.

Thaddeus sighed. "You have been too long in this country. When was the last time you had Harlem cooking?"

"What do you mean? What's Harlem cooking?" Jamie asked.

"Soul food, boy, soul food. Maybe I'll make you something. Black-eyed peas, short ribs, sweet potato, corn bread. I'll show you pork. You got a good butcher in this town?"

"I don't know."

"I'll ask Ramsay," Thaddeus said.

"Ramsay? When's he coming?"

Before Thaddeus could reply, a breathless Ramsay appeared at the front door and barged into the Lighthouse House. He was wearing a red sweater and had his jeans tucked into his socks. He had obviously bicycled over from Portmuck.

"You just missed them," Jamie said.

"Who?" Ramsay asked, panting.

"Your brother, my mom," Jamie replied.

"Forget them, I got something to show you . . . Oh, hi, Thaddeus, how's Ireland treating you? Ah, see you've been at the pork scratchings. Wait till you try black pudding. Hey, we'll have to have that game of chess sometime . . . Jamie would you mind stepping outside with me for a moment."

Jamie examined Ramsay's wild eyes.

He knew that something was up.

With a pounding heart he followed his friend into Anna's little garden.

Ramsay unfolded a copy of the *Irish Independent* that he had shoved under the saddle of his bicycle.

"Let me guess, they published your story," Jamie said.

Ramsay shook his head.

"No, although that *is* why I've been getting the paper every day. Good job I did too. Take a look at this."

Ramsay thumbed through the paper until he found page five.

He pointed at a small article with the headline ARMADA TREASURE TROVE above a picture of a bespectacled man grinning broadly in a wet suit.

"What's this?" Jamie asked.

"Just read," Ramsay said.

Jamie read the article.

> In shallow waters off the north Antrim coast, an archaeological dive team from Queen's University Belfast and Trinity College Dublin have discovered what they believe to be the scattered remains of a ship from the Spanish Armada. In 1588, after the invasion of England was repulsed, the Spanish fleet headed north and west around the British Isles, where it was destroyed by Atlantic storms. Several galleons have been located over the years, the most famous of which, the *Girona*, was discovered almost intact in a similar spot off the coast of Northern Ireland. Although this find is not as spectacular as the *Girona*, several small objets d'art have been retrieved.
>
> Professor McGarraty of Queen's University's Department of Archaeology and Palaeoecology was particularly excited by a small metal fish sculpture

unlike anything ever seen before in Spanish metallurgy.

"We think this lovely bejeweled fish might be Central American in origin. Perhaps plunder from Cortéz's conquest of Mexico. It appears to be an original Aztec totem that, unlike much of that nation's heritage of gold working, was not melted down into bullion, maybe because of its extraordinary beauty. It's a very exciting find indeed," Prof. McGarraty said from his Belfast office. McGarraty is sending the Aztec totem to Edinburgh University for laser analysis tomorrow. "The results will be very exciting," he added.

Jamie passed the newspaper back to his friend.

"I don't get it," he said. "Why is this of any interest to me?"

Ramsay sighed impatiently.

"Look at the photograph. Look at the fish in the diver's left hand."

Jamie examined the grainy black-and-white shot of the ecstatic diver. There, covered with silt, in the man's left hand, was unmistakably the Salmon of Knowledge, the device that allowed you to leap through wormholes from world to world.

* * *

Dawn smeared the eastern horizon. Improbable violets, pinks, purples between the clouds. Day was stealing into the edges of the continent, and Europe was waking up.

Here, though, in an alley in a city on the continent's western fringe, all was quiet. The snow, that brief ghost of winter, was gone. In fact it was the vernal equinox today and spring was just around the corner.

Sergeant Dunleavy of the Police Service of Northern Ireland smiled and lit his cigar. These early-morning patrols were a doddle. No one around. No crime. Hardly anything to do at all. Perfect for breaking in a new officer—which was exactly what he was up to on this particular vernal equinox.

"Let's go down that alley, and keep your eye open for anyone trying to nick anything from a parked car," he said to Constable Peter Simmons.

"I don't see anyone at all," Constable Simmons replied.

Sergeant Dunleavy regarded his protégé dispassionately. He was a spotty, blond-haired youth who looked as if he would have had trouble arresting the Teletubbies.

"Aye, well, just keep your eyes open," Dunleavy said

gruffly, and attempted to relight his cigar without setting his moustache on fire.

They weren't too far from the Lagan, and all around them river and seabirds were hanging on telegraph wires and the eves of nearby churches. There was a sea breeze and a smell of oranges from a stack of packing crates.

A fragment of music drifted down from an upstairs window.

"I know that one," Dunleavy muttered and hummed the melody to himself.

"What is it?" Constable Simmons asked.

"Before your time, son. 'The Star of the County Down,' it's an old s— Wait a minute, look over there, do you see something? What's that behind those boxes?"

Constable Simmons drew his revolver.

"Put that away and get out your truncheon," Dunleavy whispered.

Simmons holstered the revolver and walked over to what appeared to be a dead body lying in the alley. A murder on his very first day on the job. How exciting.

General Ksar opened his eyes.

Two inches from his nose a pigeon was waddling through an oily puddle and above it a black raven was staring down at him from a telegraph pole. Ksar had only been out of his coma for about twelve hours but he already knew that he hated these nasty, flapping things that were everywhere on Earth. The planet was swarming with the brutes. And to go with these visions of terror, in the distance he could hear the horrible early-morning grumble of rolling machines, unknown on his world.

He closed his eyes.

He felt the sun warm his face.

Sooner or later he would have to get up. The alley was secluded but at any moment one of the humans could—

"You there, yeah you, I see you breathing, get on your feet," a voice said.

Ksar turned to see a pair of tall humans in dark green uniforms. One of them was pointing a stick at him. They were obviously soldiers of some kind and they carried muskets on their hips. Ksar groaned. He wasn't feeling up to yet another fight. He was hungry and the chill from the river had settled deep into his soul.

The adventures of last night had ended only a few hours ago.

After he had drowned the human he followed the Lagan all the way up into this enormous metropolis, and at the first sign of people, he had hidden here. He hadn't known where he was going to go or what he was going to do next. And now he was discovered.

"Did you not hear me? On your feet, tinker," the bigger of the two men said.

Ksar attempted to process the command.

"He's not doing it, Sergeant," Simmons said.

"This will learn him," Dunleavy said before gently kicking the Alkhavan twice in the legs.

Ksar cringed in agony, his whole body writhing in pain.

"It wasn't that hard . . . Now, do you want some more?" Dunleavy asked.

"No," Ksar said.

"Then get to your feet."

Ksar stood.

Gone was the defiance of last night. He felt weak and ill. He couldn't know that his strength of yesterday had come from the adrenaline. And naturally he was suffering the inevitable aftereffects. Ksar no longer wanted Earth to tremble at the mere mention of his name. Now all he wanted was a quiet corner where everyone would leave him alone.

"Sheesh. Look at him, Sergeant, look at those ears, what is he?" the younger of the two policemen asked his superior.

"Him? Plain as the nose on your face, Constable Simmons. He's a tinker, an Irish gypsy . . . a *Traveler* we're supposed to call them in these politically correct days. Probably a thief. Drunk and on the run from some jam more than likely."

"Aye, but look at his ears. Never seen a tinker with ears like that," Constable Simmons said.

The older man nodded and leaned in toward Ksar to get a good look.

"Yeah, jeez, look at thon. Did it to himself I'll bet. Or got a shady plastic surgeon to do it. I suppose you think that's very clever getting your ears done like Mr. Spock. I suppose you're one of those people always trying to be different. Ya probably have piercings all over your body too, don't ya? And look at you, drunk in an alley in the middle of Belfast. You're a disgrace, that's what you are. You're not 'cool.' You're a bloody disgrace," Dunleavy said in a hectoring tone. He'd been speaking so fast, Ksar had barely understood a world.

"*Kasa la vaa tamak,*" Ksar muttered, which meant, "I surrender."

He couldn't fight them, not when they had guns. And perhaps these two fellow military men would help him if he cooperated.

"Oh, that's the way it's going to be, is it? You're going to pretend you don't know English. Well, I know you know, so you can leave off with the Shelta or the Gaelic. I know you can understand me. Now put your hands behind your back. Booking you for vagrancy," the older man said.

"Food," Ksar said.

Dunleavy took out his revolver and pointed it at Ksar.

"See, Constable Simmons, told ya they can speak

English. They all can, really . . . Now you, enough of your silliness, put your hands behind your back."

Ksar considered trying to make a run for it but he was far too weak to resist, and anyway the men had made the decision easy by drawing their muskets.

"Food," he said again.

"You'll get some food. Get those arms behind yer back. Won't tell ya again, tinker," Dunleavy barked.

Ksar put his arms behind his back.

The two police officers cuffed him and led him to a police Land Rover that was parked on Donegall Place. It was early and there were few commuters. The shops weren't open, and even Starbucks had yet to get the coffee on.

They pushed Ksar into the back of the Land Rover and closed the door.

"Are you really going to book him for vagrancy?" Constable Simmons asked his superior.

The older cop shook his head.

"Nah, all that paperwork over a homeless tinker? You must be joking, mate. And if we bunged him in a cell, I guarantee you we'd have to delouse it the very next day. And we'd find that a lot of the things in the station had mysteriously gone missing, and, well, there's the other thing too . . ." Sergeant Dunleavy said with either a wink or a nervous twitch shooting across his face.

"What other thing?" Constable Simmons asked.

"Well, I'll tell you, they can do things, tinkers can, things that aren't quite right, you know what I mean?"

Simmons shook his head.

"My ma went to see one who read palms. Every single thing that woman predicted came true. I'm not saying I believe it, mind, but I want to be on the safe side. Don't want any tinker's curse on me. Even if it's not true, it's the sort of thing that can play with your mind," Dunleavy said.

Constable Simmons nodded.

"So if you're not going to book him, what are you going to do with him, Sergeant?"

Sergeant Dunleavy rubbed his chin.

"Take him to that big tinker camp in Carrickfergus. They'll look after their own. Tell him to keep his nose clean and stay out of Belfast," Dunleavy said.

"And if we do that, we won't get cursed?" Constable Simmons asked, with a worried expression on his face.

"Yeah, we'll be fine," Sergeant Dunleavy assured him.

They got in the car and drove north out of Belfast along the shore road.

Ksar could see nothing in the back of the armor-plated Land Rover. He sat on a cold metal bench, shivering, while the strange carriage bumped him down along the road.

Perhaps he had made a mistake coming here to Earth in the first place.

Things were not turning out quite as he was expecting.

Sergeant Dunleavy drove the police Land Rover through Belfast and turned left on Victoria Road, the major thoroughfare to Victoria, one of Carrickfergus's toughest estates. They headed north past red-brick council houses, pubs, and off-licenses until Victoria Road became Victoria Lane and the view on either side of the muddy track was of brambly hedges, boggy cow fields, and crumbling stone walls.

They came at last to the tinker camp.

Irish Travelers, though unrelated to Romany-speaking gypsies, essentially filled the same role as their cross-water counterparts. A nomadic, tribal people of unknown origin, they were often the victims of prejudice and had to move whenever relations with their host community went bad.

When they first arrived in a town or village, many people, especially the local children, were happy to see them. They brought horses, chip vans, sometimes a mini carnival, fortune-tellers, and, best of all, skilled black-smiths who could repair watches, cars, and other machinery.

This camp was no different.

For Simmons it was remarkable.

There were two dozen small caravans, several large tents, scores of horses, and ragamuffin children running about everywhere in a large boggy field.

A small Ferris wheel was turning in one corner, and everywhere there was the smell of funnel cake, chips, kebabs, and charcoal braziers, over which intent men with beards and tattoos were heating metal tools that would then be beaten into shape on anvils.

The Land Rover pulled to a halt and the two police officers got out.

Sergeant Dunleavy opened the rear door and took out General Ksar. By the time he had undone Ksar's handcuffs there was already a small crowd gathered around the policemen.

"Who's in charge here?" Dunleavy asked.

A surprisingly young man wearing a green trench coat covered with badges and wildflowers pushed himself to the front of the crowd. Dunleavy looked him up and down. Apart from the eccentric coat, he was wearing a tatty brown sweater, army surplus boots, and a filthy, shapeless hat that did little to contain his shoulder-length brown hair. He was pale-skinned and red-bearded and he couldn't have been more than twenty-five or twenty-six.

"I'm the Gypsy King, what do ye want with us?" he asked in lilting country Irish voice.

"One of your own here. Drunk and disorderly in the city. We were going to lift him, but we thought we'd give him a second chance. Can youse keep him out of trouble?"

The Gypsy King took a long look at General Ksar. He certainly didn't look like any tinker he had ever seen before.

"Buri talosk," he said in Shelta, the Travelers' cant that was a mishmash of English and Gaelic.

Ksar nodded at this obvious greeting.

"Aye, we'll have him. Get him cleaned up, fed, so we will. Come on, you. I'll bet you're starving so ye are," the Gypsy King said.

General Ksar nodded eagerly.

The Gypsy King took Ksar by the sleeve of the dead man's shirt.

"No more getting drunk and crashing in Belfast alleys," Sergeant Dunleavy cautioned.

"I'll take care of him," the Gypsy King said, and shook Sergeant Dunleavy by the hand.

The policemen nodded, climbed back in the Land Rover, and drove off. When the vehicle was out of sight and halfway down Victoria Lane, the Gypsy King examined the watch he had stolen from Dunleavy's wrist.

"Hmm, not bad, get a few quid for that," he said, and gave the watch to Ksar. Ksar took it, unsure what it actually was. The Gypsy King dispersed the crowd of children hanging about him. "Go on, you lot, get out of here," he said.

Ksar looked at the watch in wonder.

"What is this?" he asked.

"Compensation. OK, let's go. You seem a bit shaken up. Don't worry about it, mate, we've all been nicked from time to time. Let's get some food down your neck."

The Gypsy King led Ksar to a fish-and-chip van parked at the edge of the field. He ordered a plate of fish-and-chips, and when it came they sat down on the grass to eat it.

Ksar devoured the hot fried potatoes with relish and enjoyed the deep-fried cod even more.

"Nice bit of work on the ears there, mate, if you don't mind me saying so. Very different," the Gypsy King said.

Ksar nodded and continued to wolf down the food.

"I'm Rory. No, don't shake me hand, keep eating there, looks like you're starving. Hmm, so what can we do with you? Things are a bit hand-to-mouth here. You have to earn your keep. What can you do?"

Ksar shrugged.

"What skills do you have? Can you fix machinery? What are you qualified to do?"

Ksar's eyes narrowed. He could sail an iceship onto a foreign shore, he could besiege a city, he could order men to their deaths, he could storm a castle, he could terrify subordinates with a single glance.

"Nothing," he said.

"Nothing? Hmm. OK, let me see, you seem to like the chips . . . Have you worked with hot oil?"

Ksar's men had been bombarded with hot oil on their invasion of Aldan City. Many had died, many more had suffered terrible burns.

"Yes," he said.

"Good. Well, in that case, after ye get a kip and a wash and some more grub down yer neck, we'll get you working in the chip van."

"The chip van?" said Ksar.

The Gypsy King banged the vehicle parked next to them with the palm of his hand.

"Aye, the chip van," he said.

Ksar returned to his fish supper, and when he was done the Gypsy King ordered another.

They sat in silence and ate.

Chapter V
THE COOK

A SKY MADE OF SNOWFLAKES. An uneasy song from the herds of pack animals. A long moment of expectation. Time ebbing itself out in folded seconds . . .

The Thirty-third Witch Queen looked at the Lord Protector with deep sadness in her eyes.

"We have failed them, then," she said.

Lord Protector Krama winced and adjusted the scarf covering his mouth.

"That word is perhaps a little too final," he croaked into the relentless north wind.

The Witch Queen considered this for a moment.

"No, I think it is appropriate. We have failed," the Witch Queen said, her voice descending into a whisper.

She knew that she felt this pain more than the others. More than the Lord Protector, whose home city was a hundred leagues south of here. More than the civilians who had been kept here against their will for decades. More than her personal retinue.

More than all of them, because she would be losing her home, her revenue, and her throne.

For how could you be queen of a city that shortly would no longer even exist?

She had only been ruler of Balanmanik for a brief time. Less than a year.

All her life she had dreamed of rising to the very top of the order of the Black Sisterhood, and now at the very apex of her career, she saw how empty and meaningless it all was.

It had been harder for her than for most. She was a peasant who'd risen to this exalted position through cunning and hard work. Her grandmother had served the famous Twenty-seventh Queen—the great lady who had done so much to secure the future of Alkhavan people. She herself had been the personal attendant to the Thirty-second Queen, the sister of the former Lord Protector. A strong, proud woman who had been so brutally slain by the Prince of Oralands. Though perhaps it was fortunate that the Thirty-second Queen had died when she did and that she had not lived long enough to see the glacier's ultimate triumph over her beloved city.

The Queens of Balanmanik had ruled this portion of Alkhava for over a thousand years, but now their power base, their home, was on the verge of destruction.

With the surprising death of the Thirty-second

Queen, Tara had quickly poisoned two other candidates for the Queenship, killed a third in her sleep, and finally, after a few bribes and a few threats, she had gotten herself elected to the purple throne. All that trouble and conspiracy, all those months of toil to become the very last ruler of this doomed city.

In fact, the bigger picture was even more depressing— all those centuries of scheming, scrabbling for survival, all those wars, treaties, alliances, sneak attacks, raids . . . all come to naught.

The Witch Queen was lost in thought when suddenly there was a loud groan from the battlements.

"It won't be long now," Krama said with resignation.

Tara looked up.

He was right. It *wouldn't* be long now, and the small crowd of bodyguards and attendant servants watched with some measure of mixed horror and fascination as the great Gag Macak glacier shoved again at the Vancha Tower of Balanmanik.

Yes, it was cold out here on the exposed road to Balan Port, but this was an epoch-ending moment, this was something you'd tell your grandchildren about.

The monstrous glacier had already overwhelmed the Balanmanik city walls, crushing them, undermining them, ultimately destroying them. And every season since, it had moved closer and closer to the city center.

Annihilating the makeshift defenses, rolling over the markets, temples, houses, wiping the slate clean of everything.

And now after wreaking havoc on the helpless city it had pushed up against the Black Tower itself.

"My lady, the former Queen, hated the phrase 'Black Tower,'" Tara muttered, more to herself than anything.

"Indeed?" Krama said, interested.

"Yes, she said that it was called the Vancha Tower, that only the uneducated or foreigners referred to it as the Black Tower, that it was a holy place built by the Old Ones."

Krama nodded. Whatever name you called it would soon be academic. It wasn't going to be here tomorrow.

The tower had been here in this spot since before recorded history had begun, and now history was going to end with the tower's destruction.

Evacuation had been inevitable for the final few months, but the Witch Queen had delayed it until the very last possible day. Only her court, a squadron of soldiers, and, in a show of great courtesy, the Lord Protector and his party would be witness to the conclusion.

"In Afor we will build you a new tower. The institution of the Queen will go on, your order will . . ." Krama began, but the Witch Queen silenced him with a hand.

"No, no," she smiled affectionately. "None of that will be necessary. My sisters and I will retire to a quiet corner of the castle to await the inevitable there too."

Krama nodded. The inevitable. He knew that the glacier would not be content with swallowing Balanmanik. The thing was insatiable. It wanted all of Alkhava for its own. After Balanmanik then Balan Port, then all of the Besha coast, and then it would march south to take Carra and finally Afor and its surroundings.

None would be safe.

Just as his old mentor Ksar had predicted—it wasn't merely Balanmanik that was imperiled. It was the whole country. The whole Alkhavan people.

He adjusted the furs around his shoulders and sighed, his breath condensing as ice on his beard.

Another large groan came from the base of the tower, and in the distance a messenger *ranta* cried out in terror.

"But it doesn't have to be that way," Krama muttered to himself.

No, he mused, *things are not yet so dire.* They weren't beaten quite yet. The third royal personage who was here this melancholy morning would help see to that.

"There, look!" one of the younger Black Sisters cried.

And sure enough, the south side of the Black Tower had begun to sway.

The watchers gasped as the tower's angle of tilt increased first to ten degrees, then to thirty, and then to a dizzying forty-five.

The thousand-foot-high structure was being bulldozed to the ground by the awesome and unstoppable power of the ice.

"If you insist on retiring to a quiet corner, then your retirement must be brief, Queen of Balan, for we will need your help," Krama said to the beautiful Tara.

She looked at him.

"Indeed, Lord Protector?" she wondered.

"Indeed. I have learned much at the feet of the late Lord Protector Ksar, and since his unfortunate disappearance I have learned much more. I have consulted the guilds. I have read books in the Lord Protector's library. Even the forbidden books, *The Book of Stories* from Earth and the observations of the Star Watchers. I have learned much. I have learned that nature is not malevolent, Queen Tara. It is not evil. It has no sinister purpose. It is what it is. There are laws that govern the movement of the heavens, laws that explain how much water is displaced from the tub when you enter for your yearly bath, even laws regarding life and death."

The Queen looked at him with interest.

"Why do you tell me this?" she asked.

"The Aldanese and perhaps even the old Lord Protectors would have claimed that this catastrophe was a punishment on the Alkhavan people for some transgression against the ice gods. But no, that is not the case.

This is merely the cold, merciless operation of nature at her most indifferent. We are not being singled out, we are not being punished. Our future is what we will make of it," Krama said.

The Witch Queen nodded.

"I think I understand," she said carefully.

"You do understand, my Queen. And perhaps you see why I have invited here Prince Lanar of Oralands to witness this event."

The Witch Queen said nothing.

Prince Lanar was the direct heir of King Laman. It was his son who had killed the Thirty-second Queen; but for the rules of etiquette regarding a guest (and also his retinue of heavily armored guards), she might have been tempted to slay him in revenge.

The Prince was mounted on a *draya* and heavily wrapped in *hoxney* fur. As soon as the tower fell, she knew that he would return to his state coach, where a brazier and hot food was awaiting him, as royal personages from balmy Oralands felt the cold much more than the tough peoples of Alkhava.

"I long to hear of your plans, Lord Protector Krama," Tara said softly.

Krama smiled.

Her cheeks were red and her blue eyes radiant. How had he never noticed her beauty before? He grimaced and checked these thoughts before they got started. This was not the time for distractions . . .

"No, we are not being singled out by the ice gods . . . I know that this is a view held among the minority of us gathered here this morning, but it does give some crumb of comfort, eh, Queen Tara?" Krama said.

The Witch Queen allowed a smile to appear on her lips.

And there they waited.

Prince Lanar retired to his carriage early.

Shortly after noon the sun briefly appeared.

Then it began to snow.

The Black Tower of Balanmanik had been built well and it wasn't until almost dusk that it finally broke at the base and smashed into the ground with a tremendous roar.

At first no one could quite believe what they were witnessing, but as the terrible grinding crash reached the observation hill on the Great South Road, a mighty wail rose from the throats of the watchers.

"Oh! Oh!"

Dust rose in black vortices over the city like evil specters—and even the disciplined *kalahars* of the Queen's escort whimpered in distress.

Summoned from his wagon, the third royal visitor present mounted his well-groomed *draya* and rode over to the Lord Protector.

"Well, it's done," the Prince of Oralands said in passable Alkhavan.

"Yes, it is finished," Krama replied in English.

"Now what?" Prince Lanar said, stifling a cough.

"Art thou well?" Krama asked.

"Perfectly," the Prince said, knowing he could not afford to lose face by showing just how miserable he felt.

Krama nodded. "Now what? Now, my dear Prince, we must discuss the future."

Lanar smiled. "I hope, honored Lord Protector, that this has not discouraged you or led you to have a change of heart."

"On the contrary, it has made me more determined," Krama insisted. "As you can see, we Alkhavans have little to lose and much to gain."

Prince Lanar sniffed. "I do not mean to be insulting, Lord Protector, but your predecessors' successes in this field have been somewhat . . . limited."

Krama nodded. He knew well that Lanar was hinting at the failed invasions initiated by both previous Lord Protectors.

"This time we will not fail. The Aldanese cannot withstand assault from our armies simultaneously," Krama said.

"And the Ui Neills?"

"It is the assessment of our spies that the Ui Neills will not return for many centuries," Krama said.

"A pity, I would like to have dealt with them by mine own hand," Lanar said bitterly.

Bitterly, Krama knew, because Lanar blamed the Ui Neill for the death of his youngest, least promising, but favorite son, Lorca. Indeed, on assuming the mantle of Lord Protector it had been one of Krama's very first orders to find the body of that dashing prince. That achieved, he then sent emissaries to Oralands with the tragic news that the beloved young royal had been murdered and his bride stolen by Jamie, Lord of the Ui Neill, in an example of that high-handed cruelty so typical of the Ui Neills in their dealings with Altairians.

Lanar had been unable to do anything at all to avenge the death of his son until the ill-starred accident that had befallen his own father during a drinking binge. The old King had had some kind of stroke and was now in an irreversible coma. Rumors that King Laman had been poisoned were immediately quashed—and those who spread these rumors had met with untimely and unfortunate ends.

But now that he was Crown Prince of Oralands and commander of the imperial armies and navy, Lanar was in thrall to no one.

He could do as he wished.

And what he wished was to see justice for his poor dead son.

With an honor guard and in a specially commissioned iceship, Acting Lord Protector Krama had sent back Prince Lorca's body in a coffin made of crystal blue ice.

Lanar's eyes filled with tears recalling that moment.

By the moons and stars, the boy had looked as if he was only sleeping! Ice on his beautiful eyelashes and a frown on his blue lips.

And the Ui Neill had killed Lorca in order to steal that daughter of Aldan, Wishaway. He had never trusted her. Doubtless she had been a willing victim.

Now the people of Aldan, those Chosen People who had been the favorites of the Ui Neills for the last millennium, would feel the wrath of a grieving monarch.

"Shall we ride to Afor?" Krama said to Lanar. "On the journey, I wish to inform the Witch Queen of our plans. Her acumen will be of assistance to us."

"Yes, we shall go," Lanar agreed.

Any place was better than this blasted wasteland.

"Vaama kak, essessa kak!" Krama ordered and almost immediately the desultory caravan of wagons, *kalahars*, *drayas*, and foot soldiers began the march south to Balan Port.

Crown Prince Lanar rode boldly next to the Lord Protector for half a league without asking for his additional fur cloak. He even refused a goblet of mulled Kafrakillan wine from his retainers. He wanted his head to be clear. In fact he inwardly vowed there and then that he would touch no intoxicant until the mighty and oh-so-proud people of Aldan were at his mercy.

Our mercy, he corrected himself.

For the plan was that the western portion of Aldan would be given to Alkhavans as their new home. The eastern portion—from the Great Forest to the sea—would become a vassal of Oralands. The Aldanese men, women, and children would be enslaved, or, if they proved difficult, put to the sword.

And this time the invasion would not fail.

The Alkhavans would ride in Oralands ships and the two countries' combined forces would destroy the capital in a surprise attack.

The Aldanese would have no chance.

For a moment, Crown Prince Lanar was able to block the *draya*'s snorts and the terrible wind and the wailing of the Witch Queen's sisterhood and let his mind wander to a time in the future when all would bear witness to his triumphal entry into the city of Aldan.

He would ride through the streets in a golden chariot just as the Romans had done in Morgan of the Red Hand's *Book of Stories.*

"Sire, your mirth is attracting attention," an aide

whispered in his ear. And sure enough, when he opened his eyes he found that the Witch Queen and Lord Protector were staring at him.

He nodded grimly.

"A terrible tragedy. But soon you will have a new home for your people," he said in a loud, confident voice.

The Lord Protector nodded.

But after a minute Lanar's mind began to drift again . . . yes, soon it would be nothing but triumphs—gold, riches, and a pretty Aldanese maiden as a concubine or even a wife. With the will of Kel he would have a new daughter or a new darling son to love and cherish above all others.

And perhaps then, over time, his grief and the dull ache in his memory would be wiped clean, just as this icy northern world was cleansed by the awful inevitability of the Gag Macak.

Constable Simmons peered at the CIA man anxiously. He wiped his sweaty hands on the back of his jeans.

"Have I done anything wrong?" he asked.

Michael Lee shook his head.

"As far as I know you've done nothing wrong," Lee said. "Except for obstructing a murder inquiry."

"It wasn't my job to file the report about the homeless

man, I'm not even officially a police officer yet," Simmons said. "Sergeant Dunleavy said that weird homeless dude wasn't important. He said we could just forget it."

Lee nodded and looked about the constable's small Belfast apartment. There was nothing remotely distinguished about it. A tiny television set, a stack of rock CDs, a CD player. The room was dull, ordinary, and pedestrian. Posters on the wall: Zep, the Raconteurs, the Arctic Monkeys. A bookcase full of unread volumes, spines broken only a third of the way through. A desk, a computer, a guitar. The only interesting thing was a globe of the heavens and a small lockbox near the TV.

"Interested in astrology?" Lee asked, picking up the globe.

"Astronomy. I did my bachelor's in astronomy. Don't know how I ended up in the police. I don't really like it, actually," Simmons said.

Lee smiled. "Only recently I've become interested in astrology myself. Telling the future, all that," he said.

"This is astronomy, it's quite different," Simmons said meekly.

Lee put down the globe. "Is it indeed?"

"Yes."

"So what did you do with this homeless man who looked so very strange?"

"We put him in the van. Sergeant Dunleavy roughed him up a bit, and then we took him to a Traveler camp in Carrickfergus."

"Travelers?"

"Gypsies."

"Gypsies? Interesting. And where exactly is this camp?"

"Go to Carrickfergus, turn left up Victoria Road, keep going to the end. Can't miss it," Simmons said.

Lee nodded.

"Can I ask why the CIA is interested in this man?" Simmons wondered.

"You can ask, but I'm not at liberty to tell you, I'm afraid," Lee said.

Michael Lee leaned back in the chair and looked at the nervous young police officer. He had gotten Constable Simmons's home address from the PSNI computer. And of course he had known that this twenty-one-year-old trainee constable was going to be a softer touch than his veteran sergeant. A very soft touch. But there was no point in killing him. It was unlikely that he would talk.

"This is a confidential matter, Simmons. After I leave, you are to discuss this with no one," Lee said.

Constable Simmons nodded.

"And I'm not really in trouble, am I?" Constable Simmons asked.

Lee yawned. "You know, I've just flown in from Beijing, I really could do with a cup of coffee. Could you possibly make me a cup of coffee?" Lee asked.

Constable Simmons jumped up.

"Of course, no problem," he said. "I'll just go into the kitchen."

It took him five minutes to make the coffee, which was more than enough time for Lee to break into the lockbox by the TV and discover Constable Simmons's service revolver and spare ammunition.

Lee put the revolver in his pocket and closed the lockbox again.

Constable Simmons came back with the coffee.

Michael Lee stood.

"On second thought, I think I'll skip the coffee. I better try and find this homeless man of yours. Remember, don't discuss this with anyone. I'll see myself out. Good-bye."

"Good-bye," Simmons said, and watched the assassin walk out of his apartment and into the waning Belfast afternoon.

It was not very often that Thaddeus Harper was at a loss for words. World War II and thirty-five years of teaching in New York City public schools had prepared him for most things in life. Or so he thought.

"What do you mean you traveled to another world?"

he asked, his facial expression as neutral as he could possibly make it.

Jamie knew that there was no going back now, they had to soldier on with their explanation. If they were going to get the Salmon of Knowledge back, they were going to have get Thaddeus's permission to travel up to Belfast tonight, and quite possibly they would have to enlist his help in their scheme. Thaddeus might be old, but there was no way they could ever pull the wool over his eyes in an operation like this. They were finally going to tell Thaddeus the truth and really, as tricky as that might be, the truth was always a good thing.

"OK, Thaddeus, listen. Remember when we were supposed to go on the ski trip and we told Mom that we went to another planet?" Jamie began.

Thaddeus nodded.

"Of course, that's what you said initially but then she got the real story out of you," Thaddeus said with satisfaction.

Jamie shook his head.

"No, no, that's the point. The real story was the first story. We found this device that makes wormholes through space and we went to a planet called Altair for a week and Mom didn't really ever believe us until she went there too. The wormhole device has been found by Queen's University and we want it back," Jamie said with confidence and authority.

"Your mother went to this other planet too?" Thaddeus muttered, a little disappointed that Jamie would come up with so bold and so easily falsifiable an untruth.

"It is true, Mr. Harper. I know that you already suspect I am not from Iceland," Wishaway chimed in. "That is because I am not from Iceland. I am from a land called Aldan, a republic that lies in the Middle Sea on the planet of Altair."

There was such a look of relief on her face that Thaddeus was almost convinced.

Almost. He walked to the front door and opened it.

Outside the Lighthouse House a light rain was beginning to fall and a wind was rustling through the heather.

"And you, what's your take on this concoction?" Thaddeus asked Ramsay.

The big Irish boy shrugged his shoulders. "We went to another planet. Twice. But I know we're just kids and kids say some crazy stuff, so why don't you call my big brother and Jamie's mum in London and ask them what the truth is."

"I was thinking the very same thing," Thaddeus said. He closed the door and returned to his seat.

Jamie sat next to the old man on the sofa. "And if they confirm the story, will you help us get the Salmon back?"

"If they confirm the story that y'all went to another

planet, and that Wishaway is an alien, will I help you get the alien device back? Of course," Thaddeus said cheerfully.

He strode to the telephone and removed the emergency contact sheet from his jacket pocket.

This hoax had gone on long enough.

Without even looking at the children, he dialed Anna's cell phone number. It rang for a long time before Anna picked up.

"Ugaa, whaaa, hello?" Anna said.

"Good evening," Thaddeus said.

"Heeeiiii," Brian said in the background.

"Who is it?" Anna asked.

"It's me, Thaddeus," the old man intoned.

"Thaaaadeus! How's the kids?" Anna said, slurring her words.

"The kiiids!" Brian yelled.

Thaddeus frowned. They seemed to be intoxicated.

"I need to ask you something," Thaddeus said seriously.

"Ask away, suppose you wanna know about London. Laandan. The Big Smoke. We're having a lovely time, simply lovely, lovely, laavely. Been to London, Thaddeus? 'Course you have. During the Blitz. You told us. Yeahhhh."

"Yes, anyway, Anna, I wanted to ask you something

very important, perhaps if you could listen for one
mom—"

"We went up on that London Eye. Whoo! Crazy.
And Brian dragged me round the Science Museum. He
can be quite charming, Brian, you know. Don't worry, he
just left the room. Yes, I know what you're thinking, he's
a little younger. But it's not as if he's a lot younger. Five
years. And that's not much these days. Look at Ashton
and Demi. There used to be an expression when I was
young, 'What's sauce for the goose is sauce for the gan-
der too,' you know that one?"

"What's what for the what?" Thaddeus said, beginning
to feel that he was losing his grip on the conversation.

"The goose!" Anna yelled. "You should know that
one, it's from your day, goosey goosey, goosey."

Thaddeus frowned at the telephone, which unfortunately did not have any noticeable effect on Anna.

"Goosey, goosey . . ."

"Look, Anna, this is important, I want to talk to you
about something."

"OK, forget the goose, forget the goose, the point is
. . . well, I don't know what the point is, are the kids OK?"

"The kids are fine."

"Put Jamie on, I want to see if he's behaving himself
and—"

"No, if I could interject for a moment, Anna, Jamie

has been telling me some wild stories about a planet called, um, Altair . . ."

"Oh, Altair! I haven't heard the name of that place in a while. Don't let them take you. It's freezing there. Really. Freezing. No, no, no, I'm going to have to put my foot down. You aren't allowed to go there. You're not a young man anymore. Yes, yes, I know that you were in the Battle of the Bulge and believe me, Jamie made me sit through that episode of *Band of Brothers,* although I didn't see many African American soldiers, not that I'm doubting you for a moment, Thaddeus, I saw your citation, I just think that someone should have told them there were black tank crews, you know . . ."

"Anna, yes, but if I could bring you back to the issue of the planet Altair. Jamie says that there's this thing called the Salmon of Knowledge and—"

That was a crash on the other end of the phone and a muffled fumbling for a moment. A longish interlude of sitar music followed and then some uncontrollable giggling before Brian came back on the phone.

"Sorry about that, Anna fell over. Couldn't agree more with her though, um, Thaddeus, you can't go to that terrible place. And even if you wanted to, we've lost the Salmon. Bottom of the Irish Sea. Bottom of the ocean. Along with the UFO too. 'Course. Our only proof. Always the way. But you're just as well, Thaddeus. It's a horrible planet. Cold, windy, bad food, people being mean to you all the time, bit like my first year at MIT."

"Gimme that back," Anna said, and began singing a medley from the Fairport Convention album *Liege and Lief.* Her voice was not quite the haunting alto of Sandy Denny, but it did disturb Thaddeus enough that he hung up the phone.

Jamie looked at him.

"Well?" Jamie asked.

Thaddeus cleared his throat.

"They may have had slightly too much to drink," Thaddeus said cautiously.

"But they confirmed everything we've been saying, right?" Ramsay asked.

Thaddeus returned the phone to its cradle and sat back in the armchair. The three children were all looking at him. Apart from seeing Buzz Aldrin give a talk once at the 92nd Street Y, Thaddeus's previous experience of those who had been to other worlds was limited to his friend Henry. Henry worked as a social worker in a terrifying part of the South Bronx and after one particularly bad November chock-full of unpleasantness and with the highly stressful Christmas holidays coming up, Henry had simply disappeared off the face of the Earth for a few days. Intriguingly, Henry explained his absence by saying he'd been abducted by aliens. The aliens took him to a world where no one was ever murdered, the police never had to be called, and no one ever had to do complicated paperwork in triplicate.

He was given six months paid leave and came back tanned and healthy and no one spoke of the aliens again.

This, however, seemed to be a little different.

It didn't at all have the feel of a delusion or a practical joke or a hoax.

Clearly *something* had happened to the three kids, Brian, and Anna.

Of course there were such things as mass paranoia, group hypnosis, and that sickness that made you sincerely think you were having an out-of-body experience.

"OK, I'll go for it. What do you think happened to you?" Thaddeus said to Jamie.

"We found this machine in the old lighthouse that allows us to go to a planet called Altair. There we rescued Wishaway, I got my arm back, we took Brian and Anna, and we flew back from there in a flying saucer," Jamie said without even taking a breath.

"And you're supposed to be an alien?" Thaddeus said to Wishaway.

Wishaway held up her four-fingered hand.

"Well, yes, that I noticed," Thaddeus said. "But that hardly constitutes proof."

Wishaway nodded, got up, went to the kitchen, came back with a knife, and poked it into the first of her four fingers on her left hand.

Blood came out, as Thaddeus had known it would.

It was a little slow in clotting, which was a tad peculiar, but the really weird thing was that it was bright purple.

"You see?" Ramsay said.

"I see," Thaddeus said.

"We have to get the Salmon back. That guy at Queen's thinks its from flipping Mexico. Thinks it was part of the Spanish Armada's treasure fleet. The article said that he's sending it to Edinburgh. And they're going to probe it with lasers. Burn a hole into it. He's no idea what he's dealing with. He's going to wreck it," Ramsay said.

"Yes, and the important thing is that he's sending it off to Edinburgh tomorrow. Tomorrow, Thaddeus," Jamie said.

"Which means that if we're going to get it back, we've got to do it tonight," Wishaway added.

All three children nodded.

Thaddeus knew that he was going to regret this. He sighed heavily, and then with all the gravity he could muster, he leaned forward in his chair and said: "OK, kids, what do you want me to do?"

❁ ❁ ❁

Dandelions pushing up through the barley grass. White clouds in an eggshell-blue sky. Smoke curling from cooking fires. The smell of fish frying in beef fat. The hum of generators powering a carousel.

The field was occupied by some kind of mini carnival. Tombola stands, fortune-tellers, a very popular chip van.

Around the fringes there were tents, caravans, donkeys, and horses. A huge truck for carrying the animals that had been painted with likenesses of the sun god Apollo and Ganesh from the Hindu pantheon.

As it began to get dark, thunder sounded somewhere to the west, and a few raindrops began to drop halfheartedly from the sky. No one paid the rain any mind at all. A kid kicking a ball drifted close to the assassin's observation post and he slid back between the trees. The kid retrieved the ball and muttered something to himself in Irish about kicking it better the next time.

The assassin put down his pistol and picked up his binoculars again. He adjusted the focus and once again scanned the gypsy encampment. But once again he didn't see anything out of the ordinary.

He leaned against a hazel tree and breathed the moist, clean Irish air—so different from the muck he'd been swallowing in Beijing for the last eight months.

Michael Lee was a city boy from San Francisco, but

he'd been up to Muir Woods a few times and once to the wet, spiderwebby Olympia National Forest. He could tell old trees from new plantations and this was definitely an ancient wood—a small survivor from Ireland's primeval forest—that had probably been here for thousands of years. Imperial oak and hazel and a few witchy hawthorn trees. Nice. No wonder the gypsies wanted to camp near here.

And they were careful too. Whenever they went to gather kindling for their cooking fires, Lee noticed that they never cut anything down; even the small children gathered fallen branches only from the forest floor.

Obviously a remarkable people.

He took out his BlackBerry and activated the voice recorder. The thing ate megs, but it was too dark to type an e-mail.

"Interviewed the lead detective in Astatin murder case. No progress. Lead detective not particularly creative or intelligent. Should swallow whatever story we invent. Hacked PSNI daily log, saw the following entry: 'Homeless man found on Belfast streets, wet and in disheveled state, early morning.' Followed up. Report filed in police blotter by trainee Constable Peter Simmons. Found constable at his home, showed him CIA clearance. Interviewed him. Found that neither he nor his sergeant took the trouble to inform murder detectives about 'homeless man.' Homeless man not even arrested. Simmons informed me that the man was released to the custody of what constable called 'Traveler Camp' in Carrickfergus. This might be nothing, but the constable noticed the man had pointed ears and a very small nose as well as other unusual features. This matches description of coma patient given by CIA psychics. Drove to Carrickfergus. Arrived gypsy camp 6 P.M. Greenwich Mean Time. Observing since then, no sign whatsoever of suspect. End."

Lee put the BlackBerry back in his jacket pocket. When he got a bit more, he would send the unedited dictation as an e-mail attachment to Dan Connolly. Dan liked to get information early and without gloss. And he would surely be impressed at how quickly Lee was working on this thing.

If he could find the "homeless man" tonight, Lee would really be in Dan's good books and possibly even in the running for a promotion.

Lee yawned and examined the sky. It was getting late. And now the gypsy camp was packed with children and their parents, who were lining up at the carousel or eating fish-and-chips.

More than enough of a crowd to slip in.

But he didn't go just yet. He was patient and stayed in the forest until the last of the sun dipped behind the blue hills of Antrim and night made faces harder to spot. More difficult to find his suspect but also trickier for any of the locals to spy a stranger.

Lights came on at the fortune-teller stand and another generator powered up a cotton-candy machine.

"Time enough," he said, and he climbed out of his hiding place and mingled into the crowd. After walking around for half an hour he began to feel a little disappointed. Yes, this was picturesque and a hint of the Old World in twenty-first-century Ireland, but there was nothing out of the ordinary; there were no strange men offering herbal remedies, no odd people crying about the end times, no magicians, no horse whisperers, nothing unusual at all. And no sign of his suspect.

He was getting hungry. Maybe some fish-and-chips would be nice.

Just then he saw him, working the deep fat fryer at the chip van. A chef's hat was covering his ears, but you couldn't disguise his thin nose, weird eyes, and pinched forehead.

Yes.

Lee was a man who trusted his instincts and his instinct told him that the person in the chip van was the homeless man who had been picked up by the Irish cops, the same person who had been in the coma, and the same person who had killed Victor Astatin.

Lee took a quick picture of him with his BlackBerry and slipped back into the crowd.

Nothing happened for several hours.

But then something did happen that confirmed everything . . .

It was nearly eleven o'clock, and most of the kids were heading home when a couple of locals approached the chip van demanding fast service.

"Get a move on there, mate. Where'd ya learn to fry a chip? Slowtown?" one of the drunken locals said—a tall, rangy character with teardrops tattooed on his cheek.

Behind the counter of the chip van, and having served food all day, General Ksar was close to his breaking point.

"I consider myself blessed never to have fried a chip before this afternoon," Ksar said haughtily, and removed the humiliating chef's hat from his head.

"Look at them ears. Too good for ya, are we, Spock? Well, don't be getting airs. We don't like uppity tinkers round here," the second local said—a big bearded Sasquatch of a man in white jeans and a Metallica T-shirt.

The Gypsy King appeared at the back of the chip van and gave Ksar a look. Ksar nodded, and said, "Two fish suppers. That shall be four of thy pounds and fifty pence, please."

"Four quid fifty?" the bearded man said incredulously.

"Four of thy pounds and fifty pence," Ksar repeated.

"I'll give you two quid and you'll be happy to take it, mate," the man said, slapping two pound coins down on the chip van's counter.

The other grabbed the fish suppers that Ksar had already wrapped in newspaper.

"I think not," Ksar said, and reached for the steel-handled chopping knife under the counter, clutching it tightly in his four-fingered right hand.

"You think not, eh, tinker? Well, we're taking our money back. We'll consider these fish suppers on the house," the first man said, removing the pound coins from the counter and putting them in his pocket.

Ksar's brows knitted in fury. "You will give me the correct tally or you shall pay dearly," he said.

"Not bloody likely, mate, you tinkers are on thin ice as it is," the man said. He turned to his friend and both began walking back across the field toward Victoria Estate.

With the deft movement of a trained killer, Ksar leaped through the chip van's hatchway, landed on his feet, and grabbed the bigger of the two customers around the chest. He threw him to the muddy ground, and placed the knife at his throat.

"You owe me monies," Ksar snarled, leaning on his

helpless victim and letting the point of the knife's blade tease the man's carotid artery.

The place was already winding down for the night, but suddenly everything in the fairground went deathly quiet. The only sound was the faint chug-chugging of the generator and a gentle trickling noise, which may have been Ksar's victim wetting himself.

Michael Lee watched the little diorama with a great deal of fascination, almost forgetting to take a couple more photographs with his BlackBerry.

"The tinker's pulled a knife," the thinner of the two hoodlums said, aghast.

"You will pay me your debt," Ksar said, pushing the knife a little deeper into the man's throat.

"You, you—" the big eejit began, but he was silenced by his primordial survival instincts, honed over the millennia.

The silence probably saved him.

With the knifepoint still on his artery, and with tears welling up in his eyes, the bearded man reached into his pocket and took out a five-pound note. Trembling, he passed it to Ksar.

"Keep the change," the man said, his North Belfast tough-guy voice now strangely transformed into an impersonation of Mickey Mouse.

Ksar looked at the note, saw the number five in the

top right-hand corner, and released his prisoner. On Altair, he almost certainly would have killed the man, but this was not Altair.

The bearded man dropped his chips and ran to his friend. They both started jogging across the field, an activity clearly neither had done since high school PE class. When the pair of them were out of knife-throwing range and had recovered their breath, they began hurling insults.

"Ya pikey scum, we'll have you . . . We'll be coming back . . . We're coming to get all of you . . . Aye, you wait and see. Thon horses are gonna be ours. Get your gutties on, freaks. We're bringing our friends . . . You wait and see . . ."

Ksar yelled something back about dungeons, braziers, pikes, and hot pincers—things that would have terrified them had they known of the general's prediliction for torture and had they spoken Alkhavan.

When the men were gone and people had begun going back to their normal activities, the Gypsy King approached Ksar.

He took the five-pound note from Ksar's hand.

"Well, that was an interesting first day on the job," the Gypsy King said.

"Yes," Ksar replied.

"My fault. I showed you how to work the deep fat fryer, I showed you how to batter the fish, I even told you how to put out a chip-pan fire. But the one thing I forgot to tell you was the golden rule. You know what the golden rule is?"

Ksar shook his head.

"Never, never, never kill a customer," the Gypsy King said.

Ksar nodded.

"I will remember for the future," he said.

The Gypsy King shook his head. "There's not going to be a future. At least not for a while. Did you hear what those guys said? They're coming back with their friends. And I believe them. They're all going to have to go to the pub first to get their Dutch courage up, but they'll be back. Whole heap of them. We're going to have to get out of here. Move on. Pastures new."

Ksar shook his head. "You have tried to help me, human, but I shall not be traveling farther with thee. I have another destiny," he said, his eyes glittering in the moonlight.

The Gypsy King nodded, as if he had expected as much. "And what might that be now?" he asked.

"I seek the Ui Neill, Jamie Ui Neill, Laird of Muck, Guardian of the Passage. I seek him, for I must slay him," Ksar said.

"Well, mate, there will no more slaying tonight, but we'll give you a lift. Now come on, help me get things packed away before the angry mob arrives from Carrick," the Gypsy King said softly.

An hour later the gypsy camp had been stripped. The Travelers were in their vehicles and ready to move on to a new destination.

The Gypsy King and Ksar climbed into a big Toyota Land Cruiser that was pulling an empty horse box.

Michael Lee seized the opportunity, climbed into the horse box, and hid himself in the hay. Wherever they were going, he was going too.

As they put the car into gear he used the BlackBerry to Google "Jamie O'Neill," "Laird of Muck," and "Guardian of the Passage."

Trolling through Burke's Peerage online he found that Jamie O'Neill was a boy from New York who had inherited the title Laird of Muck and now lived at Muck Island, Islandmagee, County Antrim, Northern Ireland.

The assassin smiled to himself as the horse box joined the caravan of gypsy vehicles and began moving toward an unknown destination.

Michael Lee was excellent at his job, but even for him this was pretty good.

After only a few hours in Ireland, he had found Victor Astatin's murderer and he had discovered Jamie O'Neill, the boy the CIA psychics believed would bring the apocalypse.

This was beyond mere e-mail now. He dialed Dan
Connolly at CIA headquarters and, finding him not in
his office, decided to call him at home.

This was news. This was worth interrupting dinner
for. And more than likely, Dan would tell him to kill
both of them before the sun rose on another Irish day.

Chapter VI
THE BURGLARS

THE NIGHT WAS COLD. Nineteen-fifties cold. Freight-train-across-the-country cold. Kerouac cold. Thaddeus's feet were freezing. He tried wiggling his toes but that didn't do any good at all. When you got into your eighties your blood circulation wasn't as wonderful as it used to be.

He adjusted the Volvo's heater but for some reason only frigid air was coming out of the vents. He fiddled with the dials, and as soon as they got off the steep and rather precarious hill leading away from Portmuck village, he started banging the heater with his clenched fist even though he was driving.

"That's not going to work, Thaddeus, you're not the Fonz," Jamie said.

"Not the who?" Thaddeus asked.

"Yeah, not the who?" Ramsay wondered.

Jamie looked at Wishaway in the mirror.

"Wishaway, you know who I'm talking about, don't ya?"

Wishaway gave him a sympathetic shake of the head.

"Alas not, Jamie. Is this Fonz important to you?" Wishaway asked.

"No one in this car knows who the Fonz is? Wow, how quickly they forget. It's depressing," Jamie said.

"Tell you what really is depressing. This stupid thing. I mean, you'd think that of all cars a Volvo would have a better heater," Thaddeus said to Jamie.

"Why?" Jamie inquired innocently.

"Because they're Swedish and if I was a Swede and lived a couple of hundred miles from the Arctic Circle I'd make sure all the cars I manufactured had decent heaters," Thaddeus said bitterly.

Jamie did not reply. Thaddeus seemed irritable and nervous. It was probably better not to let the old man sucker him into an argument.

"Yeah, you're right," Jamie said.

Ramsay, however, lacked Jamie's perspicacity.

"Volvo's standards have declined since they were bought by Ford, an American company," Ramsay said from the backseat.

Fortunately for him he was removed from Thaddeus's wrath by a row of seats.

"Let me tell you something, sonny. Ford built the tanks and planes that won the war and deterred the Soviets from invading Europe during the Cold War, so you get yourself educated first before you make another crack like that," Thaddeus said forcibly.

"I think you'll find that it was the T-34 Soviet tank that won World War II and not anything that came out of the Ford production facil—" Ramsay began, and he probably would have continued in this vein until Thaddeus turned around in his seat and clobbered him, had not Wishaway pinched him very hard on the calf, effectively shutting him up. Ramsay swallowed the remainder of what he was going to say, huffed for a moment, and then took out his laptop and worked on it silently for the rest of the journey.

A good thing too.

Thaddeus was a so-so driver at the best of times, and turning around in his seat to swipe a fifteen-year-old boy on a frosty Irish country road might have proved tragic.

Like most Americans, Thaddeus was loath to admit that he was not brilliant behind the wheel. He'd learned to drive a Sherman tank long before an automobile, and although the Sherman was liable to explode when hit by an 88 mm, it never had problems with parallel parking. Decades of living in Manhattan had not given Thaddeus much opportunity to improve his skills.

The kids, though, were oblivious to the jeopardy they were in, and each sunk into his or her own respective thoughts.

Thaddeus was glad of the silence.

"Everybody better just keep out of my way," he unconsciously grumbled aloud in irritation.

Jamie caught Wishaway's eye in the mirror, and using hand gestures he made her check that her seatbelt was securely fastened.

To be on the safe side Thaddeus drove them carefully at 40 mph the whole way up to town. There was some drama when they came to the roundabout for the M5— Thaddeus nearly took them around the traffic circle the wrong way into a massive eighteen-wheeler, but luckily he swerved the car off a slip road and into a gas station instead.

He filled the Volvo's fuel tank with diesel; although it was originally designed to run on this petroleum derivative, the diesel and the fish-and-chip oil did not sit well together. Yet the Volvo made it from Islandmagee to Belfast without exploding or Thaddeus killing anyone.

They arrived shortly after nine P.M. and Thaddeus was pleased to see that Queen's University was in a nice part of town with plenty of parking spaces.

They parked and got out.

Thaddeus retrieved his hat from the trunk, and when no one was looking he said a silent prayer of thanks to any deity who was listening.

After asking only a few dozen students for directions the group finally found one who was sober enough to show them the way to the archaeology department.

"Just at the end of that street there," the student said.

"Thank you very much," Thaddeus replied, and looked to where the young man had pointed. The Archaeology and Palaeoecology Department appeared to be housed in a large Victorian house at the end of a red-bricked terrace near the student union.

When the student had gone, Thaddeus gathered the kids into a circle to discuss the situation.

"We can't do anything until we know the terrain. You lot wait here while I go down there and case the joint," Ramsay said.

"Nonsense. We'll all check it out together," Thaddeus insisted.

"No, no, we're too obvious as a group. We look like we've just come from Sesame Street," Ramsay insisted. They did too. The old African American man in a three-piece suit; the blond alien girl; Jamie, the nondescript street kid; and Ramsay, whose wild, curly hair was straight out of the seventies. For the burglary, Ramsay had dressed himself in a one-piece black catsuit, which didn't help them blend in much either.

"We stick together," Thaddeus insisted.

They walked down the street, and after they had obtrusively sauntered past the building a couple of times, Thaddeus called them over for another pow-wow.

"OK everyone, pros and cons," he said.

"Pros, there's a door on the ground floor, I don't see anyone inside, and there are no lights on," Jamie said.

Thaddeus nodded with satisfaction.

"Good," he said. "Now, cons?"

"Cons, there's a lot of pedestrian traffic outside and if you look across—no, don't everyone look at once, dammit—you'll see a lot of students sitting on the stoops of their houses," Ramsay said.

Thaddeus nodded. "Yeah, I noticed that too," he said with a frown.

Jamie looked at Ramsay with expectation. Thaddeus was the weak link here. If he got discouraged, the whole scheme could quickly go down the U-bend.

"So, what's the plan?" Jamie said enthusiastically to Ramsay.

"What plan?" Ramsay replied.

"In the car I saw you writing stuff in your laptop. I assumed you were working on a plan," Jamie said.

Ramsay shook his head.

"No, no, I wasn't working on a plan. I was rewriting my Wikipedia entry on 'Expedition to the Barrier Peaks,' one of the best modules they ever made for Dungeons and Dragons. Of course it was very controversial in its day and—"

Jamie sighed. "Fascinating I'm sure, Ramsay. Now, do

you have any thoughts on how we're going to get into the building?"

"Yes. Yes, I do, actually. Everyone hold on a minute," Ramsay said, his face suddenly taking on a look of extreme cunning.

He winked at them and tiptoed up the steps to the front door of the archaeology department. He tried pushing on the handle. It was locked. He pushed harder. It was still locked. He walked back down the steps to the others.

"OK, I'm fresh out of ideas. Anyone else?" he said.

"I think I might be able to squeeze through that open window," Wishaway said, pointing to a narrow gap on the left-hand ground-floor window.

Two obstacles immediately presented themselves to this scheme. First, the window was placed precariously over a cast-iron spiked railing; and second, even if she wasn't impaled horribly on the spikes, everyone on the other side of the street would see Wishaway climb through the opening.

"You really think you can get through the gap without being seen?" Jamie asked, concern flitting across his face.

Wishaway nodded. "Easy-peasy," she said.

Ramsay wagged his finger at her. "What have I told you about using slang? 'Easy-peasy' is very elementary school."

"What we'll need is some kind of distraction. Thaddeus, any thoughts?" Jamie said, ignoring Ramsay completely.

"A distraction? No problem, mate. We can MacGyver a solution right here. Some flints, a little gasoline, I'll make a distraction that'll have them talking about it for years," Ramsay said.

"Any ideas, Thaddeus?" Jamie repeated.

Thaddeus nodded slowly.

"Yes, yes, I think I do have some thoughts," Thaddeus said. "When we drove through Belfast the other day I couldn't help but notice all the street preachers on the sidewalk, and again today I saw them. Now, I wouldn't say that I am an ardent believer, and I certainly have never been called to testify, but I've been going to church for eighty years and I believe I can sermonize with the best of them. If I went to that corner on the other side of the street, I think I could attract a crowd long enough for young Wishaway to get through the window."

Jamie looked at Ramsay as if to say, *See, I told you he was cool.*

"OK, great, do you need a soapbox? Need any prep? When will we go?" Jamie asked.

Thaddeus looked at Wishaway.

"What do you think, honey?" Thaddeus asked.

She nodded at him.

"OK then, now it is," Thaddeus said. He straightened his tie and walked to the corner of the street. He was wearing a conservative blue suit, but carrying a silver-tipped cane and wearing a purple felt fedora. It was unlikely that anyone not involved in a Noel Coward play or ballroom dancing contest looked as elegant as Thaddeus that night in Belfast, and that gave him confidence.

He found a spot on the sidewalk and cleared his throat. He'd seen this done but it was not going to come naturally. He'd been brought up as an Anglican and as a result he'd always had a bit of High Church disdain for dynamic preachers, though he would have been the first to admit that Jesus Christ himself had been something of a hippie and rabble-rouser. And of course it was true that all successful religions had to have an element of theater.

He cleared his throat a second time and began. "Brothers and sisters of Belfast, blessed are you that can hear my voice. Blessed are you. This is the luckiest night of your life. Oh yes. This is a night when your life is going to take a new path. Brothers and sisters of Belfast, I am not selling anything. Nope. Tonight I'm giving something away. What am I giving away? I am giving, free, the secret to eternal life . . ."

Within five minutes Thaddeus had a small crowd of

the curious. He made everyone shake hands and then hug the person next to them. A very un-Belfast thing to do. Then when they were loosened up he made them say "amen" at the end of every one of his sentences, and of course he told them repeatedly that he couldn't hear them and they had to say it louder.

"Does he think God is deaf?" Ramsay whispered sarcastically.

Jamie ignored him and started walking to the open window of the archaeology department.

"What are you doing?" Wishaway said, putting her hand on his shoulder.

"It's not safe for you to do this mission. I'm going in there," Jamie said.

"What are you talking about?"

"Look at those spikes at the window. One slip and you're toast. It's up to me," Jamie said.

"I'll do it, both of you will screw it up," Ramsay said.

"It was my idea," Wishaway protested.

"Yeah, but I'm the natural hero," Ramsay insisted with a grin.

Jamie laughed but Wishaway shook her head. "Yes, you're very heroic, Ramsay, but what you don't seem to understand is that I'm the female lead. I'm the spunky heroine. I have to go for it," Wishaway said.

"But you might be killed," Jamie protested.

"I can't die, at least not until the end of the third act," Wishaway insisted.

"But maybe this is the third act and you just don't know it," Jamie said.

"This, the third act? Are you crazy? We've barely got going. I'm not going to get killed now," Wishaway said.

"Your whole theory is misguided," Ramsay added vociferously. "You ever see *Psycho*? Janet Leigh thought she was the female lead and *bang!* They top her twenty minutes in. Didn't see it coming. *Wheech, wheech, wheech,* bread knife in the shower, blood in the drain, dead eye staring straight into the camera . . . Drew Barrymore in *Scream* is another example of—"

"No, no, Drew Barrymore just had a cameo in *Scream*. Janet Leigh carried the whole movie for the first half hour," Jamie said.

Before the conversation turned, as it always did, to Ramsay's views on *Star Wars*, Wishaway took the opportunity to slip away. She climbed the steps leading to the archaeology department and threaded her body nimbly over the cast-iron spikes and through the open window.

Wishaway found herself in a messy office filled with books and papers. She made her way through a maze of teacups and stacks of *Archaeology Today*. She discovered a light switch, turned it on to get her bearings, and then turned it off again. She opened the office door, found herself in a lobby, and bent down to pet a small black cat that was rubbing itself against her legs.

"As a watch cat, you're ineffective," Wishaway told the kitty.

It meowed a response.

"Well, I better let in the others. We have a Salmon to steal," she said.

She undid the chain and the dead bolt and opened the front door.

The door opened easily and set off a silent burglar alarm, which in turn triggered a less silent alarm in the Shaftesbury Square police station a quarter of a mile to the north.

Wishaway, of course, was unaware of any of this and walked back down the steps to Jamie and Ramsay with an enormous grin on her face.

". . . you see, Jamie, the message of *Star Wars* is essentially a very conservative one. The choices we are offered are between competing brands of theocratic monarchism. Princess Leia and the Jedi on one side, Lord Vader and the Emperor on the other. There is no secular voice or—"

"I opened the door," Wishaway said.

Jamie looked up the steps and saw that she was right.

"Hey, good job," he said delightedly.

"Thank you," Wishaway replied, a very beautiful twinkle appearing in her eyes. Jamie reflected that he hadn't seen her this happy for weeks.

"We have to do more stuff like this," he said.

"Breaking and entering?" Wishaway asked.

"Yeah. You know . . . adventures."

"Yes," Wishaway said, and squeezed his hand. His cheeks reddened.

"OK then. Well, if there's no one looking, let's go," Jamie said.

Ramsay checked on their distraction at the end of the street. Thaddeus had now gotten the dour Irish folks singing and shouting the occasional "hallelujah."

"He's doing a good job," Ramsay said. "At any moment I think people are going to start speaking in tongues."

"Come on," Jamie said, and seizing the opportunity, they went up the steps into the building.

A helpful notice board told them that Professor McGarraty's office was on the third floor.

"Third floor," Ramsay said in case the others had forgotten how to read.

"Let's go up," Wishaway replied.

"Me first," Ramsay said quickly, and sprinted ahead of them, gleefully expecting danger at every turn and taking the stairs three at a time.

His grin faded, however, when he reached floor number three without incident.

For a university branch that dealt with ancient ruins and artifacts, the Queen's University Department of Archaeology and Palaeoecology was disappointingly lacking in secret doors, booby-trapped staircases, or giant granite balls that rolled down on top of you from hidden alcoves.

"It's nothing like Lara Croft," Ramsay muttered, checking the ceiling anyway to see if there were any swinging swords, like in the iconic Tomb Raider 1, Level 5.

"Wait a minute! What's this? What's this?" Ramsay cried, spotting a strange obelisk filled with stones on the floor near the top of the staircase. On closer examination, however, it turned out to be a litter box for a cat.

"What were you saying?" Jamie inquired upon reaching the top of the steps.

"Nothing," Ramsay muttered.

Professor McGarraty's door was pretty uninteresting too. It had been painted white sometime in the previous century and had nothing on it but his name and a bumper sticker that said ARCHAEOLOGY ROCKS!

"It's supposed to be a joke," Jamie explained to Wishaway.

"'Geology Rocks!' would be better," Ramsay said.

"Well, we are presented with another problem," Jamie said. "How are we going to get into the office?"

Ramsay looked at the closed door.

"In the Scouts I learned a little bit about picking locks. Wishaway, do you happen to have a hairpin?"

Wishaway looked puzzled. "A what?"

"It's a thing from the thirties that women used to keep their hair pinned back. It was useful for picking locks. A staple of early detective fiction."

"Sorry," Wishaway said.

Ramsay sighed. "Now that we are in the era of scrunchies and barrettes the lot of the amateur lock picker is a much more difficult one. OK, we'll have to improvise. Let's look for a box of paper clips."

While Ramsay and Jamie began their hunt for useful office supplies, Wishaway turned the door handle and went into Professor McGarraty's office.

She didn't have to hunt around for the Salmon.

A FedEx package in the middle of Professor McGarraty's desk was marked "Armada Finds." She examined the delivery label and found that it was heading for Edinburgh University.

"Jamie, Ramsay!" she called.

"How did you do that?" Ramsay asked, looking in wonder at the unlocked door.

Wishaway pointed at the FedEx package.

"This is it? Well, that was easy," Jamie said.

"Too easy," Ramsay said, looking suspiciously around the room for further evidence of booby traps. No obvious holes in the floor, but there was a crack in the wall that could easily be a repository for poison darts.

"No!" Ramsay cried as Jamie lifted the box off the desk.

No darts of any kind came shooting out of the wall, and Ramsay reluctantly realized that it was just an ordinary split in the plaster.

Jamie pulled the quick release tab on the FedEx box and there, lovingly protected by several rolls of bubble wrap, was the Salmon of Knowledge—that wonderful device made by an unknown race of aliens that allowed you to leap across the light-years of space all the way to the planet Altair.

Even though it had been lying at the bottom of the Irish Sea for a year, it still was pristine and beautiful. All three children gasped and even Ramsay remained speechless for half a minute or so.

"We've got it back," Jamie said.

"Yeah," Ramsay agreed.

And maybe this was what had been missing in their lives. The Salmon had brought them all together and when they had lost it, it had been like losing a part of themselves.

"Let me touch it," Ramsay said.

Jamie passed it to him.

"Good as new," Ramsay muttered. "Even the internal power source seems to be fine. This is some piece of equipment. How could anyone think this was from the Aztecs? Professor McGarraty's not very good at his job, I can tell you that."

"May I touch it too?" Wishaway said.

Ramsay nodded and passed it to her.

For Wishaway, Jamie reflected, it was even more significant. This was her link to home. To a world a hundred light-years from Earth. It must be really hard for her, being adrift from Altair in twenty-first-century Ireland. Especially here. In this country, of all places on Earth, you could really lose yourself in melancholy. New Yorkers weren't happy but most of them were too busy to be introspective about this state of being. In Ulster, however, time moved slower and the Irish were experts in the poetry of unhappiness. The whole history of Ireland were one long ballad that the Celts obviously loved, embellishing the epic with each new telling and adding their own sad verses to the dark, unbroken song.

And wasn't that part of why he was so sad? The atmosphere. Maybe there was nothing wrong with him. Maybe it was just the Irish vibe. And perhaps the Salmon would change things. Perhaps the Salmon would jolt him out of his negative thoughts, and if they returned to Altair he would appreciate how fortunate he really was.

"OK, I've got the fish, let's get out of here," Jamie said, putting the Salmon in his jacket pocket.

"I'll wipe off our fingerprints," Wishaway said.

"And I'll grab the roll of bubble wrap in case we get bored in the car ride back to Islandmagee . . ." Ramsay added.

Constable Simmons was on his way home from second duty when he got a call on his cell phone.

"Simmons, are you home yet?" Sergeant Dunleavy asked.

"Nearly," Simmons said.

"Good, are you near Eureka Street?"

"I'm just turning the corner. Why?"

"Excellent, go down to the Queen's University Department of Archaeology. There's a good lad, and have a scoot around. Someone or some thing has just tripped the front door's burglar alarm," Sergeant Dunleavy said.

"Can you not get someone else? I'm actually off duty," Constable Simmons said.

"Policemen are never off duty. Their job is to serve the public, always," Sergeant Dunleavy growled. "Did I ever tell you about the occasion when I was on holiday and yet I grabbed that pickpocket in Chicago?"

"Only about a dozen times," Constable Simmons muttered.

"Go, and do thou likewise," Sergeant Dunleavy said.

Constable Simmons hung up the phone. He walked past a street preacher telling a small crowd that they were all doomed or going to hell or something and strolled along the sidewalk until he came to the archaeology department.

For once this didn't seem a false alarm.

A window and the front door were open.

He walked up the steps only to be met by three children coming out of the building.

Ramsay looked at the rather short, nerdy man blocking their path. Obviously a student come to do some late-night work on Stonehenge or the pyramids or something of the kind. "Hold it right there," Constable Simmons said.

"Shove off, Frodo. Don't you have a ring to destroy?" Ramsay said, trying to push past him.

"Wait a minute. What were you three doing in there?" Constable Simmons said.

"We came in to feed the cat. We feed it every night," Wishaway said sweetly.

"The cat?" Constable Simmons inquired.

"Yes, the cat," Wishaway insisted.

"What's his name?" Constable Simmons asked.

"Aldan, and it's a she," Wishaway said.

Constable Simmons's phone rang. He answered it.

"What's going on?" Sergeant Dunleavy asked.

"Um, it appears to be a false alarm," Constable Simmons said.

"Yes, it is. Now excuse us, shortarse, we have things to do," Ramsay said with an exaggerated shake of the head.

Tears welled up in Constable Simmons's eyes. First the gruff CIA man. Then his missing revolver. And now this.

"Who was that?" Sergeant Dunleavy said over the phone.

"It's three kids and they're being rude to me," Simmons said with a sniff.

"How rude? High-school-chemistry-teacher rude or snooty-Starbucks-barista rude?"

"Starbucks-barista rude," Simmons said, and wiped his eyes.

"We didn't mean to upset you," Wishaway said.

"That's all right, I'm used to it," Constable Simmons replied.

"Pull yourself together, man," Sergeant Dunleavy snapped.

Constable Simmons blew his nose and looked at the three children. They seemed harmless enough.

"OK, you can go," he said, trying to assert his authority.

Ramsay, Wishaway, and Jamie walked as calmly as they could to the end of the street and joined the crowd gathered around Thaddeus.

Jamie gave the old man the "OK" sign.

Thaddeus nodded and decided to wind things up.

"Well, folks, I've enjoyed mightily this time we've shared together. But I have to be heading on to pastures new. Time's wingèd chariot is drawing near and all that, and I must be off."

His followers watched in a state of mild shock as he climbed into the Volvo with the three kids and turned the engine on.

"But you can't go now, teach us more," someone yelled.

"Please lead us," another person begged.

Thaddeus put the car into reverse.

"You've left them all pretty unsatisfied and discontented," Ramsay commented.

Thaddeus nodded. "Good. Next time they'll know better than to listen to life lessons from some lunatic off the street."

"Show us the way," a woman cried but Thaddeus ignored the pleas, reversed messily out of the parking space, clipped the bumper of a white Mercedes, and drove off contentedly into the Belfast night.

The Gypsy King pulled the Toyota Land Cruiser into a car park at the bottom of the hill.

He killed the engine.

Ksar looked out of the window. They appeared to be in a small village near the water. The rest of the Travelers were not with them. Ksar and the Gypsy King were alone.

The Gypsy King got out of the car and lit himself a cigarette. He offered one to Ksar, who refused the foul-smelling weed.

"Where are the others?" Ksar asked.

The Gypsy King nodded to himself. "I sent them on ahead, to a campsite a few miles up the coast in Ballygalley. We go there now and again. We can stay there for a while without being hassled by anyone. Up in the Glens of Antrim they're a wee bit more sympathetic to our people than down in Belfast or in Dublin," the Gypsy King said.

"Why do we not go with them?" Ksar asked.

"Well, to tell you the truth, Ksar, I didn't want anyone else to be privy to this conversation."

Ksar nodded. He too was suspicious and trusted very few people. Whether he could trust the Gypsy King himself, however, was still in considerable doubt.

"What do you want to say?" General Ksar asked.

The Gypsy King threw his cigarette onto the damp ground and stamped it out under his hobnailed boot.

He looked out at the sea and stroked his beard.

"Ksar, tell me something first. Have you ever been to America?"

Ksar shook his head. "No," he replied.

"I have, went out there a few times. Manhattan. Worked as a groom for the horse-drawn carriages in the park. Two years I was there."

Ksar had never heard of Manhattan and he grunted with impatience. What was this fellow getting at?

"I slept in the stables. Had to do a lot of work with those horses. It's not like here, you know. Out there the poor cratturs get spooked at night. Too much stuff going on all the time. The traffic, the noise, but more than that. The bears, coyotes, wolves, they can smell all that. They can smell a bear from twenty miles away. You don't believe me? Well, it's true. A horse walking around the pond at Central Park can smell the black bears in the Jersey woods on the other side of the Hudson. And the reason they're nervous is that they don't think we can keep them safe. In fact they know we can't keep them safe. They know that we're afraid ourselves, because they can smell that too. But that's not the case in Ireland. Irish horses like dusk. They like night. Night is a time to stand or lie upon the ground and feel the earth and scent the air and rest. There are no tormentors in Ireland. We eradicated the bears and wolves centuries ago and the horses know that we did it for them. That's why they're relaxed. That's why they can rest easy . . . And that's why the way they reacted around you made me very surprised."

"How did they react around me?" Ksar asked.

"They reacted like the American horses. Around our horses were tremulous with excitement. You are something brand-new to them. You are nothing their mothers knew about, nothing their siblings knew about. You are something they've never encountered before in their lives. Even the dull-witted Irish cows get spooked by you. You are a prodigy. Did you watch the horses in the camp? I did. I saw what they were like when you walked past. Their back hair stood up. They started to shake. To sweat. They were feared and yet curious to know you better—to know what you are."

"I did not notice that," Ksar said, wondering if horses were those large brown creatures that everyone made such a ridiculous fuss over when they were packing up the camp.

The Gypsy King smiled.

"And yet you know why the horses were so confused by you, don't ya, Ksar? It's not a mystery to you, is it?"

Ksar hesitated for a moment but then nodded.

"No, it is not a mystery to me," Ksar said.

"Tell me the truth. Don't be shy. Tell me," the Gypsy King said.

Ksar looked at the man. Could he tell this human the truth? The Gypsy King seemed stronger than the man he had drowned in the river the other night. Breaking this one's neck might be harder than it looked.

"I-I-I am not of this world," Ksar said at last.

The Gypsy King nodded as if this was the most natural statement Ksar could have made.

"Tír na nÓg, then, is it?" the Gypsy King asked, his eyes narrowing with expectation.

Ksar looked quizzical.

"The land across the sea, the land of the faeries," the Gypsy King said.

Ksar shook his head. "No. No. I came here in a ship that voyaged between the stars. A boy, one of your great Lords, brought me. Jamie of the Ui Neill," he said.

A spaceship? The Gypsy King leaned against the car to steady himself. This was not the answer he'd been expecting. He lit himself another cigarette.

"Jamie of the Ui Neill. The one you mentioned earlier? The Laird of Muck?" the Gypsy King asked.

Ksar grimaced. "I-I feel that I must slay him. He has caused great harm to my people. And further . . ."

"What?"

Ksar hesitated. "I seek the Ui Neill because I desire him to use his power to return me to my own world."

The Gypsy King laughed. "You can't kill him and then ask him to take you back to your planet," he said. "I mean, you see the contradiction there, don't ya?"

Ksar nodded grimly. "Yes. I see it."

They listened to the sea lap against the shore of the gravelly beach for a while. On the other side of the water, in Scotland, the lighthouses began to come on one by one.

"So you came here in some kind of spaceship, is that what you're telling me?" the Gypsy King asked.

"A sky ship. The Ui Neill discovered a sky ship and brought me here. The ship wrecked itself in the ocean and I was saved," Ksar said.

"And you've decided you don't like it here?"

Ksar thought about it.

"Earth is not the place that I imagined it to be. In Morgan's *Book of Stories*, men of honor are treated with respect. Great warriors are recognized for what they are. But this world, this world is . . . is . . . petty."

The Gypsy King nodded.

"Aye, the concept of honor has become obsolete. I can see how that would depress you. And your world still has it?"

"Indeed."

A sly look appeared on the Gypsy King's face. "I'd very much like to visit there meself," he said.

"How can we get back?" Ksar asked.

The Gypsy King smiled. "Cast your eyes about you," he said.

But one part of Ireland looked pretty much like another part of Ireland to General Ksar. This hamlet on the seashore did not seem particularly special or interesting.

"Where are we?" Ksar asked.

"We're in the village of Portmuck on Islandmagee," the Gypsy King said significantly.

"Why are we here?"

"Why are we here? Well now, I'll tell you why we're here. You said you wanted to see the Laird of Muck, did you not?" the Gypsy King replied.

"I did."

The Traveler grinned in the moonlight.

"You're a very lucky man, er, faerie, er, alien, whatever you are. Very lucky. I doubt that there are more than a few hundred people in the whole of Ireland who have heard of that title. *The Laird of Muck.* It's an old 'un. One of the ancient titles of Erin."

"The Lord Ui Neill is not well known?" Ksar asked, greatly surprised.

"No, no, I'm afraid not. We're done with all of that stuff nowadays. Along with any notion of honor, we don't put much hold in titles or where someone came from. We live in a meritocracy. What matters is what you can do, not where you came from. It's a good thing on the whole, Ksar. Talent, like cream in the churn, rises to the top. 'Course it means that those at the bottom are called lazy rather than unlucky. They're hated a wee bit more than in the old days."

"It sounds awful," Ksar said with disgust.

"Well, I suppose you'd think so. People are obsessed with their rights, but no one thinks about their duties anymore. Everyone wants to know what they can get out of society but nobody wants to hear about their respon- sibilities as part of that society . . . Anyway, I didn't bring you here to talk philosophy. I brought you here because I know who the Laird of Muck is, and what's more, I know where he lives."

Ksar grabbed the Gypsy King by the lapels of his long trench coat.

"Ye jesteth with me!" Ksar said excitedly.

"I jesteth not, me old mucker. The Laird of Muck is a wee lad called Jamie O'Neill. You can look him up in Burke's if you'd like, but I don't have to. Like I say, I know all the old titles of Ireland. All the old titles, all the old histories, all the old songs. You know, a lot of us

Travelers can't read and a lot of us don't have any skills, but all of us know where we came from and we know our story and our place in the great conversation of mankind. You see that island off the coast there?"

"Yes."

"That's Muck Island and that house on it is called the Lighthouse House. That's where the Laird of Muck lives. When the tide goes down we can drive over there. I think he's only a wee lad. From America originally. But he might be the one you're looking for. It'll be interesting to find out," the Gypsy King said with satisfaction.

Ksar slammed his fist into the palm of his hand with unconcealed delight.

And a few yards from him, in the horse box trailer behind the Toyota Land Cruiser, Michael Lee was also feeling rather delighted with his day's work.

He had heard the entire conversation between Ksar and the Gypsy King, and although he was still of two minds as to whether he believed it, it was certainly confirmation of much that he had been told by Dan Connolly.

An alien?

A spaceship?

Well, at the very least, Astatin's murderer sincerely believed that he was from another planet.

He was in the middle of e-mailing a report to Dan when the BlackBerry vibrated.

"Yes?" he whispered.

"So, you've found the boy?" Dan said.

Lee turned down the volume.

"Yes, I've found the boy and Victor's killer."

"Good work. Very good work. You've done an amazing job," Dan said excitedly. "The whole psychic team is very relieved. I'm relieved. I never believed it was true until Victor got killed. These two have to be stopped."

"You don't need to tell me my job. I'll do it," Lee said.

"It's not going to be pretty, um, dealing with a child, but I know you're, uh, capable of t—"

"I am," Lee said coldly.

"Where are you now?" Dan asked.

"I'm in a village called Portmuck on Islandmagee, Northern Ireland. Apparently this is where Jamie O'Neill lives. Victor's killer led me right here. The psychics were right about that."

"You've got the boy and the killer under supervision?"

"We're waiting for the tide to go down and then we're going to drive over to Muck Island, which is where the boy lives," Lee said.

"So you think you can, um, eradicate, this, um, problem soon?" Dan asked.

"I think so."

"Good. The higher-ups are starting to take an interest. I want to present this as a fait accompli before there are too many questions. Can I take it that the situation will all be over by morning?"

"I don't like to be rushed, Mr. Connolly, but I'll take care of it. I haven't let the department down once in five years, though I think it's a lot for one man," Michael Lee said.

"You're getting help. We're sending out a pair of agents to pick up O'Neill's mother. So you only have to handle the kid."

"I will . . . Damn it, I'm going to have to go. My targets are coming back to the car and I am concealed in the back of their vehicle," he said, and hung up the phone.

He thought about it for a minute but then he decided not to send the e-mail about Ksar being an alien.

It might hurt his future career prospects.

"All right then, let's be having you. Get inside," the Gypsy King said.

"Where are we going?" Ksar asked.

"There," the Gypsy King said, pointing at the dark Lighthouse House.

The Gypsy King and Ksar got inside and drove the Toyota and the horse box over the causeway to Muck Island.

They parked behind a ruined tower and the assassin settled in to await the return of Jamie O'Neill, the boy who was to cause the end of the world.

* * *

Satellite-cold ocean. Blue black of an Irish night. Lee checked his gun and peered out of the horse box. Muck Island was a small, boggy piece of terrain that seemed to contain only one house and a ruined tower. A misty rain was falling now and it had turned cold.

Ksar and the Gypsy King were sitting on the porch of the Lighthouse House.

There was no sign yet of his primary.

What was a kid doing out this late in the middle of the week?

Lee shivered.

His BlackBerry began to vibrate again.

What is it now? he thought irritably.

"Yes?" he said.

"Is it done?" Dan Connolly asked.

"I'll let you know when it's done," Lee said with annoyance.

"So the boy's still alive?" Dan asked.

"He hasn't even come home yet," Lee said.

"Maybe he's fled. He may be on to us. He's probably clever. If he brings about the destruction of the Earth, he must be some kind of evil genius," Dan said.

"Look, will you just relax, I'll take care of it. I'm hanging up now," Lee said.

"No, wait a minute, I wanted to tell you something," Dan said.

"What?"

"It's confirmed. We've had the boy's mother and her boyfriend arrested in London," Dan said.

"So you're definitely going to kill her too?" Lee asked.

"I suppose we'll have to," Dan said.

Lee shrugged. "OK, that's your business. Now please get off the phone."

"OK, but I just wanted to—"

Whatever Dan wanted to was lost because at that moment Lee spotted two lights on the causeway. Finally a car was coming to the island. Lee ended the call immediately and then switched off the device.

He stood and stretched. He checked his police revolver.

The halo around the headlights drew closer until the Volvo drove up in front of the Lighthouse House.

"We did it, Jamie, we really did it," Ramsay said, getting out of the car.

"Yeah, Ramsay, we really did it," Jamie replied.

"Well, this is more than enough excitement for one night. I'm going to bed and I suggest you kids do the same," Thaddeus said.

Lee examined the crew. A girl, the boy Jamie, a tall Irish lad, called Ramsay, and an African American about seventy or eighty years old with thick white hair. Handsome for an old codger.

"Why don't you stay with us tonight?" Thaddeus said to Ramsay.

"Well, I don't know, I suppose that—"

"*Go mbeannai Dia duit.* Hello to you all," the Gypsy King said in Irish and English.

"Good day," General Ksar said.

"Oh my God!" Ramsay cried. Jamie dashed protectively in front of Wishaway.

"I see that you know each other," the Gypsy King said.

"He's not dead," Wishaway gasped.

"No, Lady Wishaway, I am very much alive," Ksar replied.

"What do you want, Ksar?" Ramsay snarled.

Ksar began walking toward them.

"Stay right where you are," Jamie said, opening the Volvo's trunk and removing a wooden baseball bat. Ramsay rooted around the trunk and found a long metal tire iron. He brandished it menacingly.

"Keep your distance, Ksar," Ramsay said.

"As you can see, Lord Ramsay, I am not armed," Ksar replied, holding out his hands.

"What do you want?" Jamie asked suspiciously.

"I wish to return to my own world. This place is too, too . . . I do not like it here," Ksar said. "I wish you to send me back."

"I don't believe you. You've risked everything to come here," Jamie said.

Ksar sighed. "I made a mistake. This world, for all its wonders, is not my home. It is my desire that you send me back."

"You don't like Earth? Are you nuts? Your planet is a hellhole," Ramsay said, a little defensively. "We've got planes and antibiotics, you haven't even invented the steam engine."

"Nevertheless," Ksar insisted.

Jamie examined him. This did not seem like a trap. Ksar, apparently, was telling the truth.

"Why should we do anything for the person who has caused us so much trouble?" Ramsay snapped.

Ksar shook his head. "I can think of no good reason, but if you allow me to return home, you will be rid of me forever."

"We could just kill you," Ramsay said.

"Yes. You could try, but why not just let me go?" Ksar said.

"How are you even here? How are you alive? You survived the crash?" Jamie asked.

Ksar nodded. "Obviously," he said.

"Who is this man?" Thaddeus asked.

"This is the Lord Protector," Jamie said with initial distaste, but then remembering his manners he went on. "General Ksar, allow me to present my friend Thaddeus Harper. Thaddeus, this is General Ksar of Alkhava."

"Pleased to meet you," Thaddeus said.

"Likewise," Ksar replied. "And allow me to present my friend, the King of the Gypsies."

The Gypsy King bowed.

Everyone said hello and there followed an awkward silence for half a minute.

"You have heard what I have to say, Lord Ui Neill. I wish to return to my own land. Will you take me back?" Ksar said at last.

Wishaway shook her head. "No, Jamie, he will only cause havoc to my people."

Ksar nodded. "I give you my word, Lady Wishaway, that I will raise no army nor bring any harm to the people of Aldan. I swear it on the blood of my fathers . . . Permit me to return, Lord Ui Neill. I am a proud man. In my life I have always taken what I wanted. But now I ask."

"You think you could take it if you wanted to?" Ramsay said, waggling the tire iron. "You against the four of us?"

Ksar smiled. "I do not wish to cause you further

trouble, Lord Ramsay. I ask merely that you send me back to Altair."

"And I'd like to go along too," the Gypsy King said. "If that's all right. Always wanted to go to Tír na nÓg or whatever you're calling it these days."

Jamie looked at Ramsay.

"We have got the Salmon back," Jamie whispered. "What do you think, Wishaway?"

"I don't know," Wishaway said.

"Thaddeus?" Jamie asked.

But Thaddeus was still trying to take it all in and had no response. Jamie knew it was up to him.

As usual.

"OK, I'll take you back to Altair," Jamie said.

Lee stepped out of the horse box and pointed his loaded revolver at the two groups of people.

"No one's going anywhere," he said.

Chapter VII
THE SACRIFICE

THE SITUATION WAS FLUID. Lee knew that he had to take control of it immediately. He pointed the pistol at Ramsay and Jamie.

"Drop your weapons now!" he shouted.

After a moment's hesitation, Ramsay and Jamie did as they were told. The baseball bat and the tire iron clattered to the ground.

Lee turned the pistol on Ksar and the Gypsy King.

"Now, you two, come out from the doorway and walk slowly over to the car," Lee ordered. Ksar and the Gypsy King joined the others by the Volvo.

"Good. Now everyone get your hands up in the air and keep 'em up there," the assassin ordered.

When they had done that, Lee took the safety off the revolver and cocked back the hammer.

"What is the meaning of this?" Thaddeus demanded.

"Be quiet, old man. This is not your concern," Lee said.

"I'm responsible for these children. This is exactly my concern. Put that gun down immediately. What kind of person points a gun at children?"

"Shut up or I'll shoot you first."

"What fresh impertinence is this?" Ksar asked.

The Gypsy King sighed. "The man has a gun and that's all that matters right now."

"That's right. I'm the man with the gun. Now step forward, Jamie O'Neill!"

"Have I done anything wrong?" Jamie asked, and his voice was so sincere that Lee knew he would have to give him some sort of explanation.

He cleared his throat.

How best to put this?

"Um, look, nothing wrong, not as such . . . It's like this, I work for the CIA and we employ a group of psychics who can see into the future. They've determined that at some point in the next few years you are responsible for the destruction of the planet Earth and so I've been sent here to stop you."

"Are you crazy? How can you see into the future? It's bloody impossible. No one can see into the future," Ramsay said.

"We can," Lee assured him.

"How?"

"By using aspects of nonlocality. It's something to do with the arrow of time. You know, time is curved and all that," Lee said.

"You've no idea what you're talking about," Ramsay said.

"As a matter of fact, I do. I would never have agreed to go on this mission if I didn't believe in it. Apparently, after a quantum event, probability waves go forward and backward in time. Our scientists reckon that someone with a sufficiently elevated consciousness might be able to read these probability waves. So, after September 11, a Special Projects group of psychics was put together by the CIA to see if they could look into the future."

"And you believe all this nonsense?" Thaddeus said.

"It's produced some results," Lee said.

"How do you raise the consciousness?" Ramsay asked, moving a little bit closer to Lee. Jamie saw what he was doing and began inching a little bit closer too. If they were gonna jump him they'd better do it together.

"We've tried various things. Peyote. Trances. In China they use the *I Ching* and yarrow stalks," Lee said, almost talking to himself now. To convince himself. "I know it sounds far-fetched, but my bosses believe it and they saw, very clearly, that a person called Jamie O'Neill will bring about the end of the world."

"There must be more than one Jamie O'Neill," Jamie said.

"There is. But you're the one we're after," the assassin said.

"So you've come to kill me," Jamie said.

"I'm afraid so."

"Are you hearing what you're saying? Are you out of your mind?" Ramsay asked.

"I'm perfectly sane," the assassin said.

"How are you going to live with yourself if you do this?" Thaddeus asked.

"I have a difficult job. But my duty is to my country," Lee replied.

"You'll never get away with it," Jamie said.

"We've already gotten away with it. Earlier this evening we arrested your mother in London, and this place is isolated and perfect—no one knows that I'm here on this island with you. There are no witnesses."

"So it's more than just me then, isn't it? 'No witnesses' means that you've come to kill all of us," Jamie said, trying to keep the fear out of his voice.

Lee nodded. The kid was smart. He liked that. "Yes," he said coldly. "And Jamie, you and your friend better stop moving forward or you'll both die right now."

Ramsay and Jamie froze in their tracks.

"Damn," Ramsay muttered. That was his only plan. Now what?

"Look, there must be some mistake," Thaddeus said, trying to be reasonable.

Lee frowned. There was no point drawing this out. It was better to get it over with sooner rather than later. It wasn't going to be pleasant and the longer he waited the more chance there was that the tide would change and leave him stuck on this island.

"I'm sorry," Lee said, and leveled the revolver at Jamie.

The Gypsy King stepped out in front of the kids.

"Out of the way," Lee said.

The Gypsy King shook his head. "I don't think so, me darling. See, it occurs to me that what you've got there is a six-shot revolver, and there are six of us, so you really can't afford to miss," he said.

"I never miss," Lee said.

"Well now, let's see about that," the Gypsy King said. He sprinted as fast as he could and jumped on top of the assassin.

Lee shot him twice in the stomach but the Gypsy King's momentum was enough to carry him forward. He crashed into the hit man, knocking him to the ground.

"Run, the lot of you," the Gypsy King said.

Blood filled his mouth.

He smiled.

He was never going to get to Tír na nÓg, and that worthless wretch Michael Finnegan was going to be Gypsy King now, but the faerie would get back and the kids would be safe.

"Run," he croaked, and held the assassin tighter. Lee pumped another round into the Gypsy King and squirmed out from under his grip.

"The car," Ramsay said, and they sprinted toward the Volvo.

"You've lost," the Gypsy King hissed to the assassin as the strength left his body.

"See about that," Lee said, pushing the blood-soaked Traveler from him. He slithered out from under the dying man and fired wildly at the kids.

"Come on, come on," Jamie said as they reached the Volvo.

"Too late!" Ramsay cried.

Behind them the assassin was back on his feet and reloading his gun.

"This isn't going to work," Ramsay said breathlessly. "If we're going to drive off the island, we're going to have to go past him and he can shoot Thaddeus or whoever's driving right through the windscreen. And then when the car crashes he'll easily kill the rest of us."

"So what do you suggest?" Jamie said.

"Still got the Salmon?" Ramsay asked.

"Of course! Come on, everyone, we're going to the lighthouse," Jamie said.

Thaddeus was breathing hard.

Jamie looked at Ksar. "You and Ramsay are the strongest. The pair of you make a chairlift and carry him."

Ksar nodded and crossed his palms. Ramsay grabbed the eight-fingered alien's hands and they made a chair.

"Get on, Thaddeus," Ramsay said.

"I'm fine, I just need a—"

"Get on, old man, you are slowing us down," Ksar said.

Thaddeus sat on the pair of crossed hands and they ran with him to the lighthouse.

Lee finished loading his pistol, wiped his bloody fingers on the side of his jeans, and began walking calmly toward them.

"There's nowhere to run to," Lee shouted. "It's over."

Jamie found the key under a rock, unlocked the lighthouse gate, and sent Wishaway up the spiral staircase first.

"Ramsay, you next. Help Wishaway find the ladder," Jamie said. Ramsay hurried up the staircase, followed by Ksar. Thaddeus took a deep breath.

"Are you OK to go?" Jamie asked him. "Want me to help?"

"I'm fine. I can go up myself," Thaddeus insisted, and hurried up ahead of Jamie.

"Watch out for the trip step halfway up," Ramsay called up from somewhere on the staircase.

Jamie closed the gate behind him and took up the rear. "It's a pity the gate won't lock from the inside," he muttered as the assassin approached the lighthouse. Jamie then ran the steps two a time, and when he got to the top floor he saw that Ramsay had discovered a couple of flashlights and turned them on.

"OK, what do we do now? We're trapped here," Thaddeus said breathlessly.

Jamie ignored him and helped Ramsay put up the stepladder.

"There a secret chamber up there. Go, now," Jamie said to Thaddeus.

"I still don't see how that helps us get—" Thaddeus began, but Jamie cut him off.

"Just go," Jamie said.

Thaddeus climbed the ladder as fast as he could up into the hidden chamber. The room was empty except for a pillar in the center. He didn't even have time to catch his breath before Wishaway's head appeared behind him at the top of the ladder. He helped her up into the room.

Down below, Jamie looked at Ksar.

"Can we trust you this once?" Jamie said to him.

Ksar looked at him. His friend, the Gypsy King, had sacrificed himself to save Jamie and the others. It would be a betrayal of his honorable death to try and kill Jamie now.

"I give you my word that I will not attempt to harm you," Ksar said.

"OK, then go," Jamie said, and Ksar also climbed the ladder.

The assassin had now reached the bottom of the spiral staircase. Believing that they were trapped, he wasn't sprinting after them, but all the same they heard him slip and fall on the trip step.

"That stair gets them every time," Ramsay said with a grin.

"Enough yakking, get on then," Jamie said to Ramsay.

The big Irish boy nodded and climbed the ladder.

Jamie followed him just as the assassin was entering the room. The assassin fired his pistol twice, both bullets striking the aluminum stepladder.

"Bye," Jamie said, and pulled himself up onto the upper floor. He kicked the ladder away.

"You think that will stop me?" the assassin said with a laugh, and repositioned the ladder under the hole that led to the upper chamber. With all the athleticism of a trained government agent he bolted up the steps and onto the floor above, all the while keeping the gun in front of him in case any of the trapped rats tried anything desperate.

As his eyes adjusted to the dim light he saw all five of them huddled together in the center of the room, standing around a pillar.

Lee smiled to himself. Now they really had no place to go. Things couldn't have worked out better, in fact. This would be a perfect place to kill them and leave the bodies—up here where they wouldn't be discovered for a long time, especially with all the ambient mildew and guano stink.

"Please don't," Thaddeus said.

For a moment Lee's heart was touched with pity.

But then he regained his focus and recocked his revolver.

All of them were holding onto a peculiar gold device that looked like a freshwater trout from the deli counter.

Lee pointed the barrel at Jamie.

"It's time," he said.

"No," Jamie mouthed, and holding fast to the Salmon, he closed his eyes, pushed the red button on the device's tail, and leaped with the others across the light-years of space to the other side of the galaxy.

When Thaddeus Harper opened his eyes in the lighthouse on the planet Altair, he had to fight hard to keep down his panic. This was definitely not the room where they had been a moment ago. If he could believe the information his eyes were sending to his cerebral cortex, somehow they had teleported to an entirely different place.

Through the large lighthouse window he could see a cold, distant sun, and near the horizon there were two moons in the daytime sky.

So it was more than a different place. They were on a different world.

He breathed.

Nowhere in the solar system was there an oxygen-rich atmosphere, except for Earth, which meant that they were in an entirely different star system.

It was all too much to take in. First they'd had some lunatic with a gun raving about seeing into the future, and now he'd actually experienced a teleportation event. It was all a bit like one of those *Amazing Stories* comics he used to read back in the forties.

His knees began to knock.

His head was spinning. In the last week, starting with that terrifying jaguar, he'd suffered more shocks and surprises than in the previous five decades. Nothing so far compared with what he had witnessed in the Battle of the Bulge, but that had been so long ago it was almost as if it had happened to a different person.

He breathed again.

He felt a hand on his shoulder.

"Are you OK, Thaddeus?" Jamie asked.

"Where are we?" Thaddeus replied.

Jamie led him to the window of the lighthouse on the Sacred Isle. He pointed out to sea, where huge blue icebergs were grinding up against the shore.

"It's like I said, Thaddeus, we're on Altair, where Wishaway came from."

Thaddeus nodded. Yes, either Jamie was speaking the truth or he was having some kind of stroke. He chose, for the moment, to believe the former.

Wishaway stood next to the old man and took his hand.

"As I understand it, Mr. Harper, the Salmon took us here," Wishaway said.

"It's an ancient piece of alien technology. It does that," Jamie explained.

Thaddeus smiled. "OK," he said.

Ramsay looked at General Ksar with disgust.

"All right, Jamie lad. We're here. We're safe, but we've still got problem number one—what are we going to do with Ksar?" Ramsay asked.

"Nothing for now, he gave us his word," Jamie said.

Ramsay balked. "At least we have to tie him up. First chance he gets he'll stab us in the back."

"That I will not do," Ksar said.

Jamie looked at Wishaway.

"What do you think?" Jamie whispered to her. "Better safe than sorry, or trust his word?"

Wishaway regarded the Alkhavan general, the man who had despoiled her city and tried to kill her father. His face was neither pleading nor recalcitrant. Yet his eyes were clear and seemed to be filled with honest intent.

"I think we can trust him . . . for now," Wishaway said.

"Leave him alone then," Jamie said to Ramsay.

Ramsay nodded and leaned close to Ksar.

"Don't think you're off the hook, pal. You're not. I seen what you did in Aldan City, I know you," Ramsay whispered.

"All I have done is try to fulfill my duty," Ksar replied.

"Duty? Aye, you're a soldier and all that, but it was wrong of you to kill those innocent councilors in the arena," Ramsay whispered.

Ksar shook his head. "In time of war we do things that are not acceptable in time of peace. I had to do my job . . . but I—I do regret some things," he said in what for him was about as strident an admission of guilt as anyone was ever going to hear.

Ramsay looked at him with suspicion.

"Yeah, well, for the moment you've convinced Jamie that you're on the side of the good guys, but I know better, and I'll be watching you, mate, I'll be watching you," he said.

Ksar nodded. "I am sure you will, Lord Ramsay, I am sure you will."

"OK, let's get some fresh air," Jamie said, and together they walked down the lighthouse steps.

"I think we're pretty lucky to have ended up here," Ramsay said as they hurried downstairs. "I mean, with the destruction of the White Tower in Aldan, the only jump points left on Altair are here and the tower in Balanmanik. We still don't really know how to work the Salmon, so I guess it was fifty-fifty that we came here rather than the heart of enemy territory."

Ksar shook his head and stroked his angular, scarred face. His eyes narrowed.

"I doubt thy hypothesis," he said.

"Why?" Ramsay said petulantly.

"I have been sleeping for over a year. In my 'coma.'"

"And?" Jamie asked.

"And thus over a year has passed on Altair," Ksar said.

"Think so, yeah," Jamie said.

"Then the Black Tower of Balanmanik is no more. The Gag Macak glacier was already threatening the foundations when I last was there. The guilds estimated that it would only be a few more months before it would be destroyed," Ksar said.

"Yes, but you don't know any of that for sure, and I think you'll find that—" Ramsay began, but Jamie cut him off. As interesting as this discussion was, it was hardly pertinent to the situation they were in now.

Night was coming. They needed to get a fire started, and if there really was no food on this islet they were going to have to figure out how long they could stay here before jumping back to Earth. The assassin would still be there for a while but surely he wouldn't wait for them indefinitely . . .

An hour later Thaddeus had recovered a little from his shocks, and the others had thoroughly explored the bleak environs of the Sacred Isle. Things were worse than on previous occasions when they'd come here. The sea ice that had been bobbing off the shore to the north was now fused to the land along all the northern beaches of the tiny island. And despite the fact that it was clearly the Altairian summer, it seemed a good bit colder than the last time they'd been at this latitude.

All of them, save Thaddeus in his three-piece suit and black overcoat, were woefully underdressed.

Although there were no supplies of food, fortunately Wishaway's artesian well, protected from the elements by a thick cast-iron lid, was filled with cold, stagnant, but quite potable water.

"Is it good to be home?" Jamie asked her as they sipped from the well's bucket.

Wishaway's smile broadened.

"Yes," she said.

"We might need to hang out on this island for a few days just to make sure that guy back on Muck Island has gone," Jamie said.

"I would like that," Wishaway said with a winning smile.

Jamie grinned too.

This was nice.

It was a pity everyone else was here too. Even without grub it might have been very pleasant to spend a weekend with Wishaway, going for walks on the frosty beach, or gathering heather for the fire, or—

Ramsay ran up to them from a spot on the east headland.

"Something to show you," he said breathlessly.

"What?" Jamie asked.

"It's a message painted on the exterior of the lighthouse. On the far wall. Don't know how we missed it on the first pass. We were too close, I suppose. But if you take a few steps back you can see it. Dead obvious. In fact it's the most obvious place on the whole island to leave a message."

"How old is th—"

"Seems reasonably fresh," Ramsay said.

"Definitely a message?"

"Yeah, a message or a warning, something like that."

"What does it say?" Jamie asked

"Don't know, it's written in some foreign language."

"Well, it can't be for us then. They know we only speak English," Jamie said.

"Maybe Brainiac here can figure it out," Ramsay said, punching Wishaway lightly on the shoulder.

"Where are Thaddeus and Ksar?" Jamie asked.

"I told them. They went to check it out," Ramsay said.

"You left them together?"

"I don't think Ksar will try anything," Ramsay said a little guiltily.

"Let's go fast," Jamie said.

They hurried from the well back to the lighthouse.

Ksar met them halfway.

"What do you want?" Ramsay asked.

"I have deciphered some of the inscription painted on the lighthouse wall. It is for the Lord Ui Neill," Ksar said.

"Impossible. They do messages to him in English," Ramsay scoffed.

"No. Not this time. It is written in archaic Aldanese, presumably in an attempt to fool any wandering Alkhavan sailors who are endowed with only a smattering of education. They might know English but not ancient Aldanese," Ksar said.

"What does it say?" Jamie asked.

"That I cannot tell, but I was able to read your name, Lord Ui Neill. Doubtless the Lady Wishaway will comprehend it. The writer must have known that if the Lord Ui Neill would come back to this desolate spot, he would bring with him his consort," Ksar said with impeccable logic.

Wishaway blushed at the word *consort* but Jamie barely noticed it.

"Who would write a note like that?" Jamie asked.

"It must have been done on the order of the Lady Wishaway's father," Ksar suggested.

But Ramsay had other ideas.

"Wait a minute, maybe it's a trap. Maybe you did it while we were off exploring the island," Ramsay said, jabbing his finger into Ksar's chest.

"Poke me not, Lord Ramsay," Ksar said, removing Ramsay's finger.

"Don't touch me!" Ramsay said, swatting away Ksar's hand.

"Cut it out, both of ya," Jamie said.

When they reached the lighthouse, Thaddeus was grinning at them broadly. He pointed his stick at the curved stone wall in front of him.

"Look at that. Alien writing. I've never seen anything like it," he said happily.

Jamie examined the graffiti written on the lighthouse. It was completely incomprehensible. A collection of signs, symbols, and weird, unearthly hieroglyphs.

"Well?" Jamie asked, turning to Wishaway.

"Ksar was right, it is for you," she said.

"Don't keep us in suspense."

Wishaway bit her lip. The news wasn't good.

"Come on," Ramsay said.

"'Hail, mighty Ui Neill, Lord of the Isles, Guardian of the Passage, Defender of the Shore. We write this in the old tongue in the expectation that ye will come to us a final time in our hour of need. The Lord Protector of Alkhava and the Crown Prince of Oralands have landed a fleet on the southern shore of Aldan. They march on Aldan City. We are prepared for a long siege and will await thee until the end of time. I have placed a boat in my daughter's old hiding place on this island. I entreat thee, Lord Ui Neill. Please come. And may we be worthy of thy aid . . . Callaway,'" Wishaway said.

"What's the matter with these people? They're being invaded again? Don't they ever learn? It's like France in the Third Republic. Bloody eejits," Ramsay said.

Jamie turned to Wishaway. "What does he mean 'a boat in the old hiding place?'" he asked.

"The cave on the eastern shore," Wishaway said simply.

Thaddeus examined the wall. "How old do you think this paint job is? Maybe they wrote this message months ago. Everything could be all over now," he said.

Jamie nodded. Thaddeus was right. "But we don't have any choice, do we?" Jamie said. "We can't go back to Earth for at least a few days until that nutcase goes away. We can't stay here without food. We might as well go to Aldan and see what's going on."

No one could think of an objection to this remark, so they walked in reflective silence as Wishaway led them the short distance to her old hiding place—a tidal cave on the eastern shore of the island.

Cunningly concealed inside the cave was a small sailing boat. A single-masted steep-sided vessel, only about fifteen feet long, it would be a tough squeeze for all five of them.

"Maybe Thaddeus should wait on the island," Ramsay said, looking at the old man.

"And miss the chance to see an alien civilization first-hand? You must be kidding me. You can wait here if you want, but I'm going in the boat," Thaddeus said.

Ramsay shook his head at Jamie, but Jamie knew that there was no convincing the old man. And besides, it wouldn't be right to leave Thaddeus here by himself.

"Ksar, what do you want to do?" Jamie asked.

"I will accompany you," he said.

"OK. Well, I suppose we'll all go," Jamie said.

"That's it then, Jamie? You've decided and that's it," Ramsay said, looking angrily at Ksar.

"Yeah," Jamie said.

"You're not as cocky as this on Earth," Ramsay commented.

"No, I'm not, more's the pity," Jamie agreed, and moved on breezily. "So what should we do? Light a fire, rest up tonight, and then head to Aldan first thing in the morning. What do you think, Wishaway?"

Wishaway looked doubtful.

"We are close to high tide now, Jamie. I do not see what purpose can be served by waiting until tomorrow. Why not go now? I know the route very well. Indeed it will be easier to navigate there at night," she said.

Jamie nodded. "I suppose," he said skeptically.

"We're going to jump into that tiny boat and make our way through an iceberg-filled ocean at night? Am I the only one here that's learned any lessons from the movies?" Ramsay asked.

"Thaddeus, what do you think? Do you want to rest up for the night?" Jamie asked.

Thaddeus wanted nothing more than to warm his bones by a fire, but he didn't wish to appear to be the weakest link.

"I say if we're going to go, then let's go. I'm assuming you kids have done this before and know what you're about," Thaddeus said.

"Ksar?" Jamie asked.

"You're asking him for his opinion?" Ramsay said, horrified.

"If you wish to go immediately, I will assist you," Ksar said.

"Bet you will. Bide your time until you can dump us all overboard," Ramsay muttered.

Wishaway looked at Jamie.

"Do we need provisions?" Jamie asked.

Wishaway examined the boat. There were skins filled with water and some dried meat and biscuit-bread. It wasn't much but there was nothing on the island that could add anything to it.

She shook her head.

"OK then, let's go," Jamie said.

Jamie helped Thaddeus into the boat first. Wishaway climbed in next, while he, Ramsay, and Ksar pushed the small wooden craft into the freezing, frothy water.

"Bloody hell. Five minutes in here and you'd be toast," Ramsay muttered as the icy sea cut off the circulation around his ankles.

They pushed the boat all the way out of the cave and when the craft floated they climbed aboard, Ramsay with clumsy strength, Jamie with an awkward stumble, and Ksar with surprising alacrity.

Wishaway hoisted a small blue sail and almost immediately they began heading for an iceberg.

She turned the boat into the wind.

"We'll never get through the ice," Ramsay said.

"We will," Ksar said, and moved to the front of the boat. He turned to Wishaway. "Since I was a boy I have sailed among the ice monsters off the Alkhavan coast. I will be able to thread us through this field."

"If we crash into one of those things, that's it," Ramsay said to Jamie. "We'd literally be putting our lives in his hands."

"Come on, let's go," Jamie said, and nodded at Wishaway.

She turned the tiller and the boat gathered headway again.

Ksar grabbed an oar that looked like a long barge pole and went to the very tip of the prow.

"Lady Wishaway, reduce the sail, and slowly take us between the ice mountains. I will fend them off with this oar," Ksar said.

Wishaway reefed the main by about a third and retook the tiller.

The boat handled well despite being overloaded with people. Wishaway nudged it out into the floes. As they got closer to the big iceberg dead ahead, Ksar pushed it away from the boat with the wooden oar.

"He's very strong," Thaddeus commented.

"Yeah, I see that," Ramsay agreed.

The boat was making only a couple of knots and progress was very slow; still, as Wishaway pointed out, they could consider themselves lucky—if this had been the winter they wouldn't have gotten much of anywhere on the frozen sea.

As it was it took them a whole day to finally free themselves of the maze of ice and make their way into the open ocean.

The sun sank in the east.

The moons glistened.

The peculiar constellations formed themselves in the Altairian sky.

Jamie relieved Wishaway at the tiller and let her rest. He had steered to Aldan City once before and he knew the way: Keep the blue star on the port side and the right to three points off starboard.

Wishaway lay down on the foredeck, curled into the fetal position, and after a few minutes was asleep next to the exhausted Thaddeus.

A meteor shower appeared in the inky blackness to the south.

Jamie considered waking Thaddeus to show him but he decided against it. The old man was going to need to keep his strength up. Ramsay, of course, was far too excited for sleep.

They watched the meteors for an exhilarating ten minutes before the planet's atmosphere burned them all out of existence.

It made Ramsay think about mortality.

"What do you think that dude meant when he said that you were going to cause the end of the world, Jamie?" Ramsay whispered.

Jamie shrugged. "I have no idea. Maybe he got me mixed up with you. All those potions and weird cocktails you're brewing up in your bedroom, maybe one of them mutates into a bug that destroys the human race."

Ramsay shook his head. "No way, I don't make stuff like that."

"If you say so."

"Do you believe he was really from the CIA, or was he just a nutter?" Ramsay asked.

Jamie rolled the sleeves of his black sweater down over his hands. He was very cold but he was trying not to show it.

"Why is it every single time we come to Aldan we're underprepared and underdressed?" Jamie asked.

"Don't even try to change the subject, mate. I know your ways. Come on, it's OK. I know he freaked you out—freak anybody out—but I was only asking. I personally don't believe you will destroy the world in the future. Even if you become president of the United States or something, which is pretty unlikely. He must have been just a crazy person, don't you think?" Ramsay said.

"Didn't seem like one to me," Jamie said. "He seemed far too calculating for that. I think he was the real deal. Definitely CIA. Or something."

They sat in silence for a while.

"Nah, the CIA would never hire someone like that. He had to be off his rocker," Ramsay said at last. "Just another madman with a gun. You've got plenty of them in America, unfortunately."

Jamie nodded. "Well, you're right about one thing. He was American, his accent confirmed it. Northern California, if I had to guess."

"Do you think he really had your mum arrested?" Ramsay asked.

"I don't know," Jamie said.

"Call her up on your cell phone," Ramsay suggested with a grin. "She'll get the message in about ninety-six years."

A chunk of ice crunched against the side of the frail wooden boat. Thaddeus groaned in his sleep and woke disoriented. He sat up and stifled a cough. He looked around and then shuffled down the deck into the cockpit next to Jamie and Ramsay. He coughed again.

"Are you OK, Thaddeus?" Jamie asked.

"Will you stop asking me that! Don't I look OK?" Thaddeus said irritably.

"Yeah, you look great," Jamie replied.

Yes, I am usually very good at concealing my terror, Thaddeus thought. For the truth was he hated boats. He had never really learned to swim and the last time he had been on any kind of vessel was the Staten Island Ferry in a choppy ride across New York harbor—and the time before that was in a troop ship that carried him from Europe to America at the end of World War II.

"While you were resting you missed a meteor shower. You should check out the sky," Jamie said. "There's lots of cool stuff up there. Different constellations, nebulae, you name it. Did you see the moons?"

"I did, two of them. Like Mars. Only those are real moons, not just captured asteroids. Millions of years ago, when they were closer in to the planet, the tidal forces must have been incredible," Thaddeus said.

"Yeah, isn't it amazing to be on another world?" Jamie asked.

Thaddeus nodded. "It is amazing. Yes. It is. I never really believed that there were other worlds out there in the universe with sentient beings walking around on them. I guess I was wrong."

"Yup," Ramsay said.

"Is this the only one? Are there other planets out there like this?" Thaddeus asked.

Jamie shrugged. "I don't know, Thaddeus. The Salmon only lets you jump between Earth and Altair. Ramsay reckons that if a long-lost race of aliens made it and the towers on the two worlds eons ago, there might be portals to other parts of the universe, but he's just speculating. He doesn't have proof."

"Well, it's informed speculation," Ramsay said.

"No one on this planet made the Salmon?" Thaddeus inquired.

"Nah, I doubt it. They're pretty backward," Jamie said. "We found an alien spaceship the last time out, but it was definitely not from any civilization currently on Altair. We reckon it was from the Salmon makers. Like, maybe that was their old technology before they perfected this whole teleportation lark."

Thaddeus nodded.

"And where are those aliens now, do you think?" he asked with a shiver.

"I don't know. I never really thought about it," Jamie said. "Probably dead."

"Or hibernating," Ramsay said.

"Dead," Thaddeus said sadly.

Probably dead, the First said with a trace of irritation.

Or hibernating, the Second countered.

Or hibernating, the Third agreed.

They are the ones who are "probably dead," the First said.

Soon to be dead, the Second corrected.

Yes, that is more correct. Soon to be dead, the Third said. *Every last one of them.*

The whole human race, the First said.

And not just the humans. Every living thing on the whole planet, the Second said.

Every living thing on the whole planet, the Third said with a deep, cold, and infinite sadness.

Chapter VIII
THE LIZARDS

ICE AND PAIN. A wound on his arm cauterized by frost. His feet frozen. A wind howling out of the north, sea spray all around him on the cursèd bark.

"How are you doing up there?" Jamie yelled from the back.

He fended off a big chunk of drifting sea ice with the oar. The berg was so thick it cracked and creaked like the boards on a ship.

"I am well," Ksar replied.

He was far from well. His muscles had atrophied in the coma ward. He was a shadow of the man he once had been. But every day that he lived and breathed he was a little bit better than before. And he was determined that he must never show weakness. While the others sat at the back of the boat, huddled in blankets, he stood on the prow with the oar, pushing off the icebergs, seemingly oblivious to the biting winds or his chilled hands.

His body was getting stronger but his thoughts were not so single-minded.

Jamie of the Ui Neill had brought so much personal

destruction into his life. For the last two years, since first the boy had thwarted his invasion plans, he had been determined to exact his revenge upon him. But now he had given Jamie his word that he would not harm him or his friends. And princes did not break their word.

And it wasn't just that.

There was something else too.

All his life he had thought of Earth as this magical, wonderful place right out of Morgan's book. If he got to Earth everything would be put to rights. He would be feted as a hero. He would lead the life of heroes, the virtuous life. He would live and prosper. But now he'd gone to Earth and it hadn't been magical or wonderful. It had been hostile and bleak and the only person who had been kind to him had been murdered by one of his own.

Where did that leave him now?

What should he do now?

Did his life have any purpose left?

"Ksar," a voice said.

The Alkhavan general turned.

Thaddeus, defying his own fear, had walked along the slippery, icy deck to the front of the boat.

"Here," Thaddeus said, handing Ksar some dried *gassi* meat. "Thought you might be feeling hungry."

Ksar popped the delicacy in his mouth.

"I don't know what it is exactly, but Wishaway claims that it's good for ya," Thaddeus said.

"It is a small animal that lives in tidal pools. The Aldanese smoke the flesh in vats and give it to their sailors," Ksar said.

Thaddeus nodded and took a bite. It was a bit like caviar but with the consistency of crab meat. "Definitely an acquired taste."

Ksar nodded and ate. "In the iceships our sailors were given salted animal fat. This is better," Ksar said.

"If you say so," Thaddeus muttered.

They stood there for a while without saying anything. Wishaway had taken all the reefs out of the main sail and the little boat was making good progress. Thaddeus was no expert but if he had to guess he reckoned they were probably up to about twelve or thirteen knots.

"The ice floes seem to be thinning out now as we head south, so you can come back to the cockpit and join us if you want," Thaddeus said.

Ksar shook his head. "I will remain here, at least on lookout. If we were to hit even a small ice island, we would be in grave peril."

"Yeah, down with the old canoe, huh? When I was a kid everyone still talked about the *Titanic* like it happened yesterday. This was before all the picture shows. Suppose you've never heard of it."

"The what?"

"Doesn't matter . . . OK, it's getting a bit nippy. Well, if you want to come back to the cockpit we'd love to have you."

Thaddeus gingerly walked along the deck, which was now some twenty degrees from the horizontal. For once he wished he was wearing sneakers rather than his expensive Brooks Brothers leather shoes. They looked good on the outside but they didn't have much grip and they certainly let the water in.

"What were you doing?" Jamie asked when Thaddeus returned to the cockpit.

"Giving Ksar some food. He's been standing there for hours," Thaddeus said.

"Plotting, no doubt," Ramsay said.

"Stopping us from crashing into an iceberg, more like," Thaddeus said.

"You wait. You just wait," Ramsay muttered.

"He seems like a decent fellow," Thaddeus countered.

"Yeah, after he mutinies and clubs us all on the head and you wake up in the bowels of an iceship heading for the slave markets of Afor, you'll remember my skepticism," Ramsay said.

Thaddeus frowned. Ramsay might be right, but his flip tone was not appreciated. In Thaddeus's day kids were seen and not heard and none of them would have dared talk to someone of Thaddeus's age as if they were equals.

"Look, a *juula*!" Wishaway cried, but when everyone turned the big amphibian's snout was dipping beneath the gray sea.

"What was that thing?" Thaddeus asked Jamie.

"We don't really know. Wishaway's never been able to describe it properly. Some kind of fishy octopus," Jamie said.

"Well, I've never seen anything like it. It puts my jaguar to shame," Thaddeus said, forgetting his irritation with Ramsay. "I hope Ksar saw it too."

Ramsay looked at Jamie and shook his head. Thaddeus was a nice old bird but he was obviously very naive.

"Thaddeus, you know you should just stay away from that guy," Ramsay said, pointing at the Alkhavan. "He's likely to do us all a mischief. Remember Sméagol? All lovey-lovey, but scheming the whole time to get the precious back."

Thaddeus ignored him and took some water.

"Could I have some water, please, Thaddeus?" Wishaway asked, stifling a yawn. Thaddeus passed her the skin and she took a sip.

"Are you getting tired? Do you want me to take over steering?" Jamie asked.

"No, I am tired, but I am quite content," Wishaway said with a happy smile. Jamie knew what she meant. This was the way it was supposed to be. The two of them on the high seas, off on some crazy adventure. If they got back to Earth in one piece they definitely had to do a lot more of this. Maybe not stuff where their lives were in actual jeopardy, but from now on it couldn't all just be school and homework and TV. There was a great big world out there.

"You know, in Ireland they have this thing called the Ocean Youth Trust," Jamie said. "I don't know why I never thought of it before. You'd love it. They go up around the islands of Scotland and down to France. I think we should—"

"Lord Ui Neill!" Ksar called from the foredeck.

"What?" Jamie yelled back.

"Come," Ksar said. "I wish you to see something."

"I'll go," Ramsay said, suspicion knitting his eyebrows together.

Ignoring him, Jamie walked the short distance from the cockpit to the prow of the boat.

"What is it, Ksar?" he asked. "Hey, you look cold. Are you all right?"

Ksar found that he was momentarily touched by Jamie's concern.

"I—I am well, thank you, Lord Ui Neill," he said.

"What's up?" Jamie asked.

"There," Ksar said, pointing to an enormous chunk of ice floating about a kilometer from the port bow.

"Oh, we'll easily miss that. Wishaway can steer around it, she's quite an accomplished helmsman, you know. In fact I was just thinking she'd be great in the Ocean Youth Trust. Sort of thing we should do together. Ideal for blowing away Ramsay's talk of *weltschmaltz* or whatever that word was," Jamie said cheerfully.

"No, Lord Ui Neill, we will not steer around it. It is an Alkhavan iceship. It has already changed direction once, they have seen us," Ksar said calmly.

Jamie peered again at the iceberg.

Without his telescope he couldn't tell for sure, but after a moment's hard concentration it appeared that Ksar was correct.

"What will they do?" Jamie asked.

Ksar looked grim.

"They will board us, kill the men, take the Lady Wishaway prisoner," he said.

"What about you? You can order them not to," Jamie said.

Ksar scoffed at this idea.

"I have been gone for over a year. A new Lord Protector will have risen to the top of the imperium. No one will be under obligation to obey my orders. They may even consider me to be an outlaw," Ksar said with a shudder.

"They don't treat outlaws well?" Jamie asked.

"Outlaws they bind and throw in the *firbolg* pit to be eaten alive," Ksar said.

"They have a similar thing on Earth, it's called *American Idol* . . . Come on, let's alert the others," Jamie said.

They walked back to the cockpit. Wishaway looked into Jamie's face and saw immediately that something was wrong.

"Jamie?" she said.

"OK, everybody be cool. There's an iceship off the port bow. Ksar thinks they've seen us. They'll probably board us," Jamie said quickly.

"A what ship off the what?" Thaddeus said.

"I see it," Ramsay said. "Yeah, it's definitely coming for us."

"How many would they have on board?" Jamie asked Ksar.

"It is the not largest I have seen but I would estimate that it will crew a dozen men and perhaps more," Ksar said.

"A dozen," Jamie said, "and apart from that big barge pole thing we've got no weapons at all."

"The barge pole and my fists. For the last few months

I've been studying Shotokan karate online. I reckon I'm up to yellow belt at least," Ramsay said.

"And of course you're a twelfth-level magic user in Dungeons and Dragons," Jamie said with heavy sarcasm.

"That thing is a ship? Are you sure?" Thaddeus asked.

"Yes, we're sure. Now, does anyone have any ideas?" Jamie asked.

No one spoke.

Jamie poked Ramsay in the ribs. "Come on, big fella, sorry about that D and D crack, get that noggin going," Jamie said.

"I accept your apology," Ramsay said with condescension. "And actually I do have an idea."

"Well?"

"I suppose we could try a *Mary Celeste*," Ramsay suggested.

"Let's do it," Jamie said and then after a moment's hesitation he added, "And what is that exactly?"

"A ship they found floating in the sea, with the table set for dinner but all the crew vanished. It was quite the sensation at the time. Creeped everyone out. They still don't know what happened," Ramsay explained.

"How can we vanish?" Jamie asked.

"We can't," Ramsay said. "We can't go over the side. The water's freezing. But we can all pretend to be sick or dead. If we all lie down on the deck and Wishaway lets go of the tiller, it might seem as if we all died from some terrible plague. The crew of the Alkhavan ship might not want to touch us in case they get the plague too."

Jamie nodded. "It's worth a try," he said. "Quickly, before they get too close, everyone find a spot to lie down and don't look too comfortable, you're supposed to be dead or dying. Wishaway, let the tiller float free. OK, chop-chop, we're almost in visual range. We don't want them to see any movement. Let's go."

They all lay down upon the deck or slumped forward in the cockpit.

The iceship came closer and closer until it hauled its sail when it was only a boat-length away.

Jamie cocked open an eye.

"Fraka sak saam akk!" the Alkhavan captain yelled. Obviously some kind of challenge. No one on board the little boat moved. *"Fraka sak saam akk!"* he cried again.

Jamie saw the fur-clad, blond-haired Alkhavan turn to his fellow officers and mutter something. There followed a lot of finger pointing and fist clenching, though what they were actually saying was impossible to know.

The two vessels drifted closer to one another.

A minute passed.

Two minutes.

"Damn it. It's not going to work," Ramsay hissed. "They're sending over a boarding party."

Jamie was puzzled. Ramsay didn't speak Alkhavan.

"How do you know?" Jamie whispered.

"Ropes," Ramsay whispered.

Jamie cursed inwardly. The Alkhavans had lowered two thick ropes from the gunwale of the iceship.

"Fama kiak sa!" the Alkhavan captain said, and reluctantly two burly Alkhavan marines began lowering themselves down the ropes.

"OK, new plan," Jamie whispered. "As soon as they set foot on deck we have at them. Ramsay and I will take the guy near the stern. Ksar, can you handle the dude near the prow?"

"Easily," Ksar whispered.

"But then what, Jamie?" Thaddeus asked.

"We'll improvise," Jamie said.

The current brought the ships closer and closer until they were almost touching.

The two burly marines lowered themselves tentatively down onto the deck. No doubt they were expecting to see the effects of starvation or the evidence of some dread disease on the stricken crew. What they weren't expecting was former Lord Protector Irian Ksar to leap up from a prone position, yell at them in Alkhavan, grab one marine by his thick *hoxney* belt, and toss him into the ocean. The second Alkhavan took more than a few beats to process this information, which gave Ksar ample time to continue his run along the windward side of the boat, charge the poor marine, knock him to the ground, and throw him over the scuppers into the sea.

"Up the rope," Ksar said in animated English. "Surprise is our only ally."

"Wait a minute, maybe we should—" Ramsay said but it was too late.

Ksar climbed the rope as if there was an angry gym teacher yelling at him from the bottom and in two seconds he was on the broad deck of the iceship. Ramsay climbed up after him and Jamie followed his friend.

Wishaway wasn't to be left out. "Take the tiller," she said to Thaddeus and nimbly climbed the thick rope. When she vaulted over the sticky frozen side of the iceship, she found that Ksar had already killed three Alkhavans, taken their bronze daggers, and given one to Ramsay and one to Jamie.

Whether he could be trusted or not, one thing was sure about Ksar: He was good at his job.

Ksar parried a blow from a sailor who was trying to get behind him and then with a deft thrust he plunged his weapon into the man's throat.

He withdrew the dagger and attacked two more Alkhavans coming at him with axes.

"I am Irian Ksar, of the Ninth House of Alkhav.

Surrender thy ship to me or thy blood will join thy fellows' on the deck," Ksar said in High Alkhavan.

"Impostor!" a sailor yelled at Ksar, and swung a stone hand axe at Ksar's head. Ksar ducked the blow, stepped to one side, and stabbed the sailor between the ribs.

The blond captain hesitated for a second but then lunged at Ksar with a large curved sword. The point knicked Ksar on the lower arm but that wasn't enough to upset the former Lord Protector.

He parried the sword away, kicked the captain in the knees, and as the burly sailor was falling to the deck he drove his own blade into the man's heart.

"Enough!" Ksar yelled in Alkhavan. "Surrender thy ship!"

With six of their fellows dead at their feet and another two dead in the sea, the remaining four crew members begged for quarter.

"Drop thy weapons," Ksar said.

The sailors dropped their assorted knives and axes and put their hands in the air.

"You did it! Well done," Wishaway said to Ramsay and Jamie.

"We didn't do a thing, it was all Prince Valiant over there," Ramsay complained.

"What now, Lord Ui Neill?" Ksar asked. "The ship is your lawful prize."

"We don't want the ship. It's too slow and hard to handle. Let's tie up what's left of the crew and take what supplies we might need," Jamie said. "And then we'll move on as quickly as we can."

Ksar grunted his approval. "My sentiments exactly, Lord Ui Neill," he said.

When Jamie signaled that the fight was over, Thaddeus took the Aldanese boat away from the side of the iceship to preserve its hull.

Ten minutes later Thaddeus saw the four of them call him over. He steered the boat next to the iceship again. Wishaway threw a grappling hook to the smaller vessel and made them fast together.

Jamie and Ramsay climbed down the ropes, carrying ships' biscuit, jars of fresh water, and some of that dried fat that apparently tasted so disgusting. Wishaway and Ksar followed with swords and a couple of strange-looking crossbows.

Wishaway took the tiller again and Ksar resumed his lookout position at the front of the boat.

"I see that Ksar's got a bit of a cut. He's very stoic and all but he needs something on it," Jamie said to Ramsay. "Rip off a bit of your T-shirt and I'll make him a bandage." His friend was wearing a scruffy long-sleeved T-shirt under his ridiculous black catsuit. Ramsay was incensed by the suggestion.

"Rip off your own shirt," he said.

Jamie lifted up his sweater. "I'm wearing a shirt-shirt, it won't tear. Come on, a thin sliver off the bottom," he said.

"But this is my favorite T-shirt," Ramsay protested, pulling down his catsuit to reveal Cartman from *South Park*.

Jamie didn't want to discuss it. "Give it over, the man's bleeding."

"Come on, Ramsay," Thaddeus said.

Ramsay shook his head. "For Jamie, it's ideological, Thaddeus. We disagree about *South Park*. Jamie thinks it's not as funny as the *The Simpsons*, whereas I believe that the season ten opener 'Warcraft' is the best episode of television since the classic *Trek* story 'City on the Edge of Forever.'"

"Come on, Ramsay, you're losing face here in front of Thaddeus," Jamie said with a wink at the old man. Reluctantly Ramsay tore a strip off the bottom of the T-shirt. Jamie took it forward to bind Ksar's wound.

As the boat gathered momentum and began to tilt, Ramsay sat next to Thaddeus on the lee side of the craft.

"Well, that was upsetting," Ramsay said.

"Yes," Thaddeus agreed, and before Ramsay could complain more about his T-shirt he noticed that all the color had drained from the old man's cheeks. He seemed frail and old.

"Are you OK, Thaddeus?" Ramsay asked him.

"I'm fine, just a bit stunned by the speed and casual brutality of that little encounter we just had. Is it always like this when you come to Altair?" he asked Ramsay.

Ramsay nodded. "Pretty much. And things will only get worse when we get to Aldan."

"Why do you say that?" Thaddeus asked.

"Because they always do," Ramsay said with satisfaction.

Ramsay was not to be disappointed. When they sailed into Aldan harbor later that day, they could tell that things were not good. Fires were burning in several buildings and the docks and high walls were lined with archers and musketeers firing long bows and carbines into the sky.

"What are they shooting at?" Thaddeus asked.

"There!" Jamie said, pointing at a squadron of flying things coming down from a height of about a thousand feet.

"What are they?" Thaddeus asked, stunned to see large, batlike creatures gliding toward the ground with men strapped to their backs. The men were shouting maniacally and shooting crossbow bolts at running civilians, before the big creatures reached the bottom of their parabolic descent and swooped them up again into the sky.

"Pterodactyls," Thaddeus said in horror.

"No, not as bad as that," Jamie assured him. "They're called *rantas*. Never seen ones that big before but I think they're pretty harmless on the whole."

"The Aldanese don't think they're harmless," Ramsay said.

"No," Jamie agreed. Even the trained soldiers were running in panic along the battlements, for although there were only a dozen or so of the attackers, the whole thing was the stuff of nightmares.

A few Aldanese were attempting to return fire with their rifles and one group of men had succeeded in throwing a clay pot filled with napalm into the wings of a low-swooping *ranta*.

Crying horribly, the burning creature dived into the sea with a splash of steam and spray.

Visibly shaken, Thaddeus turned to Jamie. "What's going on?" he asked.

"The city's under aerial attack from Alkhavan soldiers mounted on the backs of giant lizardlike bat things. Looks like they're firing crossbows down on them."

"They're breathing fire," Thaddeus said, aghast.

"No, no, they're not. The Aldanese are firing up clay

pots filled with napalm—a substance that Ramsay unfortunately invented on Altair two years ago."

As the giant *rantas* gained altitude for another raid on the city, a watchman at the harbor mouth finally spotted their boat coming into the port.

"What ship is that?" he yelled in Aldanese.

"We bring the Lord Ui Neill!" Wishaway replied.

There was immediate consternation on the wharves.

"Say again!" a port officer cried.

"Our boat carries Seamus of the Black, Guardian of the Passage, Heir of Morgan, the Lord Ui Neill!" Wishaway called again.

The news went through the port like wildfire.

"The Lord Ui Neill come to save us!" someone yelled, and a sporadic cheering began to be heard all over the lower city.

"Raise expectations, why don't ya," Ramsay said sarcastically. For he knew that, as usual, there wasn't much that they could do.

"Quickly, quickly, dock thy ship, mighty Ui Neill, ye must land immediately. We are in grave peril," the harbormaster, a chubby man in a bloodstained white shirt, called out in English.

While the squadron of *rantas* formed themselves into a wing to make another pass, a group of soldiers ran to the pier and pointed crossbows at their ship.

"Show thyself, Ui Neill, lest we fire at thee. We have suffered much from Alkhavan trickery," a grim-faced sergeant yelled.

Jamie knew what was required of him. He strode to the front of the boat and stood on the prow.

"It is I, the Lord Ui Neill," Jamie said, spreading his arms.

There was a huge cheer from the soldiers as recognition slowly dawned. Almost everyone remembered Jamie from his previous visits to Aldan, and those who didn't only had to look at the copper coins in their pocket to see his likeness.

"He's not shy, is he?" Thaddeus whispered to Ramsay.

"Aye, look at him up there on the front of the boat. Can't help himself," Ramsay said with a sigh. "Thinks he's DiCaprio."

A sergeant threw a hawser to Jamie, who caught it in one hand and tied it to the ship through one of the eyebolts.

"Quickly, my Lord, they come again," the sergeant cried.

Jamie stepped off the boat and onto the stone pier.

"But what can Jamie do against those things?" Thaddeus asked.

"Very little, I reckon," Ramsay replied. "I mean, it's pretty silly. And typical. One day we're going to come here and nothing's going to be going on. No wars, no invasions. They'll have a big party for us, lay out the red carpet, they'll say, 'Hey look, it's those two who saved our city, let's give them medals.'"

"What do they usually say to you?" Thaddeus asked.

"What do they usually say? What they're saying right now. 'Help us, we're in big trouble. Hurry up. Can't you think of something? Oh, please help us, help us, we can't do anything' . . . You know? With these guys it's very much 'What have you done for us lately?'"

Thaddeus nodded. "And do you always get them out of trouble?" he asked.

"Yeah. We do. Jamie kind of gets them all worked up and while he has them distracted I usually think of the solution to their latest batch of problems. He's the figurehead and I'm the power behind the throne," Ramsay said with a sniff.

The boat was tied up to the dock just in time for them to witness another terrifying attack from the *ranta* squadron.

The lizards tumbled out of the sky like Stukas, strafing the marketplace and sending the petrified Aldanese running for cover. Several of the *ranta* riders got off a few shots with their bows and one managed to hit a soldier who was attempting to return fire.

The soldier fell to the ground with an arrow protruding from his thigh.

The Alkhavans buzzed the city for another minute before gliding to the thermals to get to a higher altitude.

"Come on, let's get ashore," Ramsay said to Thaddeus. Turning to Ksar, he said, "If I was you, mate, I'd wait on board if you don't want to get lynched."

Thaddeus climbed up onto the stone pier of the harbor and stared in wonder at this extraordinary alien city. Glass sculptures, minarets, and round towers dotted the landscape—the architecture a mishmash of different cultures, eras, and even planets.

"Come on, Thad, enough gawking," Ramsay said.

Thaddeus ignored the insolence. "This is incredible . . . to be walking around an alien civilization. The wonder, the amazement," he said.

Ramsay yawned.

"Yeah, the wonder wears off quickly when people are trying to kill, torture, or enslave you all the time," he said.

"Torture?" Thaddeus asked with concern.

"Yeah. Torture. Ksar tortured us with my pocket solder. That guy there on the boat that we're all so chummy-chummy with right now," Ramsay said. "Jamie might have blocked it out, but I certainly haven't."

"Perhaps he's changed his outlook," Thaddeus suggested.

"Changed his outlook? You should have seen him on the iceship. Couldn't wait to get the killing started. Loved it."

"But he could have betrayed us there," Thaddeus said.

"Nah, not with me and Jamie right behind him. He's biding his time, believe me . . . Come on, push your way through the masses, Thad, looks like they've brought the boss to see us already," Ramsay said.

"The who?"

"Callaway," Ramsay said.

"Who's Callaway?" Thaddeus asked.

"Wishaway's father, he runs this joint. OK sort of bloke. Bit ineffectual."

"Wishaway's father is in charge of this city?" Thaddeus asked.

"Yeah. He's OK. Not great, but not a disaster. If he was on Earth he'd be driving a white BMW. You know? That kind of guy. Rich, white boomer type. The sort of person who thinks golf is cool and Robin Williams is funny."

This was no help at all to Thaddeus.

"Wha—" Thaddeus began, but found himself being guided through a throng of soldiers and citizenry until he was standing in front of a thin, white-bearded man in a yellow robe. Wishaway was giving the man an enormous hug.

"*Fana treepa laa,*" she said to her father.

"*Sama caa, Wishaway,*" Callaway replied with tears in his eyes. Wishaway had changed a great deal but he didn't care, he was just happy to see her, even under these circumstances. They held each other for a moment before Callaway collected his wits and bowed to Jamie.

"Lord Ui Neill," he said.

Jamie returned the bow with a curt nod and got straight to business.

"What's happening?" Jamie asked.

"We are under attack from these foul things," Callaway said.

"I see that. What's the strategic situation? Where are the Alkhavans?" Jamie said calmly.

Callaway seemed flustered. His eyes grew defensive.

"They are not our present concern. Our present concern, as you can see, are these terrible—"

Jamie cut him off. "Yeah, I see. Now, where is the Alkhavan army? Is it outside the gates? Is it waiting in a fleet? What's going on? Surely your intelligence has improved in the last year."

Callaway nodded. "The Alkhavan and Oralands armies are fifteen leagues to the east of here. They have landed unopposed and have fully disembarked their war engines and their soldiers."

Jamie was incensed. "Unopposed? How could you have let that happen?"

Callaway could feel the moral pressure of the small crowd gathered about them.

"We had spies keeping watch on the Alkhavan fleet, and it did not occur to us that the Alkhavans would embark their armies onboard ships of Oralands. It, um, did not seem likely . . ."

Jamie frowned.

"OK, well, it's done. Nothing we can do about it now," he said. "Fifteen leagues. That's about what?"

"Forty-five miles," Ramsay said.

"So more than a day's march from the city," Jamie said.

Just then another attack from the *rantas* sent everyone scurrying for cover. The terrible screams from the lizards and the shouts of triumph from their handlers were drowned out by the panicked yelling coming from the Aldanese. One Alkhavan swooped down over the docks, his face painted red, his howling mount demonic and terrifying. A few of Callaway's personal guard fired muskets at the fast-moving creature but none of them got a lucky hit.

The citizenry ran for cover, some even jumping into the harbor.

When the raid was over, Jamie resumed his conversation as if nothing had happened.

"OK, so if your intelligence is correct that the combined army is more than a day away, this appears to be a skirmish attack, rather than a precursor to an imminent assault," Jamie said.

"Perhaps," Callaway said.

"No 'perhaps' about it, they're probing the defenses," Ramsay said.

"What did you bring to assist us, Lord Ui Neill?" Callaway asked, deciding that maybe it was time to put Jamie on the defensive.

Jamie looked askance.

"Bring your . . . um . . ." Jamie said, his mind racing. Of course, as usual, they had brought no guns, explosives, or useful weapons of any kind.

Jamie looked at Ramsay, but his friend's face was blank.

"Oh, I know. Yes . . . We brought Thaddeus," Jamie announced, slapping the old man chummily on the back.

"What?" Callaway said.

"Who. Thaddeus is a he. This gentleman right here," Jamie said.

Callaway bowed. "Lord Thaddeus, it is an honor to meet thee," he said.

"The pleasure is all mine," Thaddeus replied.

"And Lord Thaddeus, please tell me, how can ye assist us?" Callaway asked.

"Yeah, how can he assist them?" Ramsay echoed, with only a trace of irony in his voice.

"Oh, he can do plenty, Callaway," Jamie said. "On Earth Ramsay and I are mere amateurs, but Thaddeus is a mighty general who has fought in many wars."

Callaway took the information in and looked up at the sky.

The *rantas* were forming a wing for another swoop.

"What shall we do, Lord Thaddeus?" Callaway asked.

Jamie bit his lip. He'd really put the old man on the spot. Not a very nice thing to do. Thaddeus hadn't asked to come to Altair and he certainly hadn't put himself forward as a great warlord. Jamie cleared his throat uncomfortably.

"Give him a minute to assess the—" Jamie began.

"They are coming again! What are thy suggestions, Lord Thaddeus?" Callaway asked with a touch of impatience.

"Nothing," Thaddeus said after a moment's reflection.

Jamie groaned inwardly.

"Nothing?" Callaway said.

"Nothing," Thaddeus repeated. "My suggestion is that you do nothing."

"But the creatures?" Callaway asked.

Thaddeus shook his head and pointed his stick at the sky. "Those things, what are they doing exactly? They're flying down on ya, sowing havoc, making a lot of noise, but they're not exactly a big threat, are they? A dozen men with crossbows? That's really what it amounts to. What they're trying to do is cause panic. And you lot are giving them everything they want. How many runs have they done now? I've seen them do at least four since we got here. There can't be much left in them beasts and they certainly don't have an infinite supply of crossbow bolts. I say ignore them. Don't do anything. Tell the people to continue about their business or stay indoors. If the Alkhavans see that they're not creating a big fuss, they'll probably fly back to their army. And if they don't, well then, get a couple of snipers up on the rooftops, get some good, calm cross fire going. The person who keeps his nerve the longest is going to win this encounter."

"Brilliant," Jamie whispered, absolutely delighted.

Callaway nodded, taking in the wisdom of what Thaddeus had said.

"I will do as ye say," he said.

He ordered that criers be sent out into the streets telling the people that the Ui Neill had arrived in the city and that they were saved. He further proclaimed that the *rantas* were only trying to cause panic and that concerned citizens should stay indoors.

In an hour it was over.

From his perch, Lord Protector Krama knew that the

beasts were getting tired and their raids were becoming less and less effectual.

For some reason the people of Aldan no longer seemed quite as terrified of the great lizards as they initially had been, but that was all right. They had scoured the defenses and had gained much valuable information. The Aldanese seemed to have manufactured roughly a score of muskets—far less than he had expected—and they appeared to have no heavy artillery. Best of all, their organizational skills were less than impressive.

After half a dozen more assaults and at the loss of two more men who were hit by Aldanese musketry, he gave the order to fly away from Aldan. The *rantas* found the thermals rising over the cliffs and one by one they rotated in big counterclockwise spirals until they had gained enough altitude to fly back to the outer pickets of the combined armies.

"A fine day's work, sir," one of his officers called out. Krama nodded.

"I believe that today we would have made even Lord Protector Ksar proud were he alive to witness it," Krama said to himself.

A thousand feet below them Irian Ksar skulked on the deck of an Aldanese boat, hiding his face from a population that would certainly tear to him to shreds if they got half a chance—and whether he was proud of

Krama's efforts, only time and the vagaries of circumstance would tell.

The *rantas* landed on a grassy slope on the outskirts of the invasion force. From the air the combined armies of Alkhava and Oralands were an impressive sight. Although they had been unable to bring *kalahars* or *yasis* or any of the large animals, there were at least twenty thousand highly trained soldiers warming themselves by campfires or drilling or sharpening their weapons. And that was enough to put heart into anyone's breast.

Krama gave orders that the *rantas* be fed, watered, and bathed, and after taking only light refreshment for himself, he marched to the Witch Queen's tent.

Her servants let him into the inner chamber.

The Witch Queen was recumbent upon a couch, leafing through a volume of Earth poetry. She stood when Krama entered.

"My Lord, thou art returned safely," she said with a smile.

Krama bowed.

The Witch Queen dismissed her attendants and when they had gone she crossed the tent and embraced him. She kissed him on the lips.

"I am so glad you're alive. You should have sent

someone else on this mission. We cannot lose you . . . I—I cannot lose you," she said.

"I was never in any serious danger," Krama replied, returning her affection.

"The gods did not mean us to take to the skies. That is their domain," the Queen said seriously.

Krama said nothing and sat down on the couch. He drained a goblet of chilled wine that had been left out for him.

"The gods seem to favor our enterprise. We lost only three men and we have plunged much of the city into chaos," he said.

The Queen stroked his arm.

Three men? That was a quarter of those of who had gone out on the raid. Those were not good odds.

"Ye shall not go again?" she asked with concern.

Krama shook his head. "There is no need. I have garnered the information that I sought," he said.

"And all is well?" she wondered.

"All is well," he said.

The Witch Queen found the carafe of wine and poured him another goblet. Krama thanked her and drained that cup too.

"Yes, the hardest part of the invasion is over. The Aldanese cannot withstand an assault from both of our—"

Suddenly there was a loud grunting noise from the far side of the tent. Krama sprang to his feet.

"A spy?" he wondered aloud.

The Witch Queen smiled. She took his hand and led him behind a divan. There, on the carpet, the Prince of Oralands was dozing heavily.

"What is the meaning of this?" Krama asked.

"The Prince is merely intoxicated. We may speak freely," the Witch Queen said.

Krama looked at the Crown Prince with skepticism.

"Perhaps it is a ruse," he whispered.

"It is no ruse. I have observed Prince Lanar closely. Once the sun passes the zenith, it is unlikely that he will be encountered sober. He came to see me in this condition. Two glasses of Aforian ale were enough to send him into a slumber."

"He is a fool," Krama said with disgust.

"He is, but we have need of him."

"For two more days," Krama said firmly.

"For two more days," the Witch Queen said, more dubiously.

Krama smiled. "Have no doubts, my Queen. We have two armies. They barely have one. And I personally have witnessed the chaos that exists in their ranks."

"Can we be sure of success?" the Witch Queen asked.

"We are strong and they are weak, we are bold and they are timid, we are prepared and they are unprepared."

The Witch Queen smiled.

"I am glad that you say as much. From the very beginning I have entertained misgivings about this alliance," she confided.

"Wipe the slate clean of thy doubts, Queen of the Alkhav. We must win. Either the Aldanese will be crushed or the Alkhavans as a people will be extinguished forever," Krama said as the snoring in the corner become even louder than before.

"To inevitable victory," the Queen said, raising her glass.

Krama shook his head.

"In war, nothing is inevitable," Krama said. "Let us toast to 'victory' pure and simple."

"To victory," she said, chastened.

"To victory," he echoed back.

Chapter IX
THE WOODS

D AN CONNOLLY WAS SITTING in his back garden with a pint glass half full of a frozen margarita when the FBI agents came to arrest him. Unlike Prince Lanar on the planet Altair, he wasn't drunk, but he wasn't exactly 100 percent sober either.

The house was a pleasant one with a private beach, six bedrooms, and four and a half bathrooms.

He had been sitting out here for several hours now.

Drinking. Reflecting. Trying to placate his guilty conscience. But not that guilty. What was a boy's life against the whole world?

It was a lovely spot. On a clear day you could see all the way across Chesapeake Bay to the peninsula beyond. And Earth itself was lovely, and all the precogs had confirmed that it was doomed if Jamie lived.

The FBI agents rang the doorbell, and when there was no answer they pushed their arrest warrant through the letter slot and broke the door down.

They found Dan by the rosebushes on the sundeck.

Dan looked at the three men in dark suits and sunglasses.

"Hello." he said. "Can I help you?"

"Dan Connolly?" one of the men asked.

"Yes?"

"I'd like you to stand up, sir."

"What's going on? What's this all about?"

The FBI agent handed Dan another copy of the arrest warrant. He scanned through it and handed it back.

"I'm Special Agent Wilmot. We'd like you to come with us, sir," Wilmot said, showing Dan his identification.

"I'm not going anywhere until someone explains what this is about," Dan said.

Special Agent James withdrew his 9 mm and pointed it at Connolly. Wilmot shook his head. James was new in the D.C. office. Very green. You didn't point guns at important government officials, not if you wanted to progress up through the ranks. And according to the briefing notes, Dan Connolly had been senior FBI until only a few months ago.

Wilmot didn't want any trouble.

"Put the gun away," he mouthed to Special Agent James. James did so. Dan smiled.

"Good. Now I'd like you all to leave, please, there must have been some misunderstanding," Dan said.

Wilmot nodded. He'd been prepared for this.

"Just one moment, sir," he said to Dan. He called Director Jenkins on the private number he'd been given.

"Hello?" Jenkins said.

"Sir, this is Agent Wilmot, we're at Mr. Connolly's house. I think it would be helpful if you explained to him why he's being arrested," Wilmot said.

"Give him the phone," Jenkins said.

Wilmot passed Dan the phone.

"Hello?" Dan said.

"Connolly, you're under arrest for exceeding your authority and for conspiracy to commit murder. You ordered the assassination of some kid in Ireland? You must have lost your mind," Jenkins said.

Dan Connolly smiled and took another sip of margarita.

"No. I've been seeing clearly for the first time. The world's going to end and Jamie O'Neill's going to end it. And you're too late, anyway. He and his mother and her boyfriend, they're all dead by now."

"You *have* lost your mind," Jenkins said.

"One day you'll thank me. You'll see. They killed Victor and they're going to try and kill all of us, you'll see. Mark my words," Dan said, and hung up the phone.

Wilmot took the phone back and helped Dan to his feet. He put Dan's hands behind his back and cuffed them.

"You have the right to remain silent . . . You have the right to have an attorney present during questioning. If you cannot afford an attorney, one will be appointed for you . . ." he began, but after a while Dan wasn't even listening anymore. Only he knew where the CIA hit man was. Soon, if not already, the boy would be dead. His mother, his friends, all of them wiped out. They'd thank him in time. They'd give him a citation. *I'm not crazy. I saved the world*, Dan thought. "I'm not crazy, I saved the world!" he yelled.

Agent Wilmot looked at Agent James and sadly shook his head.

Thaddeus laid out the map on the big oval table in the Council president's house. Behind him the sea glittered in the light of two moons. Thaddeus swallowed. That fact alone was enough to throw you for a loop. Two yellow moons in a magenta sky. But he was determined that he was not going to be distracted. At least there weren't a lot of people in here. Because of the presence of Irian Ksar in the room, the Council of War was being held in secret. Only Callaway, the children, Thaddeus himself, and Ksar were deciding their upcoming strategy. If the other councilors had been there, the debate wouldn't have been about how to defend the country from invasion, but rather how to prosecute Ksar for war crimes.

Thaddeus jabbed his finger into the map.

"Where are the armies?" he asked.

Callaway pointed to a large stretch of heath land to the east of Basky Wood. A day's *yomp* from the city.

"And they landed where?" Thaddeus wondered.

Callaway showed Thaddeus the broad beach where the Alkhavans and their allies had come ashore.

"Hmmm," he said, and stroked his lower lip. Thaddeus had a bit of gray beard growing there now. Jamie had never seen him unshaven before, but rather than giving him a scruffy appearance, it added to his air of quiet dignity. Yes, his hair was unkempt and his trousers were soaked from the boat but he was still wearing his dark three-piece suit and carrying his cane. He didn't look like an armchair general—he looked like a real general.

"Why 'hmmm'?" Jamie asked.

"Well, they were pretty smart in their choice of landing area. They put their troops down far enough from the city so that the Aldanese navy can't harry them, which apparently you guys did last time, but not so far away that their supply lines would be stretched thin. It's very clever," Thaddeus said.

"Krama," Ksar said from a chair near the window.

"What?" Jamie asked.

"Of all the candidates for Lord Protector, none would

be this subtle. It must be Krama, my former lieutenant," Ksar said. "A good man with a bold vision."

Thaddeus was interested.

"What can you tell us about him?"

"Now that his soldiers have landed and he has scanned your defenses from the air, he will not delay his final assault on your city. He will come soon and in force. He will attack with great ferocity in a frontal assault. If he has at his disposal the armies of Alkhava and Oralands, I do not see how your walls can withstand such an attack."

"Is that true?" Jamie asked.

Callaway nodded. "We have been sadly neglectful about the city walls. All these years we have been expecting a seaborne invasion. We have been strengthening our navy at the expense of the fixed fortifications around the city," he said.

Jamie looked around the room.

"Any thoughts, Ramsay?" Jamie asked.

"Well, not really, but if the seaways are clear and we have a large fleet and a day and a half to work with, we could evacuate the entire populace if we wanted. We could save the population at the expense of losing the city," Ramsay said.

Ksar shook his head. "At the expense of losing the country. If I know Krama he will be following my plan, not the former Lord Protector's. This time the Alkhavans come not to plunder but to settle. The land of Alkhava is a lost cause. Each year the ice comes farther south. Soon all of Alkhava will be under the Gag Macak glacier. The Alkhavans do not seek spoils of war, they seek your land, your homes, your farms. If you evacuate now, there will be no Aldan to return to."

Thaddeus grunted his approval of this remark. "Ksar's right. Let's have no more talk about retreat or evacuation. We're going to have to stop these armies here and now," the old man said.

"But how?" Jamie asked.

Thaddeus walked around the map once more and peered at it intently. He tapped his cane on the vellum several times.

"How many soldiers can you muster, Callaway?" he asked finally.

"Five thousand, perhaps another two thousand sailors if we bring them in from their ships," Callaway said.

"Yeah, by all means bring them in. We're going to need them on the land, not the sea. Seven thousand then. And auxiliaries, any auxiliaries, men who have some military training and who will be more of a help than a hindrance?" Thaddeus asked.

"Perhaps another two thousand of those," Callaway said.

Thaddeus nodded.

"So you'll have about nine thousand men. They've got at least twenty thousand trained soldiers. Hmmm. Yes. Yes," Thaddeus said.

"What are you thinking?" Jamie asked.

Thaddeus's eyes were twinkling. His face was animated. Jamie could see that something was cooking in that brain of his.

"It's like this," Thaddeus said after a pause. "If we spread our resources around the perimeter of the city, we're going to be in trouble. They can attack in force at any point along the walls. We'll be so thin on the ground that chances are they'll punch through fairly easily and then it'll be down to hand-to-hand combat in the streets. Outnumbered two to one, we're going to lose that battle through sheer numbers and attrition."

"So what *do* we do?" Wishaway asked.

But Ksar could see where Thaddeus was going.

"We must meet them outside the city. Long before the walls," Ksar said with an eager grin.

"Precisely. If they trap us in the city, they're going to wear us down and slaughter us. We need to take the initiative from them," Thaddeus said. "Please come close and look at this map."

Everyone gathered around the table.

"Now look. There are two roads from the landing

beaches to Aldan City. There's the north road, which skirts the mountains and loops into the hill country. Or there's the coastal route, which is half as long but which cuts through Basky Wood on its way here. Ksar, you know Krama—what's he going to do?"

"He will not even think twice about it. He will take the direct route through the forest," Ksar said.

Thaddeus nodded. "I would too. Along the coast and through the trees."

"What are you planning, Thaddeus?" Jamie asked.

Thaddeus sat down on an ornate marble chair. He considered for a moment. He knew he was going to have one chance to sell his plan, and sell it he must if the city was going to be saved.

"Let me tell you a story. Actually, two stories that turn into one. On Earth two thousand years ago there was a Roman emperor called Augustus. He was master of all that he surveyed except for one place called Germania. The Germans refused to join the empire, so Augustus sent his three best legions north to Germania to fight the tribes. The legions disappeared. They were never heard from again. Eighteen thousand crack Roman troops vanished, just like that, in the German forests. The Romans didn't find out what happened until decades later when they discovered the legions' standards and a few helmets and skeletons next to a forest trail. A

German leader called Arminius, or as he was called later, Hermann the German, was working as a guide for the Romans and he led the legions into a perfect ambush. The Germans attacked the Roman army in the Bavarian forest, ambushing them from both sides of a trail with bows and arrows and burning logs. The Romans couldn't form themselves into defensive squares and they were wiped out. OK. That's the first story. Now the second. This is the one that happened to me. In World War II, at Christmas 1944, everyone thought the war was over, that the Germans were beaten. But again they came through the woods, through the Ardennes forest in a surprise attack. They almost split our army in two and it took George Patton to save the line from complete collapse . . . And that's what I think we should do. I think we should leave here immediately, get to Basky Wood, prepare arrows, napalm, whatever you've got, and ambush the Alkhavan forces before they even get to the city."

Ramsay nodded. "I like the idea, Thaddeus, but there's a big problem. Surprise is going to be the key element, and surprise isn't going to work."

"Why?" Jamie asked.

"Because they have those flying *ranta* things and they'll watch our army leave Aldan and prepare the ambush in Basky Wood. They'll march their army around the forest and attack a totally undefended city. And that will be an utter and complete catastrophe."

Thaddeus shook his head.

"No. It will work. It'll work if we go immediately. Tonight. Under cover of darkness. The *rantas* have been attacking all day. Recently I've gotten to know horses. You can work 'em all day as long as you let them rest at night. All animals, including us, are the same. They're going to need to rest the *rantas* tonight. We have a window of opportunity until dawn before they'll see what we're about, and by that time we'll be in the forest."

Ksar nodded. "He is right. The *rantas* must rest. And if we are going to do this we must do it now."

"Impossible," Callaway said. "Our soldiers are not even in their barracks, they're at home with their families and—"

Jamie smacked his hand down on the table. "Do you want to save the city or not? You're acting like you have a choice. You don't have a choice. Get the army mobilized. Everyone gets their bow and their arrows, and if they don't have a bow get them to make spears. And we're going to need the men who can use the muskets you've made. Most of all we're going to need as many pots of Greek Fire as you've got. We'll want to cause chaos and confusion in the Alkhavan ranks. Muskets, napalm, arrows. We can do this. Speed is the key, though—if we're going to do it we've go to get going," Jamie said with surprising ferocity.

Thaddeus had never seen Jamie like this. It was quite the transformation from the meek, mute little boy he had known in Harlem two years ago. This wasn't a typical teenager, this was a leader.

Callaway smiled with condescension. "Jamie, listen, these things take time, there are other options on the table. Ramsay mentioned evacuation, and of course there is also the possibility of negotiation, I think—"

Jamie interrupted the Council president. "First of all, Callaway, you may not refer to me as 'Jamie.' That name is reserved for close friends only. You may call me the Lord Ui Neill—"

"I am sorry, Lord Ui Neill, I do not know what I was think—"

"And second, Callaway, I know you're Wishaway's father and I respect her and I respect you, but if you can't get this job done then by God, I'll find someone who can. Two years you've had to prepare this city for war and as far as I can see you've done nothing. It might be time to get a ruler here who can think clearly in a crisis and take action."

Callaway blanched at these words. "My Lord Ui Neill, I-I—"

"I'm not your anything. Now get off your ass and get

your army mobilized. We march in one hour. Order the men to prepare their weapons and have everyone dress in brown or green. I see one person in a yellow robe like yours and they're going in the stockade," Jamie said.

"That is too short a time," Callaway said.

Jamie walked over to Callaway and stood a few inches from him. Jamie face's was red. His cheeks burning. He wasn't pretending to be angry. He was really pissed off. And yes, Callaway was Wishaway's father, but he was still a lightweight and actually a bit of a fool. Wishaway might have his intelligence, but her depth and maturity clearly came from the other half of her gene pool. "One more word, Callaway, and I'm going to call the Council and get you removed. We'll have a snap election and get us a new Council president, one who understands matters of life and death better than you obviously do . . . Do I make myself clear?"

Callaway bowed low. "The army will be on the march within the hour," he said, and scurried out of the room.

"Well done, Jamie," Thaddeus said.

Jamie nodded.

"Yeah, good on ya," Ramsay said.

"We can congratulate ourselves later," Jamie said. "Now, let's get cracking, we have a lot of work to do."

"Absolutely," replied Thaddeus, more impressed than

ever with the boy who had become a man right before his eyes.

Krama walked to Crown Prince Lanar's litter. He pushed aside the Prince's bodyguard and pulled back the brocade curtain covering the window.

"Yes?" Lanar inquired.

"We are entering Basky Wood. The trail is too narrow for your carriage, Prince Lanar. I'm afraid that you will have to walk for this portion of the journey."

The Crown Prince looked at the Lord Protector with horror.

"My dear Krama, you are dressed for war. I am not," Lanar said.

True enough, Krama was wearing leather boots, a tough leather jerkin, and thick cloth trousers. Even though it was morning the Crown Prince was still in his night attire—flowing multicolored garments that did little if anything to cover his corpulent body.

"Nevertheless, Prince, you must walk. The trail is too narrow for your litter," Krama insisted.

"You forget yourself, Krama," Lanar said, and abruptly closed the curtain.

Krama waited ten agonizing minutes for the Crown Prince to calm down, and eventually, after a soothing visit from the Witch Queen and a glass or two of

Oralands wine, he did. "Bring me my boots and cloak," the Crown Prince demanded in a slightly tipsy voice.

"Finally," Krama said, looking at the sky. The sun was rising, and even after they were through the wood there was still a long march to the city.

While he was waiting for the Crown Prince to get dressed in more suitable clothes he read the latest intelligence reports from the *ranta* squadron. Apparently all was reasonably quiet in Aldan City. The gates had been closed and a chain placed across the harbor mouth. The Aldanese, as usual, were preparing for a siege. *A siege there may be, but it will be a short one*, Krama mused. The size of his force would prove too big for the Aldanese forces. Perhaps his army would be so overwhelming that this whole affair could be accomplished without serious loss of life. He hoped so. He for one had had enough of bloodletting.

Finally the Crown Prince appeared in a golden suit made of *juula* hide. He was wearing high-heeled boots, a full-length bejeweled sword, and, surprisingly, his crown.

Krama saw the immediate problem. Duty required him to tell the Oralands monarch of his concerns.

"Sire, perhaps you should remove the crown. It will only single you out as a target."

Lanar scoffed. "No, the crown will not single me out as

a target. It will provide me with an aura of protection. The Aldanese are not accustomed to monarchy, and if an Aldanese soldier dares come near me he will be awed by my Royal Personage. I have seen it happen many times on the streets of Carolla. Believe me, Krama, you'll see."

This answer was so idiotic that it did not even merit a response. Krama merely shook his head in quiet disgust.

"Good luck then, sir," he said, and ordered the column forward.

In half an hour he had forgotten all about their ridiculous ally and was soon further distracted by a brigade commander who needed instructions.

"Yes?" Krama said.

"Sir, the trail ahead is very narrow. Have we your permission to switch from triple to double file?" the commander asked.

Krama looked at the dense trees on either side of the path. He had not expected the forest to be quite so intimidating. In Alkhava there were few trees and no woods. This was the first time he had ever been in a landscape like this. And even though it was day, it was quite dark and visibility was poor.

"Yes, commander, permission granted. Double file is acceptable, but make sure your men keep their eyes peeled. We cannot be too careful," Krama said.

The commander saluted.

"Yes, sir," he said. "Do we know how much farther it is, sir?"

"From the air the forest is quite narrow. We should soon be through, but keep your guard up at all times," Krama said.

"Yes, sir."

Deep within the trees, on a small incline not a hundred yards from where Krama stood, Jamie and Thaddeus observed the Alkhavan army stop their approach and meticulously march their men into a different formation.

"What's going on?" Jamie asked, trepidation giving him a little crease above his nose.

"It's OK," Thaddeus assured him. "They're just changing the formation of the column, giving themselves more room to march. Don't worry. They're not retreating or anything. And look at our boys, they're itching for it."

Jamie examined the green-clad Aldanese soldiers arrayed in a long line through the forest. He could see only the troops on this side of the path but he knew that a parallel line of soldiers was on the far side too.

Thaddeus was right. They *were* itching to go, but all were quiet. They'd been given strict orders to remain absolutely silent, with no attack to begin until Jamie gave the word of command. And Jamie wasn't going to do that until the combined armies of Alkhava and Oralands were deep into the woods. If this was going to work, they would have to trap their enemies in a pincer. They couldn't afford to let any of them escape.

"The thin green line," Ramsay whispered, pointing at the Aldanese soldiers.

"How's your Greek Fire?" Jamie asked.

"We have about a hundred clay pots filled with the stuff. More than enough to cause a bit of confusion in the ranks."

"Good," Jamie said. "And the archers and crossbow-men should take care of the others. We're outnumbered at least two or three to one here so we'll need the element of surprise to pay off in a big way."

Ksar approached Jamie.

He was a wearing a hood to conceal his identity from the rest of the Aldanese, and that, coupled with a long bronze sword, made him appear only more menacing.

Ksar's mind was remarkably untroubled. He was taking arms against his own people, his own comrades, his own friends. But none of that mattered. He had taken an oath, given his word, and his word trumped all other concerns.

Instinctively, Jamie knew that Ksar could be trusted. Ramsay might doubt him, but Jamie did not.

I just hope I'm not wrong about him, Jamie thought as the Alkhavan general bowed low before speaking.

"The last of the rear guard has now entered the forest," Ksar whispered.

"OK," Jamie said, looking at the columns of obliviously marching young men. Some whistling, some talking, all of them fearful, nervous, worried for themselves and their comrades in arms.

"We await your orders, Lord Ui Neill," Ksar said.

"I know," Jamie replied, his throat dry.

Thaddeus put his arm around Jamie's shoulders.

"Now's the time, son," Thaddeus said.

"At a word from me, hundreds of people are going to die," Jamie said.

Thaddeus nodded. "It's terrible. I'm not going to argue with you about that. War is an awful, awful business. It isn't pretty and it isn't heroic and it's certainly not a place for kids. And you and I both know what's going to happen when the napalm ignites and those flaming pots come roaring in. If I could be anywhere else on this planet or any another planet, I'd rather be there than here. But I can't go off anywhere else. I'm needed here. And so are you. It's not about what we want to do, it's about what we have to do."

Jamie nodded. "I'll give the order," he said, his voice barely above a croak.

"Then give it," Thaddeus said.

Jamie cleared his throat, closed his eyes, and quickly opened them. He looked at Ramsay and Wishaway and Thaddeus. He nodded at Ksar.

"Fire!" he yelled at the top of his lungs. "Fire!"

A thousand arrows and crossbow bolts hissed through the trees of the Basky Wood.

For a second he watched in surprise and amazement as the arrows crossed the dead air, heading straight for the unsuspecting column of marching soldiers.

And just for an instant he wanted to call them back, to stop time, to make it impossible that the missiles could proceed on their journey. He remembered the paradox of the Greek philosopher Xeno, who said that no arrow could ever move because it had to cross an infinite number of increments of space before it could hit an object.

Maybe the concept of infinity would save the Alkhavan soldiers.

Maybe the arrows would never progress to their targets. Maybe.

The distance halved and halved again and again. Time held her breath.

But then—*whomp!* They struck with devastating effect. Hundreds of Alkhavans dropped to the ground, killed instantly by a lucky shot in the throat or the face or the skull. Hundreds more were hit in the leg or the shoulder or the arm. And before any of them could react, a second of wave of arrows came raining down out of the black forest, bringing more death and pain and misery.

"Greek Fire away!" Ramsay screamed, and this was the start of a fresh round of horrors.

Scores of clay vases filled with that ancient form of napalm arced through the air and crashed among the surprised Alkhavans.

The pots exploded on contact with the ground or with their human targets, bursting into an awful, sweet-smelling fire that burned through leather armor and metal and flesh without mercy. A fire that needed no oxygen, that could not even be extinguished by water.

Pot after pot burst among the ranks, sending the column into utter chaos.

"Muskets away!" Callaway shouted, and now the two dozen or so sharpshooters the city had mustered fired their weapons too. Thaddeus had instructed the musketeers to aim their carbines at officers, easily distinguished by their purple sashes, and almost instantly a score of Alkhava's most important leaders fell dead.

By this time the archers on either side of the path had reloaded.

"Archers, fire!" Jamie yelled above the screams.

"Fire at will!" Thaddeus shouted, because he knew

that soon it would be impossible to give further verbal orders.

Another deadly hail of missiles decimated the Alkhavan ranks. And then yet more Greek Fire exploded among them.

Krama looked at the situation with anguish and amazement.

He had been caught in a classic ambush. His over-confidence had betrayed him. The ineptitude of the Aldanese response had lulled him into a false sense of security. Hundreds, possibly thousands, of his men had been killed, thousands more mortally wounded.

"Help us!" came the cries up and down the line.

"You fool! You fool!" the Crown Prince of Oralands screamed at him.

Another round of arrows took out more and yet more of his men. So thick was the forest that he couldn't even see where the archers were shooting from.

An arrow struck Lanar in the back of the neck and he fell forward, dead.

Krama did not mourn for a moment.

They're shooting at us from both sides of the path, he said to himself. He knew that this meant something important but for the moment he couldn't figure out what.

Suddenly the Witch Queen was at his shoulder.

"We are lost, Krama," she said.

The Lord Protector shook his head, realizing at last the importance of what he had noticed. "No, see! They are shooting at us from both sides of the path along the whole length of the column. Along the whole length of our column! That means that the Aldanese are not formed into squares. They are not deep. We should be able to break out through their line. Yes! Stay with me, Queen, we must act quickly."

Krama called his surviving lieutenants and sergeants and brought them close to him.

"Men, we are ambushed. We must attempt to break out. We cannot stay on this path. It is suicide. On me, we will charge directly into the forest. Leave the wounded and the dying and follow me!"

"But sir, we cannot leave the—" a young lieutenant cried, his face streaming with tears.

"Follow me or die. That is your choice!" Krama yelled.

He gave the officers and sergeants a moment or two to relay his orders to the nearest elements of the column and then, gritting his teeth, he drew his sword and charged directly at the forest, up the hill, and into a hail of arrows.

"There!" Thaddeus yelled. "They are attempting to break out!"

"They're coming right for us!" Callaway screamed.

"Reload your arrows," Ramsay yelled.

Ksar shook his head. "Drop your bows and draw your daggers!" he yelled in a voice so filled with authority that every Aldanese soldier instantly did as he was told.

Ksar turned to Jamie and Thaddeus. "If we wish to win the day we must contain this breakout. The men on the flanks should keep up their barrage of arrows. I will lead the assault on the salient," Ksar said.

Jamie nodded.

"Good luck," Jamie said.

Ksar drew his broadsword, threw back his hood, and charged at the Alkhavan soldiers advancing up the hill.

He's like a berserker, Ramsay thought, deeply impressed.

Ksar's first stroke took out half a dozen men in a single devastating sweep. His second killed two more soldiers and drove back several others.

"Help him!" Jamie cried, and in a minute Ksar was joined by dozens of Aldanese bowmen using their daggers as short swords.

Jamie and Thaddeus found Callaway. "We're going to stop this breakout in its tracks," Thaddeus informed the Council president. "But your men must keep up a constant stream of fire on the column. Now is not the time to lose our heads. Relay the order."

Callaway nodded. "I understand," he said, and went to tell the others.

"Not a bad guy when he gets going," Thaddeus said to Jamie. "Now, if you think you're up to it, we go better go help Ksar."

"You're not going anywhere, Thaddeus, we can't afford to lose you," Jamie said.

Thaddeus could feel the blood rise in his forehead.

"Listen to me, sonny, you might be royal blood to these Altairian folks, but you're not the boss of me. Like to see you try and keep me out of this," Thaddeus said, unsheathing the curved bronze dagger he had been given for self-defense.

Jamie, Wishaway, Ramsay, and Thaddeus ran to the top of the incline to meet the Alkhavans head-on.

Almost immediately an Alkhavan soldier swung a stone axe at Thaddeus's head. The old man stepped to one side, let the axe carry through the air, and then drove his dagger through the soldier's leather armor and into the poor devil's ribcage.

"Be at peace," Thaddeus said as he took the dagger out of the Alkhavan's body.

Wishaway had twin swords in her hands. Schooled in combat since she was a child, she knew what she had to do.

An Alkhavan tried to hit her with a staff. She brought

her swords together in an X and parried the blow. She slashed the Alkhavan on the arm and before he hit the ground, she dealt a death blow to his chest.

She stabbed another Alkhavan in the stomach and an Oralands marine in the throat.

Not to be outdone, Ramsay shoulder-charged an Alkhavan officer, knocked him to the ground, and picked up his spear. He slashed at one soldier and smacked another in the mouth with the blunt end.

Trees were on fire now and the smoke was making it harder to see.

Wiping sweat from his brow, Jamie took his sword in two hands and sliced through the wooden club of a big shaggy-haired Alkhavan. He kicked the Alkhavan backward down the hill, where he tumbled into his fellows like a bowling ball knocking over a four-six split.

Farther along the ridge Jamie saw that Ksar was in his element.

"*Sama kaa, va lasss!*" Ksar shouted, carving a path of death and destruction with his broadsword.

Two Oralands sailors fell under Ksar's onslaught and half a dozen others turned tail and ran.

"*Sama kas, va lass!*" Ksar yelled again.

Krama looked up.

He recognized that voice.

He wiped the blood from his eyes.

Could it be? Could it possibly be?

With a quick punch to the face, he disposed of the Aldanese soldier blocking his way. He stood on a rock. Could it be?

Yes.

There on the top of the hill, in the midst of a killing frenzy, was his beloved mentor fighting on the wrong side.

Like a man possessed, Krama slaughtered his way through the Aldanese bowmen to get to the traitor. *Slook, slook, slook.* He killed Aldanese soldiers to the left and right of him as if they were made of straw.

"Ksar!" Krama called. "Ksar!"

Ksar turned. It was Krama.

Krama was leading the breakout. Krama was the tip of the spear. If Krama succeeded in punching through the Aldanese lines, then all would be lost.

Ksar lifted his sword above his head and ran at his friend.

The two experienced soldiers met at the brow of the ridge.

"I must kill you," Ksar said.

Krama swung at Ksar's unprotected legs but the former Lord Protector was too fast for him. Even with such a heavy weapon as a broadsword, Ksar had the strength to bring it down and parry the blow.

"How could you betray us?" Krama asked incredulously in Alkhavan.

Ksar lunged forward with his blade and arced it toward Krama's spine. Krama threw his sword behind his back and only just saved himself.

He spun away from the weapon and took a second to regain his balance.

Ksar thrust his sword at Krama's head but his old lieutenant had anticipated the attack and bobbed to the right. Krama feinted to the left and then back to the right and then again went for Ksar's legs.

This time Ksar was not expecting the blow. He had always taught Krama to go for the kill as quickly as possibly. The chest or the throat or the head. The legs were not a kill zone.

The sword nicked Ksar's thigh. He slipped on the wet earth and fell backward to the ground.

Ksar tried to roll out of the way but he wasn't fast enough.

Krama kicked the broadsword out of the prone general's hands and drove his own blade once, twice into the Lord Protector's stomach.

"Finish it," Ksar demanded.

Krama shook his head. "Tell me," Krama said. "Tell me why you betrayed us."

"It was a debt that I owed the Lord Ui Neill. I wished

to return here to the planet of my birth and he brought me. I would rather die here on Altair than live like a slave on Earth," Ksar said.

Krama nodded. Honor was the one thing that could explain this behavior. *A debt of honor,* he said to himself.

Krama kneeled on the ground, wiped the blood from Ksar's face, and cradled his head in his hands. "I understand," Krama said.

"Come close," Ksar muttered. His head felt light and he knew that he did not have long to live. Krama would have to be near to catch every word.

Krama inclined his head closer to the former Lord Protector.

"Listen to me, Krama, I have protected the Ui Neill, I have fulfilled my promise, but I do not wish to see the Alkhavan people exterminated," Ksar croaked, blood pouring over his cracked lips.

"What can I do?" Krama asked desperately.

"Stop the battle. Stop it now. Seek parley with the Ui Neill. Speak not to Callaway or the men of Aldan. They will show no mercy to us. But seek the Ui Neill and ask him for his protection. Though yet a boy, he is wise beyond his years," Ksar said.

"But how? In all this madness, how?" Krama asked.

"Do it! Save thy people. Save our people," Ksar said with a grimace.

Krama nodded.

"I will try," Krama said. Ksar's bloodstained hand squeezed Krama's arm and the former Lord Protector managed a smile.

"Thank you, my old friend," Ksar said. He nodded with satisfaction and breathed his last. His whole body seemed to wane, and that extraordinary light went out of his eyes.

Krama blinked the tears from his face and stood.

He ran to the very top of the muddy ridge, lifted his sword high into the air, and yelled so loudly that the sentinels on the city gates of Aldan ten miles away paused to hear:

"Ui Neill! Ui Neill! Ui Neill! . . . Parley! I seek parley with thee, Ui Neill! Show thyself! Ui Neill!"

And for a moment all the fighting ceased along the lines. Everyone, whatever they were doing or who they were battling with, suddenly turned to look at the bloodstained, wild-haired Alkhavan Lord Protector. Krama knew he would only have a second to make his case before the war resumed.

"Ui Neill! Show thyself!" Krama yelled.

Jamie climbed onto a fallen tree trunk and raised his sword too. "I am the one that you seek. I am Ui Neill," Jamie said.

Krama looked at him and bowed. "The Prince of

Oralands is dead. I am the sole commander of these forces. I have slain my master, Irian Ksar, who was in thy service. Before he died he told me to throw myself and my men at thy mercy. He told me that ye were an honorable man," Krama said.

Jamie nodded. "Tell your men to throw down their weapons and put their hands in the air," Jamie said.

Krama hesitated. "These are the last of our soldiers. The last of us. I cannot be the one who allows the Alkhavan people to vanish from the world," Krama said.

"I will treat your men with respect. On my orders I promise that no prisoners will be executed on this or any day. For as long as I draw breath your men will be neither enslaved nor put to the sword. I swear it in the presence of these witnesses, by the Salmon of Knowledge, and on the name of my forebear, Morgan of the Ui Neill," Jamie said.

Krama bowed again. He dropped his bloodstained sword on the mossy earth.

"*Remo keaass!*" he yelled to the Alkhavan army, and the clanking of falling swords rang through the air like church bells.

Krama walked over to Jamie and got down before him on bended knee.

He leaned forward in supplication and his temple touched the ground at Jamie's feet.

"I surrender," Krama said.

And with that the war was over.

Extremely well done, the First said.

Most impressive, said the Second.

He is certainly an exceptional individual, agreed the Third.

Chapter X
THE AFTERMATH

ALGAE STRETCHED from the peninsula and the broken harbor to the bend in the coast at the island. The fishing quay was covered in puffins. There were gulls on the breakwater. Seaweed, brown and black, lay draped over the stones in long, greasy strands. The tide was a green slick, a mile out over the peppered bank.

The assassin had walked from the mainland to the island and back a dozen times. He was getting bored. He had broken into the Lighthouse House and raided it of supplies. He had cleaned his gun, watched TV, even buried the body of the Gypsy King.

Someone from the CIA called Robert Jenkins had e-mailed and called several times. He vaguely remembered that Jenkins was Dan Connolly's boss. He hadn't answered the calls, and finally he'd added Jenkins's e-mail address to his spam list.

What was the point of talking to him?

The questions were always the same.

"Is it done? Are we safe? What happened?"

And anyway. What *had* happened?

The kid had done a disappearing act.

Of course, if Jamie was going to bring about the end of the world, he was smarter than he looked. It made sense. He hadn't vanished into thin air, that was for sure, but he had pulled some kind of trick.

Maybe those guys weren't just talking crazy when they mentioned aliens. Kid might even be an alien.

But now what? How much longer was he going to keep this up? Lee yawned. Dan's last few messages from Langley, before he had stopped playing them all together, had sounded frantic. *Get the job done. Get it done!*

Lee shooed away the puffins and dangled his legs off the stone pier. He let the soles of his feet touch the water. The sun was down behind the gullions, and from the east the sky was a darkening purple.

"Heck with this," he said, got up, and walked to the pub.

"You again," the barman said.

"Yeah, me," the assassin replied.

"People have seen you lurking about. They're starting to talk," the barman said, not knowing how close he was to putting his own life in jeopardy with this candor.

"I'm a friend of Anna O'Neill, and she's letting me stay at the house," Lee said.

"Hmmm," said the barman skeptically. For although

Anna and Lee both had American accents, Lee didn't look like he was the friend of anyone.

"What do you want in here?" the barman said. Lee had already told him that he didn't drink or eat hamburgers—the only food the pub had to offer.

"You want a drink?" the barman asked.

"No?"

"What *do* you want?"

"I don't know, what have you got?" Lee asked.

"Well, someone earlier today brought in a coin and swapped it for a pint. Said he found it up on the bog. It's Greek. I Googled it. Loot from the Celtic sacking of Delphi in 278 BCE. You can have it for ten quid."

Lee looked at the coin. A blond-haired boy was riding a horse.

"Alexander the Great," the barman claimed.

Lee gave him ten pounds, put the coin in his pocket, and left the pub.

"Bye," the barman said.

"Bye," Lee said.

He walked over the rocks and down the slope to the beach. The causeway was cracked and licked with salt, weed, and marram grass.

The tide would soon be on the turn.

He walked back across the causeway to Muck Island.

He went inside the house.

He turned off the TV and the radio and all the power.

He waited.

Waited for anything.

But nothing happened.

He went back outside and walked around the house and crossed a path to the boggy garden that Jamie's mother had planted. He examined the thorn bushes and rosehip and wild blackberry. Even some sweet potato.

A touch of home.

He sat on the grass. He could feel the damp begin to work its way through his jeans. He stood. His bones were aching. He stretched again. He reached in his pocket and pulled out his revolver. He examined it for a moment. Standard police job. Nothing special. But surely that dozy cop would realize that it was gone by now.

This was going to be his third night here. The barman had noticed him. The cop would eventually be on his case. Even the friends of the Gypsy King might come looking sooner or later.

"I suppose I really should go," he said aloud.

He took out his BlackBerry.

There were ten unread messages. Something definitely was going on Stateside.

"It might be time to fly the coop," Lee muttered.

But just then he saw a light appear in the old lighthouse. He heard voices.

"Well, well, well. My lucky day," he said to himself.

* * *

Jamie shaved himself in the mirror. He had never felt the need to shave before and on Altair there was no such thing as a safety razor. Callaway had given Jamie his own personal razor. With more than a hint of terror, he scraped the sharp iron blade over the two or three blond hairs that had made a surprising appearance on his chin.

"Not too hard," Thaddeus warned him.

Jamie nodded and almost cut his throat.

"Careful," Thaddeus said. "OK, I think that's enough."

"One more pass," Jamie said.

Thaddeus winced and stared out of the window at the temples and strange glass sculptures that made up the port city of Aldan.

When Jamie was satisfied he rinsed his face off in a basin of cold water.

"You look fine," Thaddeus said.

"Au contraire, as Ramsay would say, I look flaming ridiculous," Jamie replied. And with some degree of justification. While his real clothes were being meticulously cleaned, the grateful Aldanese had attired Jamie in a bright yellow and red robe—a councilor's robe, a sign of great respect.

"Shall we go in?" Thaddeus asked.

"Yeah," Jamie said.

Thaddeus opened the double doors of the Council Chamber and entered the large, spartan room.

Everyone was waiting for him and they too were dressed in red, purple, or yellow robes.

"It's like an audition for *Joseph and the Amazing Technicolor Dreamcoat*," Jamie whispered to Thaddeus.

"You're bleeding," Wishaway whispered, and dabbed his cheek with the hem of her garment.

"Everyone's here already? Am I the last?" he whispered to Wishaway.

She nodded. "We were waiting for you," she said.

"Someone could have told me," Jamie said self-consciously.

Sitting at the long oval council table were Krama, the Witch Queen, Callaway, and Ramsay. There were also a couple of burly-looking guards standing in the corner, just in case Krama was going to try anything.

They all stood as Jamie approached the head of the table, adding further to his sense of deep embarrassment.

"Sit, please," Jamie said.

Everyone sat.

The Witch Queen and Krama looked happy.

Callaway did not. Jamie knew there was going to be trouble.

"Well, have you read the treaty?" Jamie asked.

Callaway was the first to speak. "I have read it in English, Aldanese, and Alkhavan, and in all three it is extremely unpalatable."

"You're not supposed to eat it," Ramsay said.

Thaddeus shot him a dark look. Callaway continued: "Lord Ui Neill, I strongly hope that this is merely a draft proposal for a peace treaty and not the final document. For if they are your final thoughts on the subject, I really must object."

Jamie sighed.

"This is what Thaddeus and I have come up with," Jamie said. "And I think it's a pretty good solution to all these problems."

Callaway stood. "Lord Ui Neill, we won this war and yet in this document it seems as if we are being treated as the defeated."

Thaddeus nodded at Jamie. They both knew that Callaway was going to take this line. Jamie had to be firm.

"I am not to here to negotiate with you, Callaway. I am here to impose a peace. A fair and equitable peace that will last for generations. Not a peace of vengeance."

"But we are forced to give up land, while the Alkhavans are forced to give up nothing," Callaway said.

Jamie frowned. "The Alkhavans have no land to give up. Their country is doomed."

Callaway shook his head. "I am disappointed in your judgment, Lord Ui Neill," he said.

Thaddeus looked at Jamie. "If you don't mind, er, Lord Ui Neill, I'd like to say something here," Thaddeus said.

"Of course," Jamie said.

"Well, as I see it, the Aldanese wouldn't have a country at all if we hadn't shown up. You're looking at things from the wrong angle, Callaway. You're not losing any land. You're gaining your whole country back, minus a small portion needed to ensure that the Alkhavans never attack you again," Thaddeus said.

"Well put, Thaddeus," Jamie said. "Now let's look at the map."

Jamie unfolded the large map of Aldan.

Jamie's finger traveled along the southern coast of the country and stopped at the large island of Gaya. He tapped the vellum.

"But to give them the whole island of Gaya," Callaway said with exasperation.

Jamie nodded. "As I understand it, Gaya was only

recently added to your country. Even today it's largely uninhabited. You're not losing very much, Callaway."

"There are valuable fisheries, a wood, a mine, a—" Callaway began, but Jamie stopped him with a hand.

Callaway sat down and shook his head.

Jamie turned to Lord Protector Krama.

"And the Alkhavan delegation?" Jamie asked.

Krama smiled. "We are quite content with the plan."

"For decades it has been obvious that our country is in grave peril," the Queen added.

"The late Irian Ksar saw that years ago. He was a man ahead of his time. This generous solution will give us new hope," Krama said.

"A warm island, filled with trees, sounds as close to paradise as we're going to get on this world," the Queen said.

Callaway ran his fingers through his white hair. "I am not sure," he said. "If we look at all the alternatives again, then we might be able—"

Jamie stood.

Everyone else stood.

An hour later Callaway was putting a brave face on things. The "Great Treaty of Friendship Between Alkhava and Aldan" had been signed. The entire Council had given a grumbling but unanimous consent,

Krama had signed for the Alkhavans, and the Oralands ambassador was the official witness to the deal.

Jamie was pleased. Almost immediately the Alkhavans were going to evacuate their bleak northern country and move to the uninhabited Aldanese island of Gaya. The whole thing had been Thaddeus's idea. He personally had witnessed the massive population movements at the end of World War II. At first they had been terrible and many people had suffered, but in the end those movements had solved a lot of Europe's most intractable problems.

And in any case, whether the parties were fully satisfied or not, now the treaty was signed. It was a done deal, and if they knew what was good for them they had better just make the best of it.

While the wine flowed behind him and people congratulated themselves on their tolerance and foresight, Jamie found a quiet window seat and looked out to sea.

Fishing boats were putting out from the little port.

It all seemed so tranquil.

But in the back of his mind he was still deeply worried.

Thaddeus sat down opposite him.

"There you are," Thaddeus said.

"Here I am," Jamie replied.

"Don't look so troubled. Relax, Jamie. The essence of

a successful treaty is that everyone is a little dissatisfied. I think we did really good work here today," Thaddeus said.

Jamie shook his head. "That's not what's bothering me," he muttered.

"Then what is it? What's the matter?"

"It's something that that madman said back in Ireland," Jamie replied.

"What?"

"He said that Mom had been arrested along with Brian."

"Go on."

"And I know you're very keen to check out the planet and everything, Thaddeus, but I think we should get back. We've done everything that we can do for these people. They have to sort it out for themselves now. We should go back to Ireland."

Thaddeus rubbed his chin. He had wanted to spend a few weeks exploring Altair. Studying the political systems, learning the languages, drawing the flora and fauna. To go back now, when they had only just arrived, would be a serious disappointment.

But then again, Thaddeus had heard the man too.

He *had* said something about Anna being arrested. (And Jamie destroying the world.)

Thaddeus nodded.

"You're right, Jamie, we should get a fast boat back to the island. I'll see to it immediately," Thaddeus said.

For an old geezer Thaddeus worked fast. In an hour the Earthlings were in the harbor, fed, bathed, and changed back into their own clothes.

And now that they were leaving again, Callaway was all affection. He was even crying a little.

"I will miss you, Father," Wishaway said.

"And I you, Wishaway," Callaway said.

They hugged.

Callaway took her by the shoulders.

"I see that it is unlikely that you will return to us, so there is something I must ask you, Wishaway," he said.

"Yes?"

"Are you happy on Earth?"

Wishaway nodded. "Perhaps in the past not as happy as I could have been, but that will change when we return."

"Why?" Callaway asked.

"Now I know what I want," she said with confidence.

Callaway smiled.

"And what is that?" he asked.

Wishaway looked quickly at Jamie and blushed. She embraced her father and then let him go.

"Do not worry about me, Father, I will do well on Earth," she said.

"I know," he said.

Farther along the quay Krama was shaking Jamie by the hand.

"You have saved my people, Lord Ui Neill," he said.

"It is up to you now," Jamie replied. "You've got to make this settlement work."

Krama nodded. "We have many challenges ahead. But we have a new home. We will succeed."

Jamie nodded but then a cloud passed over his face. "You know, something's been bothering me. You're not just going to leave Ksar out there in the woods are you?"

Krama looked shocked.

"Lord Protector Ksar will be buried in a place of honor, I assure you of that," Krama said.

"I'm glad," Jamie said. "Well, we better go."

"Fortune go with you," Krama said.

Thaddeus, Ramsay, Jamie, and Wishaway climbed aboard a sleek thirty-foot schooner, which Callaway said was the fastest ship in the realm.

There were a few brief parting ceremonies before Wishaway piloted the boat out of the harbor. Several hundred dock workers and marines had gathered along the quays to cheer, but most of the city barely noticed their saviors leaving for the journey back to the old world.

Wishaway hoisted the main and gib sails and set out for the Sacred Isle.

When the last of the land had disappeared astern, Thaddeus sat next to Ramsay on the lee side of the craft.

Ramsay pointed at his chest.

"See what I see?" he asked.

"What?" Thaddeus replied, noticing nothing out of the ordinary.

"As per usual, we breeze into town, save their asses, set the place to rights, and do they give us medals? No, they don't. No medals. Yet again."

"You set much store by medals?"

"Well, no more than the average fifteen-year-old boy, and really, when you save a whole country from destruction, you'd think they'd give you something."

"Well, back in New Mexico I've got a whole box full of medals. Campaign medals, service medals, a Bronze Star. I don't have any kids of my own and I don't know what else to do with them. You can have them if you want," Thaddeus said.

Ramsay was deeply touched.

"Are you serious?"

"I am."

"Wow. I'd really like that," he said. "Hold on a minute. Got to tell Jamie. He'll be sick with jealousy."

Ramsay climbed back to the cockpit. At the tiller

Jamie was standing next to Wishaway. They had been holding hands.

They let go when Ramsay appeared.

"Thad says I can have his medals," Ramsay said.

"Great," Jamie replied.

Ramsay could detect a little impatience from the pair of them but he couldn't quite put his finger on its cause.

"Are you jealous about the medals?" he asked.

Jamie shook his head.

"Ahh, I know what you're thinking," Ramsay said.

"I'd be surprised if you did," Jamie replied.

"You're thinking, well, this big treaty of ours is only a temporary respite from the inevitable slow icy death of this planet. According to my brother, Altair is in a disturbed binary system, and with every passing year it moves farther and farther from its home sun. Century or two, even sunny Gaya is going to be one big snowball," Ramsay said.

"You know, I wasn't thinking that, but thanks for the cheery thought and putting everything into a crappy, awful perspective. Now, if you don't mind, we'll make better progress if you go and sit on the lee rail next to Thaddeus," Jamie said.

"Yes, please go back to the lee rail, we need more weight over there," Wishaway said sweetly.

When Ramsay was gone Jamie took her hand again.

"The Salmon seems to be working just fine. If you're homesick we can always come back here from time to time, you know," Jamie said.

Wishaway smiled.

"Perhaps," she said.

Jamie put his arm around her shoulders, and when no one was looking she kissed him on the lips.

It took them eighteen hours on a single tack to reach the Sacred Isle.

They climbed the stone steps of the tower to Wishaway's old bedroom on the top floor.

They stood together in the upper chamber, their hands tight around the Salmon of Knowledge.

Jamie looked at Wishaway.

"You want to take a last look around?" he asked.

She shook her head.

Jamie turned to Thaddeus. "We never know how long it's going to be before we get another chance to come here. Do you want to do anything else before we go back to Earth?"

"I'd stay here for a year if I could, collecting specimens and making notes, but I think you're right, we better see what's going on back in Ireland," Thaddeus said.

"Ramsay?" Jamie asked.

"I'm good to go," Ramsay said.

"OK then," Jamie said, and he pushed the button near the head of the Salmon and fell with the rest of them all the way back to his home world . . .

When he opened his eyes he could tell that it was dusk on Islandmagee.

"Everyone OK?" he asked.

They all nodded.

"Thaddeus?" Jamie asked.

"I'm fine and please stop asking me," Thaddeus snapped.

"OK, OK," Jamie said.

Ramsay found one of his flashlights and turned it on. He shined it down into the floor below.

"No sign of the madman," he told Jamie.

Jamie passed Ramsay the Salmon and took the flashlight.

"OK then, let's go down the stairs. Me first, Ramsay second, Thaddeus and Wishaway take up the rear," Jamie said.

Thaddeus wasn't having any of that.

"I think not. I'll go first. I'm the adult here. You can come after me if you wish, Jamie," Thaddeus said.

"Fine. You go first if you want," Jamie said. "Just watch out for the trip step. It's about two thirds of the way down."

Thaddeus took the flashlight and began making his way slowly down the steps. He walked carefully, holding on to the slimy stone wall with his right hand, the flashlight in his left. He got to the bottom of the tower without incident.

He shone the flashlight around the island.

There were no lights on in the Lighthouse House. However the Volvo and the Gypsy King's Toyota were both still here. It didn't feel quite right.

"Everyone wait in the tower. I'm going to check this out," Thaddeus whispered.

"I'm going with you," Jamie said.

Thaddeus nodded reluctantly. "If you must," he hissed.

"I must."

The boy and the man walked away from the ancient round tower.

As soon as the assassin had a clear shot he pulled the trigger on the revolver. A bullet whizzed past Jamie's ear.

"Get down!" Jamie yelled.

Thaddeus and Jamie both hit the deck.

Another bullet skipped past Jamie, only a few feet from his head.

"What's happening?" Ramsay yelled from the tower.

"The crazy guy is still here!" Jamie yelled. "Get Wishaway out of here. Go back to Altair!"

"Have you lost your marbles? I'm going to help you," Ramsay called.

"No! Listen to me. Get Wishaway out of here. Go back to Altair. Wait forty-eight hours and then come back. Do it! Do as I say!"

"No way," Ramsay said.

"Do it. I've got enough on my plate without worrying about you two. Get the hell out of here. Go!"

Reluctantly Ramsay climbed the steps.

"Wishaway, we've got to go. Jamie wants us out of here, he wants us safe," Ramsay said.

"We can't leave him," Wishaway said.

"I know. But we have to," Ramsay replied.

Both of them burst into tears.

"We can't leave Jamie," Wishaway said.

"He wants us to," Ramsay said. "He says he'll be safer that way."

When they got to the upper chamber of the lighthouse, Ramsay could hear more shooting.

"What's happening down there?" Wishaway asked in a panic.

"Jamie will be OK," Ramsay said, and although neither of them believed that, they pushed the button on the Salmon and jumped back to Altair.

Thaddeus and Jamie were lying on the gravel in the dead space between the lighthouse and the Lighthouse House.

"We're pinned down," Jamie whispered.

"If we could see where he's firing from we might have a chance to maneuver," Thaddeus said.

"Maybe if I could if I could get my head up and have a peek."

"Keep your head down! I'll look."

"He'll shoot you, Thaddeus."

"I'll be fine."

Another bullet struck the ground a couple of inches from Jamie's leg.

"Good, I saw the muzzle flash. I think he's shooting from behind the stone wall around the house. How many shots is that?" Thaddeus asked.

"Four," Jamie said. "I think."

"OK, well, let's gamble that he hasn't reloaded already. Think you can make it to the Volvo?"

"I think so," Jamie said. "Can you?"

"Don't worry about me. I'll be fine. Do you know how to drive?"

"Well, I've done it a couple of times. I wouldn't say I'm an expert or anything," Jamie said.

"Key's in the tray on the dash. Put it in the ignition and turn it to the right. Release the emergency brake and put it in Drive. Push on the gas. That's the pedal on the right. Drive all the way to Portmuck and get the police."

Jamie nodded. "But aren't you going to be driving?" he asked.

"No, I'm not. On the count of three, run to the car. Got it?" Thaddeus said.

"Got it," Jamie replied.

"Keep low but keep your head out of the dirt. Understand?"

"Yeah."

Thaddeus looked at Jamie and smiled. There was only one way out of this. The Gypsy King had shown him what to do. If a stranger would sacrifice his life for the kids, he had really no choice at all.

"One, two, three. Go!" Thaddeus cried.

Jamie sprang up and ran to the Volvo at the same time that Thaddeus got up and sprinted straight at the gunman hiding behind the stone wall.

"No!" Jamie cried.

"Run, you little idiot!" Thaddeus yelled.

Michael Lee saw the old man coming for him. What was that fool trying to do? Be a hero? He stepped out from behind the wall and leveled the pistol. The old man was carrying some sort of weapon. A stick. Lee put Thaddeus dead in his sights and shot him in the stomach. Thaddeus groaned.

"One down, one to go," Lee muttered.

Jamie looked over just in time to see Thaddeus stumble and fall to the ground.

"No!" Jamie screamed. "Thaddeus!"

"You're next, Jamie," the assassin said calmly.

Jamie was at the Volvo. He pulled the handle on the driver's side. It was locked. All the doors were locked.

And the spare key was inside the car on the dashboard. Jamie slapped the side window with the palm of his hand.

The assassin took careful aim at Jamie's body and pulled the trigger. It was night, there was a west wind, and Jamie was a good hundred feet away. He'd be lucky to hit him.

The bullet missed Jamie by four inches but ploughed right through the aluminum gas tank of the Volvo. In a tenth of a second the bullet vaporized as the hot lead in its outer shell ignited the petroleum fumes in the upper part of the gas tank. The combusting diesel then erupted into the nine gallons of cooking oil remaining in the bottom of the tank. The subsequent fiery explosion knocked Jamie ten feet backward onto the sand, where several shards of white-hot Volvo came within a whisker of killing him.

"Wow. Wasn't expecting that," Lee said to himself, and ducked as tires and bits of car came hurling toward him too. He laughed. "Yeah, that was some shot." He rummaged in his pocket for spare ammo.

Jamie struggled to his feet, patted out a smoldering ember on his jeans, and wiped powdered glass from the front of his jacket.

"Hey, are you still alive, little boy?" Lee shouted cheerfully, and began walking toward the burning car. "Is that you? Are you still in one piece, Jamie?"

"I'm still alive," Jamie said.

"You shouldn't be. We've already taken care of your mom and her boyfriend. Don't you wanna join them?" Lee said.

"My mother? You killed my mother?"

"Not me. But someone's done it by now, I guarantee you that. I work for the CIA, Jamie. We mean business. Now, this doesn't have to hurt, let's make this easy on you. Come out from behind that wreckage with your hands high in the air."

Jamie didn't move.

The assassin began reloading the revolver. He had gotten all six slugs into the chamber when Thaddeus's silver-tipped cane crashed down on the back of his head.

"Run, boy, run for your life!" Thaddeus cried.

The assassin sank to his knees, got up, kicked Thaddeus in the chest, and fired twice at Jamie. A bullet grazed Jamie's hand.

"Go, boy!" Thaddeus cried.

Jamie started running for the causeway. Thaddeus

knew what he had to do. He crawled to the assassin, grabbed him around the ankle, and sank his teeth into his calf.

Lee felt something bite through his tendon. The pain was extraordinary. He fell to the ground like a stilt walker tripping over a rock.

Thaddeus immediately sprang on top of him and grabbed for the gun. Lee pulled the trigger wildly and another bullet slammed into Thaddeus, this time in the upper thigh. But no punk CIA man was going to succeed where Hitler and his Wehrmacht had failed. Not without a fight.

"Yaahh!" Thaddeus screamed, and elbowed Lee in the face with such force that it broke the old man's elbow and crushed Lee's nose.

Cartilage and blood filled Lee's mouth.

"Waa!" Lee howled, stunned. Lights flashed before his head. His head was swimming.

Thaddeus punched him and grabbed the gun out of his hand. Lee recovered himself and tried to grab Thaddeus around the throat. But without hesitation Thaddeus pulled the trigger and shot Lee twice in the chest. One bullet in each lung—more than enough to kill him.

Jamie turned at the sound of more gunfire, stopped for a moment, and then continued running across the causeway. It was obvious what had happened. The assassin had finished off Thaddeus and was now coming for him. It would take him only a second or two to get the Gypsy King's car started.

Jamie had to keep going.

Had to.

The tide was turning, water was around his ankles, but not deep enough to stop the big Toyota.

"Thaddeus," he cried. "Oh my God. My mom!"

When he got to the end of the causeway he looked back. In the moonlight he could see the inky smoke from the Volvo hanging in a funeral dirge over the island, hovering like a fist before being scattered by the sea wind. Even from here he could smell the burning car—the melting tires were like the stench of death.

It began to rain.

He gave Muck Island a final look. No longer the friendly place he had come to after New York, now a house of horrors. The lighthouse sinister and terrible. The smoke from the wreckage an evil incubate oozing from the grip of the air into the shapes and turns of the gray sky.

Jamie's hand was starting to hurt and he knew that at any moment the lights would come on in the Gypsy King's car and the hit man would cross the causeway before he made it to the village.

Nothing else for it.

Jamie took a breath and headed for the hills . . .

On Muck Island, Thaddeus knelt over the CIA assassin until he knew that the insane man was quite dead. Only when there was absolutely no pulse and the assassin's face was rigid did Thaddeus put down the gun.

He rolled onto his back.

And lay for a while in the rain.

He felt the gentle precipitation drip into this mouth.

The water refreshed him a little. "Go on, Jamie, go," Thaddeus said in a whisper.

He pushed himself away from the dead body.

The contents of the assassin's jacket had spilled out. Money, a wallet, a pair of binoculars, a BlackBerry, a coin with a boy on it.

He picked up the binoculars and looked through them at Islandmagee. Pylons marked the way over the land. He saw the village of Portmuck and farther on a patch of green bracken and white heather. Beyond that fields of gorse and thistles that had turned a brilliant blue. But no Jamie.

The rain came heavier and he put the binoculars down.

On the water a smattering of vessels.

A plane.

The BlackBerry was ringing.

He picked it up.

It wasn't a call. It was an e-mail:

MOST URGENT. NEW INSTRUC-
TIONS. ABORT MISSION. ABORT
MISSION. SPECIAL PROJECTS HAS
BEEN DISBANDED. DAN CONNOLLY
HAS BEEN REMOVED. NEW DIREC-
TOR HAS RESCINDED ALL MIS-
SIONS. ANNA O'NEILL AND BRIAN
MCDONALD HAVE BEEN RELEASED.
ABORT MISSION.

Thaddeus smiled. "Well, at least that's something," he said.

And maybe he could use this thing to get help some-how. He tried pressing a few keys but now his fingers felt weak. He had lost too much blood.

The device slipped from his hand and landed beside a coin. His limbs were becoming heavy.

He could no longer feel the rain.

He grabbed the coin and held it in his hand. He looked at it: a boy on a horse. He pushed its rough edge into his palm. But its touch became more and more distant.

The oxygen was leaving his brain.

He knew that he was dying.

This was the last thing he would ever see.

The beach.

The stars falling.

The day crumpling down in floods of tears.

"I'm ready," Thaddeus said.

Chapter XI
THE ALIENS

JAMIE WANDERED IN A DREAM. The red flames didn't touch him. The crabs didn't pinch him when he crossed Larne Lough at low tide. He swam through a fog. Away from the car, away from Thaddeus, away from everyone.

Past the village of Magheramorne, up, up into the high country.

In a few hours he was lost. Hills and dales. Stone walls and wire. He walked and when the sun went down he slept on the fens. He woke up in the dew and walked again. The animals kept out of his way. He went through horse trails and fox runs. There were roads. There was so much rain that he didn't even feel it anymore.

Lightning came and he passed through a wild country to the north of Slemish Mountain.

He drank from a brown stream and chewed yellow berries from the trees and hiked farther into the bogland beyond the Glens of Antrim.

He didn't know where he was walking or where he

was trying to get to. He just wanted to keep going. If he had to stop he would have to think.

Across sheep fields and over stone walls and through more fields.

He came to a cottage. An orange glow percolating through the arrow slats and the stained glass. Candle fat and oil lamps burning in the high windows.

He went to the door and stood there for a long time. But he didn't knock.

Instead he retreated and slept under moss and heather. He coughed all night.

He found a broad river leading down to the sea.

A finger bent in the water to oppose the thumb. Pain receptors mobilized and chemical messengers did their work. The soreness was because of the pus in the volar spaces over the middle and proximal phalanges. An infection from a wound. The bullet wound. In the water a shape moved sideways. He failed to grab the fish.

A reflection in an eddy. A person. A boy. And behind him clouds. Gray, heavy.

He found a ruined famine house and built a poor relation of a fire that instead of heat merely peddled a greased smoke into the narrowest recesses of the place, choking the vermin and every manner of crawling thing.

"My mother!" he yelled. "Thaddeus," he said, and cried all night.

A gale. A cold rain out of the north.

What did it matter?

What did any of it matter?

He walked off the bog land. He came to a road. A car stopped.

In the dream, a man said, "You look lost."

The car moved and this time Jamie was inside. The man drove him to a city and gave him a five-pound note to buy himself some food.

Jamie ranged through the streets and the note fluttered from his hand.

There was a pain in his hand and he stopped and sat down on a bench. He closed his eyes.

When he opened them, the sun had burned through the low clouds.

A different man was standing in front of him. He had a pale face and a dark suit. There was something about him . . .

Jamie O'Neill, the man said. It was not a question. A statement of truth. An anchor in his dream.

Jamie blinked and the man asked him if he could stand. Jamie nodded.

This way, said the man.

Jamie followed.

Past a steeple.

A stand of bicycles.

Buskers. Students. Krishnas. Born-agains. Like shadows to him now. Nothing.

And still they walked.

Away from the city center.

The man gave Jamie a bottle of water.

And then when they were on the outskirts of the town, on the very edge of the countryside, somewhere up near Black Mountain the man said, *Wait*.

They waited.

The man made sure there were no cars and no witnesses.

Now, he said.

Jamie felt his body vibrate. He shook. He felt very, very cold. He shivered. And then Belfast was gone.

He was in a room. There were creatures opposite him. They had taken on human form, but they weren't human. A child could see that.

They projected tallness and otherness. Strangeness.

Later he would remember little of what they looked like.

And later still he would remember nothing of them at all.

Welcome, Jamie, the First said.

He opened his mouth to speak but no words came.

What was there to be said? *Mom*. That was the word. The word that wouldn't come. He was back to the beginning. Back to cancerboy, back to silence.

Welcome, the Second said.

Do you know who we are? the Third asked.

Jamie shook his head.

Do we frighten you?

"No."

A story, the First said.

Background, agreed the Second.

Close your eyes.

"OK," he said.

And he was there. On Earth, millions of years ago. Primeval jungle. Immense forests, primitive grasses, and huge reptiles living on a warm and pleasant globe. Hundreds of different species, thousands, as diverse as the mammals are today. All of them huge. Some of them intelligent.

Jamie watched.

And everything was held for a while.

Moments.

But then the apocalypse. From the sky. A comet striking the Yucatán peninsula at a place the Mayans would later call Chicxulub.

And after the terrible explosion a fire that burned for years. And then a famine. And then death.

He saw it all.

And not just death. Annihilation. Every phylum of the large dinosaurs cleansed from existence.

Gone forever save for traces in the rocks. A poor and woefully incomplete history of what once was. Ghosts.

He was cold.

"What is this?" he asked.

Facts.

Raw information.

For you.

"No, what am I looking at?"

Be assured, you are seeing what we saw.

"Why are you telling me this?" he asked.

The sun moves through the axis of the spiral arm of the Milky Way once every sixty-five million years. Each time the plane of the spiral arm is crossed, gravitational flux causes a tiny distortion in the Oort cloud—the band of icy rocks that orbit the sun on the very edges of the solar system, the First said.

Jamie looked bemused.

We have tried to calibrate our vocabulary and language to suit you. Is this getting too technical? the Second asked.

"No."

He's a clever boy, the First declared.

"Say what you have to say," Jamie insisted.

After they are knocked off their pathways and sent plunging toward the sun they become comets. They are only rocks and ice. Perhaps a hundred miles in diameter. Perhaps less. But when they hit an object such as Earth they explode with catastrophic consequences, the First said.

It's something to see, the Second added.

Sixty-five million years ago a comet strike brought mass extinction to the planet Earth. It destroyed many, many forms of life, including the first intelligent species to raise itself up off the dirt of your world. A type of dinosaur, a beautiful genus that has yet to be discovered by your scientists. It was smart, quick, moving in the right direction. Who knows what it may have evolved into? the First said.

But in twenty-four hours every single member of that species was turned to ash, the Second said.

The comet that struck the Yucatán wiped out three-quarters of all the living things on Earth. It made a niche for another species to struggle its way through to sentience, the Third said.

Yours, the Second said.

And last time we watched and let it happen, the First said.

Watched the near destruction of your world, the Second said.

We felt a little bad about it, the Third said.

There was something of an awkward pause.

"I can imagine," Jamie said.

Jamie began to feel uncomfortable, and before he could quite think it a seat appeared beneath him. He sat down.

"Who are you?" Jamie asked at last.

Oh, we were one of the first. Not the first, but one of the first.

"That doesn't explain much," Jamie said.

We haven't brought you here to explain.

"Why have you brought me here?"

We've brought you here because you activated the Salmon of Knowledge after many centuries, the First said.

Which was very impressive, the Second added.

And we believe that someone who could do that might be the person to solve a problem that we've been having.

"What problem?"

A moral dilemma.

Jamie shook his head. "You realize I'm just a kid."

We know.

"So let me get this straight. You made the Salmon of Knowledge? And the spaceship?" Jamie asked.

In a previous form, yes, we did, when there were thousands of us.

Millions.

"But you don't use it anymore," Jamie said.

The First took Jamie's hand and in a second he was floating somewhere above the Earth. It was a moment of complete terror.

You can breathe, the First said.

He breathed. Apparently he was surrounded by a bubble of air.

We are only fifty miles above Ireland. That's not too far, is it? the First said.

"Take me back," Jamie said.

He was back in the room, wherever the room was.

"I'd like a drink of w—"

A bottle of water appeared on a table in front of him.

He drank and sat back in his chair.

"OK, so now you can just think yourself places and you're there," Jamie said. "I get it . . . But wait a minute, the tower on Muck Island isn't sixty-five-million years old."

Some of our kind transcended their physical bodies. Some did not. The last of the fleshy ones vanished not too long ago, the First said.

"When?" Jamie asked.

Oh, mere moments ago.

A few thousand years.

"And now you're what's left?"

Yes.

"OK. I think I get the picture. So what exactly do you want me to do?" he said.

Solve the dilemma, the First said.

Last time the comet came and we did nothing. Which is as it should be, the Second said.

"Why is it as it should be?" Jamie asked.

In this state we can go anywhere. We can do virtually anything. With such power comes much responsibility, the First said.

"Yeah, like Spider-Man," Jamie said.

If you see things you don't like, you can change them instantly, the Second said.

You can find yourself intervening all the time, the Third said.

So eventually it was decided not to intervene at all, the Second said.

Can we show you something else? the First asked gently.

Jamie pointed at the sky. "Up there again, right?"

Yes.

"Give me a minute . . . OK then," he said.

In the blink of an eye he was floating in the Oort cloud millions of miles from the Earth. The sun was a yellow speck in the distance and not a single planet in the solar system could be discerned.

That rock there, the First said, pointing to a gigantic boulder several dozen miles long and at least a score wide.

See it?

Jamie nodded, still holding his breath.

See where it's going?

He nodded again.

The boulder was slowly rotating, heading away from the other rocks. They let Jamie get a good look at it.

Unfortunately for the human race that rock is going to rendezvous with Earth on the morning of December 21, 2012. It's hard to tell its scale out here in space but be assured that it is massive. It is so big that when the leading face of the boulder impacts with the ground, the far end of the rock will still be in space. The explosion will be greater than the event that exterminated the dinosaurs. The initial impact will make a hole in the planet's crust the size of Australia. Its debris will blacken the sky for ten thousand years. Nothing will survive this time, the First said.

Well, maybe the odd virus or two, the Second said.

No technology can stop it, the Third said.

"But in the movies . . ." Jamie began.

Mankind won't be capable of doing anything significant to protect themselves for many generations. And by that time . . .

Of course.

It will be too late.

"Take me back," Jamie said.

And with another blink he was returned to the room with the three aliens. He sat forward in the chair and waited. That wasn't it. He knew there was something else.

"There's a 'but' coming, isn't there?" Jamie said.

But it can be stopped, the First said.

Sent off course, the Second said.

Easily, the Third said.

No problem, the First said. *A piece of cake.*

There was a pause. Jamie imagined another bottle of water, sparkling this time, and it was there in front of him. He unscrewed the lid and took a drink.

"What do you want from me?" Jamie asked.

Now we get to it, the First said.

"Go on," Jamie said. "I'm all ears."

In this galaxy, the place where our race began, there are two sentient forms of life. Just two. There are many worlds with lower animals and plants, but in only two distinct places in the galaxy are there beings that have raised themselves to consciousness. We have been fascinated with these two worlds for a long time, the First said.

That was why we built the wormholes linking them, the Second said.

That was why, when we existed in our previous physi-

cal forms, we made the Salmon: so that we could easily jump between worlds, noting the progress—or lack of it—of each planet.

We lost interest for a while when we transcended the constraints of our bodies.

We explored the universe.

"And my kinsmen discovered one of the Salmons you left in one of the old towers on Earth," Jamie said.

As did you.

"Yeah."

As we said, you were the first one to use our technology in centuries, and not just the Salmon. Incredibly, you also learned how to fly one of our ancient spaceships.

"Yeah, I got a little help with that one," Jamie said.

We were impressed.

Very impressed.

So we felt that you were the person to go to to help us out of our dilemma.

"Fire away,"

Although we do not like to interfere in the affairs of other creatures . . .

There was a pause, as if the aliens were too embarrassed to go on.

"Yes?" Jamie said.

Well, after watching the human race climb down from the trees and survive countless setbacks and many near-extinctions, it distresses us to see that in a few years it will all be over. Nothing of your planet will survive the comet strike.

"Then stop it," Jamie said.

But you see, that's the problem. We don't like to intervene. We never intervene. It's against everything we believe in, the First said.

We are not gods, nor do we wish to set ourselves up as gods, the Second explained.

That is our religion, the Third said.

"But now you're thinking about changing the policy, aren't you? Otherwise we wouldn't be having this conversation," Jamie said.

He's very clever, the First said.

He was a good choice, the Second agreed.

Even with all its problems, we love the planet Earth, the Third said.

But we also love the other world we have visited for millennia, the place that you call Altair. There too they have struggled to eke out a civilization. They too are faced with a difficult climatic situation, yet with almost no metal and few natural resources they have built a culture that thrives, the First said.

And there too the people are threatened, the Second said.

"How?" Jamie asked.

Altair is in orbit about a sun that itself is in orbit about another sun. It is called a binary star system. They are very common throughout the universe, the First said.

We have visited millions of them, the Second said.

They are common, but planets in those systems are extremely vulnerable to any change or fluctuation in the orbits of the two stars, the Third said.

Two thousand years ago the Altair system passed near a black hole, which although did no initial damage, changed the gravity fields for the two stars. For the last two millennia the binary system of Altair has been in decay. The main Altairian sun has been drifting farther and farther away from the home world. In less than a few centuries there won't be enough sunlight hitting the surface of the planet Altair for plants to grow.

And without plants, all the land animals will die. Including all the sentient beings on that world.

A few centuries after that the oceans will freeze and the whole planet will be consumed by glaciers. Without plants putting oxygen back into the air, soon the atmosphere of Altair will begin to thin out and vanish. In just a few centuries the planet will become an icy, inert rock incapable of supporting any kind of life at all. All traces of the civilizations that did exist there will be buried forever under mile-thick glaciers.

Everything will be lost.

You see?

Jamie nodded. "Ramsay said as much."

Of course, death is inevitable for all of us. For the whole universe. One day all the suns in all the galaxies will go out. Eventually blackness will reign in perpetuity. Even matter will begin to break down. Atoms will disintegrate. Electrons will lose their spin, atomic nuclei will collapse. And everything anyone has ever built will fall apart. Soon the whole of creation will become a void of nothingness, a few lonely neutrinos separated by oceans of night, the Second said.

Even we will be gone by then, the Third said.

The First shook his head sadly. *But that's the future, a long, long way into the future, and we're not that worried about that. We're worried about what to do right now. And that's why we've come to you.*

"What do you want me to do?"

After a great deal of soul-searching we have decided that we will move to save one of these worlds, the First said.

For although it will mean breaking our sacred beliefs about nonintervention, it will cause us an intolerable pain to see both of these planets die, the Second said.

"Why not save both?" Jamie asked.

That would be too much. That would be acting like God. It is not our place to go around tampering with nature. The universe will take its course and we will let it take its course.

And that, Jamie, is also why we are leaving the decision up to you. One of these planets can be saved. We can move the comet or we can alter the orbit of the binary system. We can save Earth or Altair. But not both. We are compromising our system of beliefs, but we are not betraying ourselves completely. We are not acting like God. We are giving the ultimate choice to you.

Jamie shook his head.

"No, no, no. This isn't a choice for me. What you need is the United Nations Security Council or a bunch of Nobel Prize winners or something. I'm just a kid from New York. I . . . I . . . don't know anything about these big issues."

You're the one that we want.

"No, I'm not. You're making a huge mistake. Yeah, and, wait a minute, wait just one minute. Where's the representative from Altair? Where's she? I can't speak for them. I can't even speak for Earth."

You are uniquely qualified. You are one of only a few sentient creatures that have lived on both worlds.

"Wishaway, that's who you need. She grew up on Altair, but she's spent the last year on Earth," Jamie said in a voice laden with panic.

You were the first one in four centuries to harness our technology and travel between the worlds. It has to be you, Jamie. It has to be you, the First said in a voice that was so definitive that Jamie knew further argument would be futile.

He stood up.

"You can't bring yourself to save both places, so you want me to decide which planet to condemn to a terrible fate? That hardly seems fair at all. That I have to make that dreadful decision because of your bloody principles," Jamie said angrily.

We didn't say it was going to be fair, the First said.

No, the Second agreed.

We definitely never said that, the Third concurred.

We want you, Jamie. We have faith in you. One person, picked freely from the multitude. One person who would understand the issues and then speak for the rest. Not the smartest, not the most eloquent, just an ordinary specimen who would make a decision that we are incapable of.

"Me. I'm responsible for the fate of millions?" he asked skeptically.

They nodded their heads in their own fashion.

"You know who you need? You need Thaddeus. He's the wisest man I know. He can make this kind of decision for you. Maybe he's not dead yet. Find him. Get him. He's been to both worlds and he's very, very smart. I bet you he could even beat you at chess. Get him. Get Thaddeus," Jamie said.

Ah yes, Thaddeus, the First said.

Thaddeus, the Second said.

Thaddeus, the Third said.

A truly impressive individual, the First said. *But we want you, Jamie. It's up to you.*

Jamie inhaled but he didn't speak.

It was an awesome responsibility. But there was no getting out of it.

"OK. When do you need my answer?"

Now.

He closed his eyes and let the impressions come to him.

First he thought of Altair. The beauty of the place: the iceships, the mountains, the forests, the great creatures swimming in the ocean. But the horror too. The tyranny of Oralands, the bleakness of Alkhava.

He thought of the tens of thousands who lived on that world, what this would mean to them . . .

And then he thought of Earth. He thought of faces. Millions. Thousands of millions.

Africans, Europeans, Americans . . .

He imagined a balance in his head.

And not just people. All the things they had done. The pyramids. The Brooklyn Bridge. The early albums of PJ Harvey.

On one side all the great works of art and music and literature and poetry. All of it would be lost. Gone for ever.

As if it never existed.

But there was another side too.

There was also the Holocaust, war, torture, famine, and the deep evil of humanity that never seemed to leave the world.

The evil that had killed Thaddeus.

The evil that had murdered Brian and his mom.

If Earth survived, surely that evil would go with humans farther out into the universe.

Yes.

The poison that was in human beings would always be with them. The darkness trailing them around the cosmos like a twisted familiar.

Yes.

Well?

The aliens were looking at him. What could he say? How could he explain?

He closed his eyes and tried to think in the right way. Intelligently. With prudence. But the thinking process was clouded up. The only thing his mind would hold was the image of his mother. They had killed the one person on Earth who loved him without prejudice. He had cried and cried . . .

He looked at the aliens.

Well? the First repeated.

Do you need more time? the Second asked.

Jamie shook his head.

He cleared his throat.

Are you ready?

"Yes," he said.

It was clear to him. It was obvious. There could be no other resolution. There was nothing for him on Earth. They had murdered his mom and Thaddeus, and the only people he cared about now, Wishaway and Ramsay, were on Altair.

Really there was no choice at all.

"Altair," Jamie said. "Save Altair."

Very well, the First said. And what was that in his voice? A trace of surprise? Had they picked Jamie because they had assumed Jamie would save the place he came from? The planet with the richer culture, the world with more people on it? Had they rigged the game right from the start?

If so, that was their problem.

There was a cough behind him.

Jamie turned.

The First was standing at his shoulder. He put his hand on Jamie's sleeve. *If you'll come with me please,* he said.

They were on a single-track road outside of an Irish town.

Is this all right for you? the First asked.

"Where are we?"

It is a place called Larne. Not far from your home on Islandmagee. It is the nearest settlement to your home that has a hospital.

"Do I need a hospital?" Jamie asked.

You will. We are going to wipe your memory of everything that just transpired. I'm afraid that you are very likely to be disoriented for some time.

Jamie nodded.

The First turned to look at Jamie.

Thank you, he said, and escorted Jamie to the edge of a rain-blacked street near Mater Hospital in Larne.

Jamie's head felt light. His skin was tingling.

"For what?" he asked, but when he turned to see who was talking to him, there was no one there at all.

He walked ten paces down an alley, and then slipped and fell.

Ramsay looked at his watch. "Well, it's been exactly forty-seven hours," he said. "And they haven't come back."

Wishaway nodded. "We know what we have to do," she said.

"We should arm ourselves," Ramsay said.

They walked to the boat and grabbed the oars.

"A bit unwieldy," Ramsay said.

"It's the best we're going to get," Wishaway replied.

They walked together to the old lighthouse that dominated the terrain of the Sacred Isle.

"A last look around?" Ramsay asked.

Wishaway shook her head. "We must get back," Wishaway said.

They climbed to the top floor.

Nothing remained of Wishaway's old bedroom. All of it had been stripped long before.

She and Ramsay encircled the pillar. Ramsay pressed the button on the Salmon and they jumped back to Earth . . .

Rain and the noise of helicopters.

Wishaway opened her eyes.

"Do you hear that?" she asked.

Ramsay nodded.

They climbed down into the lower chamber of the lighthouse, descended the stepladder, and hurried down the steps.

When they got outside they saw dozens of police officers, a police helicopter, a BBC camera crew, and a harassed-looking Brian and Anna.

"What's going on, Brian?" Ramsay asked.

"Where have you been?" Brian asked. "You didn't pop off to Altair again, did you?"

"What's happening?" Ramsay asked, ignoring him.

"Oh, Ramsay, it's terrible. Thaddeus is dead and we just got word five minutes ago that Jamie's in the hospital in Larne. We were just about to drive down there," Anna said.

Wishaway gasped. "Is Jamie OK?"

"He's fine. He has a cut on his hand and he's heavily sedated, but they say that he should be fine. I want to be there when he wakes up," Anna said.

"We'll all go," Wishaway said.

"And in the car you can tell us what's going on," Ramsay insisted.

In half an hour they were in Larne.

Wishaway had never been there before and she was a little surprised. Larne was not the worst place on Earth. There are cities she had read about in sub-Saharan Africa that are far bleaker and more miserable. But charmless tower blocks, sectarian graffiti, and boarded-up houses were the things tourists noticed the most when they visited Larne. And for an urban center of its size and location in Western Europe, it certainly punched above its weight in unpleasantness.

The hospital, though, wasn't too bad. And the staff were low-key, helpful, and professional. In a few minutes they had been escorted to Jamie's room. They went immediately inside.

"He's just waking," a nurse said.

Anna started to cry.

"My little boy," she said.

Wishaway looked at Ramsay and Brian.

"He should see his mother first," she said. "Let's wait outside."

Jamie's eyes fluttered.

"My darling Jamie," Anna said, drying her cheeks with the hem of her dress.

"Mom!" Jamie cried. "You're alive."

"Of course," Anna said.

"But that guy, he said that you were dead," Jamie protested.

"And yet, as you see, I'm not," Anna said with a grin and a flurry of kisses.

"Where am I?" Jamie asked.

"You're in Mater Hospital in Larne," Anna said with a little laugh. It was so great to see Jamie talking and apparently unhurt.

"What happened to you and Brian?" Jamie said.

"What happened to us? Nothing happened to us," Anna said.

"That crazy person said you'd been arrested and killed."

"We were picked by the Metropolitan Police in London. They allowed us a phone call. We called a lawyer. The lawyer issued a writ of habeas corpus and got us released."

"But who was that guy?"

"Apparently he was a rogue CIA agent. He must have completely lost his mind. The CIA has denied that he was following their orders. They say he went crazy. Of course, because of all the publicity there's going to be a full inquiry."

"What publicity?"

"Well, after they found the bodies of Thaddeus and another man and the CIA man himself, all hell broke loose. The BBC came down. Not just the local BBC, the BBC in London. It's a huge story, Jamie. It's been picked up by CNN and all the networks."

"So that man *was* working for the CIA?"

"Yes, until recently. The CIA say that he was junior employee in their Beijing office. He was fired for stealing. Apparently got the first plane out of Beijing, went to London, and found his way to Ireland. No one knows why, but the latest theory is that he was just looking for a bolt-hole and he fancied the Lighthouse House," Anna said.

"And all that stuff about the end of the world?"

"Delusions. He was completely mad."

"And now Thaddeus is dead because of him," Jamie said.

Anna sighed sadly.

"Poor Thaddeus."

"He saved my life, you know," Jamie said.

Anna nodded. She stroked Jamie's cheek while he let the tears flow for his dead friend.

"He was a fine man. It was a privilege to know him," she said.

Jamie smiled sadly.

"It was," he agreed. "What did they do with his . . . his body?"

"They're flying him back to the States. He was one of the last surviving black soldiers to have fought in the Battle of the Bulge. They're burying him at Arlington National Cemetery. It's quite an honor," Anna said.

Jamie nodded. "I'm not sure he would have wanted all that fuss," Jamie said.

Anna laughed. "No, probably not."

"Where are the others?" Jamie asked.

"They're waiting outside."

"Can you go get them?" Jamie asked.

"I'll see what I can do," Anna said.

Ten minutes later Ramsay and Wishaway were sitting on opposite sides of his hospital bed.

"How's your hand?" Wishaway asked.

"It's OK," Jamie said.

"That lunatic shot you?" Ramsay asked.

"Yeah, he shot me, but I was only grazed. My mom says I should make a full recovery," Jamie said.

Wishaway looked relieved.

"And even if they did take my hand off, I promise I won't do the no-talking thing again. I'm done with that forever," Jamie said.

"But you're going to be fine," Wishaway said, and held his arm affectionately.

"Yes," Jamie said. "I'm going to be fine. Everything that's happened has really brought it home to me how lucky I am to be alive. How lucky I am to have a house and my mom and friends."

"We're lucky to have you, mate," Ramsay said.

"Yes," Wishaway said, and gave Jamie a kiss on the cheek.

"What happened back on Altair?" Jamie asked.

Ramsay sighed. "Nothing. We hung out on the island. Ate some grub."

"But what do you think's going to happen with the treaty?"

"You can never predict what's going to happen, but it seems to me that Callaway, the Lord Protector, and the Queen have reached an understanding."

"And in Oralands?" Jamie asked.

"I'm sure what's left of their army has retreated with their tails between their legs. Look, don't worry about any of that stuff. Worry about yourself. They've got a lot of challenges ahead on that world, but if they work together it's going to make everything easier," Ramsay said.

Something seemed to click in Jamie's brain. Some recollection that he couldn't quite grasp. He tried hard to force the memory but it wouldn't come.

He shrugged. "I don't know, but for some reason I think things on Altair are going to get a lot better in the future," he said.

Wishaway took Jamie's injured arm and gently kissed it. She smiled.

"I hope you're right," she said.

He frowned. He had never been able to fall back to sleep. Didn't they know how busy he was? There were more treaties to be signed. Cooperation agreements. Trade deals. All that took a great deal of mental energy. You needed to get a good night's sleep. It was absolutely essential. Every night his routine had to be the same. Have a simple, late dinner, take one cup of sleeping draft, and then go straight to bed. And he always gave firm orders that he was not to be disturbed unless there was a fire or a citywide emergency.

His servants knew his routine.

They knew how strict he was about it.

And yet.

And yet . . . in the middle of the night the

astronomer royal had burst into his sleeping chamber and awakened him.

Actually, shook him awake.

"What is the meaning of this?" Callaway had demanded of the man.

"The stars, the stars, they rise in a different place," the poor man had insisted, and then he had babbled on about the heavens for the next twenty minutes.

The third invasion in the space of a couple of years had been trying for everyone, but you'd think an important personage such as the astronomer royal would have learned to cope without finding a solution to his problems in a bottle of Kafrakillan wine.

Callaway had been sympathetic to the elderly gentleman at first but when the astronomer royal had tried to drag him outside, he had taken a definitive stand.

He had called his steward and the steward had escorted the poor fellow out of his house.

That had been four hours ago.

And of course he'd been unable to go back to sleep.

His whole day was to be ruined.

Callaway buried his head under the pillow.

"What now?" he muttered, for even though he had decreed absolute silence he could hear a loud commotion outside his bedroom door.

"Go away," Callaway shouted in base Aldanese.

The door opened. His steward entered. A bold, sallow-faced man from the mountains who had done well in the Battle of Basky Wood but had been in his service for less than a week. Clearly he was better at fighting that running a household.

"You are awake, sir," the steward said.

"Yes, I am awake. I never went back to sleep," Callaway said.

"Then you must come outside now, sir," the steward said.

"Have you taken leave of your senses? Are you telling me what to do?" Callaway asked.

The steward nodded, and insisted, "Yes, sir, you must come outside."

Callaway was too stunned to even yell at the man. Instead he found his night cloak and meekly followed him onto the stone patio.

"There," the steward said, pointing to the west.

Callaway noticed that, despite the hour, half the city of Aldan was also staring in that direction.

"What am I supposed to be looking at?" Callaway said.

"Just look," the steward said.

Callaway looked.

The temples were the same, the houses, the harbor, the fishing smacks, the ocean, the sky, the . . . the sun.

The sun was twice as big as it had been yesterday.

It was warm and huge. Yellow, golden, full of life.

"It's like the old times," the steward said with awe. "Surely this is the work of the Lord Ui Neill."

Callaway shook his head. *How could Jamie do this? How could Jamie move the planet to a new orbit about the sun?*

But then again who else could?

Chapter XII
THE END

SNOW WAS FALLING on the dome of
Armagh Observatory on the morning of
December 21, 2012. For a thousand years Armagh had
been the ecclesiastical capital of Ireland and from
monastic times onward it had housed the island's cen-
ters for record-keeping and adjustment of the calen-
dar. And perhaps that was why Ireland's most ancient
and prestigious observatory was located here, in one of
the wettest and cloudiest places on Earth.

Dr. Peter Simmons peered out of the window and
shook his head. Snow was still tumbling from low
clouds. If it wasn't snow it was rain. If it wasn't rain it
was sleet. He looked at his watch. It was almost six
A.M. Even if the snow stopped right now there would
be less than an hour's viewing time before sunrise.

The whole night was going to be a bust.

He sighed. This was not a rewarding job, but at least
it was better than being a police officer. He was glad
that he had quit the cops after the incident with the
rogue CIA agent on Muck Island.

And he was glad too that he had gone back to university and gotten his PhD in astronomy. Even if the Armagh Observatory wasn't exactly Mauna Kea or the Very Large Array in New Mexico, it was better than pounding the beat in Belfast and dealing with drunken students and homeless people.

He took a sip of his coffee and continued working at the *Times*'s Sudokuword—that amalgam of Sudoku and a crossword puzzle that had been sweeping the country for the last few months.

He gave up after a few clues, yawned, and flipped back a few pages to the international news. Tedious stuff: Starbucks had just bought two small coffee-producing countries in Central America. Paris Hilton was beating Lindsay Lohan in the race for governor of California.

Ho-hum.

He turned on the radio.

"God is no more and his priests mourn for him. In Chichen Itza and among the tellers of the royal court, each looks up, witness to the distant trail of his death mask. Aneirin sings of death which is foretold amongst the heavens and is obvious to those who know and wait—"

He switched the radio off. At this time of the morning the BBC always had some kind of religious "Thought for the Day." The BBC was obliged to cover all faiths, and usually when Simmons tuned in it was some nutter waffling on about reincarnation or life after death. It never made any sense.

He went back to the Sudokuword, filled in a clue, and then erased it when he realized that the numbers didn't add up.

He walked over to the coffeepot and was just about to consider brewing a fresh batch when he noticed something—a beeping sound coming from the telescope.

The alarm.

"The alarm!" he said out loud.

Because it was overcast on 90 percent of all viewing nights, Professor Jones had set up a laser that constantly scanned the sky, looking for a break in the clouds. When it discovered a viewing opportunity it sounded an alarm.

Simmons looked out the window.

The snow had stopped and although another system was moving in from the west, there appeared to be a gap in between two fronts.

He rushed to the big leather chair near the TV monitor. He pushed the red button and with much clanking of gears the electric motors opened the observatory roof.

Because it was so close to sunup, all the other observatories along this line of longitude were shutting down their operations about now. The South Africans, the Spanish, and all those big European telescopes on the Canary Islands.

And it was this fact that meant that Simmons and Simmons alone was the man who discovered the comet.

He flipped on his PC and ordered the telescope to scan the sky overhead for any new objects. This was the routine task they always did when they got a chance to view. After that he would go through as much of Professor Jones's prearranged orders as he could. An examination of the Andromeda Galaxy, a look at Saturn, a photograph or two of the dust storms on Mars.

The telescope began moving slowly above him but then, abruptly, it stopped.

"What's the matter with the thing?" he said to himself. He hit the gear. But it still didn't move.

"Piece of junk," he said. But the scope had stopped for a reason. It had found something. And there, right in the center of the TV monitor, was an unknown object. He almost fell out of his chair.

"What in the world is that?" he said to himself.

He focused the image and printed it out.

He couldn't believe it.

He ran a cross-check.

He printed it out again.

"Oh my God," he said when he had digested the information.

The object that he had just discovered was a previously unknown long-duration comet, and it was heading straight for Earth.

Simmons checked the wires and the astronomy blogs. No one else had seen it. He alone knew. He sat with the information for five minutes.

It began to cloud over again, and almost immediately after that the snow came back.

Simmons shook himself from his reverie. He closed the dome and called up the head of the Armagh Observatory and Planetarium, Professor Jones.

"Ahh, Simmons, it could only be you calling me at this time of the morning. What fresh insights do you draw from the tail of the beast of night? Don't tell me the observatory roof's stuck again," Jones said.

"No. The roof's fine," Simmons replied.

"Then what is it?" Jones asked.

"I think I saw something out of the ordinary," Simmons said as calmly as he could.

"Just now?"

"Yes."

"How could you see anything. It's nearly morning."

"Well, I did. And it's a big one. The big one. I think I've found a new object."

"What object?"

"I think I've found a comet," Simmons said in a whisper.

"You're joking."

"No. No joke. A comet. A bloody great huge one too," Simmons said.

"Are you sure?" Jones asked.

"Yeah, actually I am. Absolutely sure."

"Did you confirm it with any of the observatories on the Canary Islands?"

"No. They've all shut down for the night."

"Hold the fort. I'll be right over," Jones announced.

"What do you want me to do?"

"Think of a name for your discovery. You're going to be famous."

When Professor Jones arrived, still in his slippers and with a raincoat on over his pajamas, he saw that Simmons was not pulling a practical joke.

Far from it. The Simmons 2012 Comet was the biggest one anyone had discovered in a long time.

How the comet had gotten so close so quickly without being observed was a mystery, but not a big one. It had come at a trajectory from behind the sun, staying hidden in the sun's penumbra. Furthermore it appeared to be made of a very dark material that absorbed sunlight and had kept it concealed until its small tail had formed.

Jones called up NASA and Space Command in Colorado Springs.

The news buzzed around the world.

For a terrifying few hours many people were worried that the comet was actually going to hit the Earth.

This would not have been good.

The comet was so big that if it had impacted anywhere on the globe it would have set the atmosphere on fire, boiled the oceans, and killed everything on the planet.

But after exhaustive computer modeling and double-checking, and much to everyone's relief, it was discovered that the comet wasn't going to hit Earth at all.

In fact it was going to miss the planet by about eighty thousand miles, which was next to nothing in stellar terms. A hair's breadth.

A very narrow escape indeed.

But an escape nonetheless.

Jamie knew nothing about any of this when the phone rang in the common room of his dorm at Queen's University Belfast.

Groggily he climbed out of bed and pulled the curtains back from the window. He was up in the tenth floor of the residence hall and had an unobstructed view over the whole city.

It was snowing in Belfast. All the way from Cave Hill to the old shipyards at the mouth of the Lagan.

"Snow."

Maybe they were going to have a white Christmas. *That'll be nice*, Jamie thought.

He looked at his watch. It was eleven o'clock.

It was late.

He padded into his small bathroom and looked at himself in the mirror. His eyes were bloodshot and his thick blond beard could do with a trim. In fact he was probably going to have to shave it off before his mom got back from America. She'd have a fit if she saw him looking like this.

In the common room the phone was still ringing.

He brushed his teeth and picked bits of fluff out of his mustache.

He opened his door.

"Isn't anyone going to get the phone?" he shouted into the corridor. He waited for a response.

Nothing.

"Sheesh. If you want something done, you gotta do it yourself," he muttered. He put on a pair of slippers, grabbed his dressing gown, and walked down the hall.

He went into the common room.

He could hear the phone ringing but he couldn't see it. He knew that it was in the vicinity of the coffee table, but the coffee table was littered with newspapers, dirty dishes, and old pizza boxes.

He hunted around for a bit and then finally discovered the phone actually inside a take-out container from a Chinese restaurant.

Disgusting. He wiped a gooey brown substance off the antenna and pressed Talk.

"Hello?" he said.

"Jamie," his mom said.

"Hi, Mom, what time is it in America?"

"It's just after six in the morning."

"You're up early."

"Yeah. Brian got me up. He remembered that old Mayan prophecy that today was supposed to be the end of the world. So we got up to see if it really was going to end," Anna said.

Jamie nodded. "That's today? Yeah, I remember Thaddeus talked to me about that once. He said how could a race of people who didn't even invent the wheel know anything about the fate of the universe."

Jamie could feel Anna smiling down the phone. If it had been his cell phone and not this cheapo university job he could have seen her smiling on the streaming video feature.

"Thaddeus," Anna said.

"Thaddeus," Jamie agreed.

"He was quite a character," Anna said.

"He certainly was."

"So you're OK?" Anna asked.

"I'm fine . . . How's Brian?" Jamie asked.

"He's good. He's complaining about the workload of lectures and seminars and the like. But he's only mouthing off. You can tell he loves it."

"Yeah, it's a good gig for him. Assistant professor of physics at MIT. Ramsay's eaten with jealousy, you know . . . And how's Cambridge?"

"It's beautiful here. We went to Cape Cod over the weekend. I love it too. I could stay here forever . . . Oh, but don't get me wrong. We're still looking forward to coming back to Ireland for Christmas."

"When are you coming back?" Jamie asked.

"The day after tomorrow."

"Good . . . 'cause, uh, I miss you, Mom."

"I miss you too, Jamie. I'll see you soon. OK, I better go. Glad we're all still alive," Anna said.

"Yeah, me too. Bye."

"Bye."

Jamie hung up the phone.

Ramsay appeared in the common room. He too looked a bit rough. His hair was tousled and he had put his beloved Cartman T-shirt and pajama bottoms on backward.

"I feel terrible. We had way, way too much to drink last night," Ramsay said.

"We had to celebrate the end of term. You know. It is traditionally a time for celebration," Jamie said.

Ramsay groaned. "We shouldn't have got into that drinking game with those students from Trinity College Dublin," Ramsay said.

"Then let it be added to the ancient knowledge. 'Never get in a land war in Asia,' 'Never cross a Sicilian when death is on the line,' and now 'Never get in a Guinness-drinking competition with students from Dublin.'"

"Well, I'm staying out of the pub for a long time," Ramsay said. "Alcohol kills the brain cells and I need all the brain cells I can get if I'm going to get that scholarship to graduate school at Harvard."

"What are you worried about? You're top of our class," Jamie said.

"Yeah, that's the trouble, mate. The only place for me to go is down," Ramsay said gloomily.

"Oh, be quiet and put the kettle on for a cup of joe," Jamie said.

When the coffee was made and they were tucking into microwaved pieces of last night's pizza, Wishaway appeared in her nightgown.

Of course even at this early hour of the day she looked stunningly beautiful. Her glacial eyes, her pale skin, her hair like spun gold on an ancient chalice.

She came over to Jamie and kissed him.

"How do you feel?" Jamie asked.

"I have a bit of a headache," she said. "I don't think we should spend the whole of the last day of term in the pub, even if it is an Irish tradition."

"I agree," Ramsay said.

Wishaway grabbed a cup of coffee and sat next to Jamie on the least dodgy cushion of the common room sofa. Jamie put his arm around her.

"You smell nice," Jamie said.

Ramsay groaned again. "Don't start, you two, please." Then to change the subject he asked, "Hey, who called on the phone?"

"Aha! So you did hear the phone," Jamie said. "And yet I had to get it. I always have to get it."

"Who called?" Ramsay asked again.

Jamie stood up to get some more coffee. "My mom," he said.

"What did she want? Brian get in another punch-up with Chomsky or something?" Ramsay asked.

Jamie shook his head. Disconcertingly, a couple more things fell out of his beard.

"Nothing like that," he said.

"Is she coming back for Christmas?" Wishaway asked.

"Day after tomorrow," Jamie said.

"I miss her," Wishaway said.

"Yeah, me too," Jamie agreed.

"Why did she have to call so early? Must have been five in the morning in Boston," Ramsay said.

"Oh, um, it's the solstice today, December 21. She wanted to check that the world hadn't come to an end like the Mayans predicted it would."

Ramsay yawned. "It hasn't, has it?"

Jamie looked out the window. The sky was cloudy but singularly lacking in comets, mushroom clouds, or horsemen of the apocalypse.

"What do you see? Has the world come to an end or not?" Ramsay asked.

"If it has, it's doing a pretty good job of faking it," Jamie said.

"That's good enough for me," Ramsay replied.

"Me too," Jamie said, and sat back down on the sofa. And slowly they got their act together. They read yesterday's papers and drank coffee and ate old pizza, and then when they were fully awake they showered, packed up their stuff, and drove back to the Lighthouse House for a well-deserved holiday.

❋ ❋ ❋

The oxygen leaving his brain.

He knows he's dying.

This is the last thing he'll ever see.

The beach.

The stars falling.

The day crumpling down in floods of tears.

"I'm ready," Thaddeus says.

A final look at the ocean.

The water migrating toward the other side of the lough in obedience to the moon and the pull of the sun, which is not yet up, but no doubt is already boiling east of here, over the rice fields, factories, and jasmine trees.

"But I'll never make it to the dawn," he says.

The belched smoke from the burning car rises and then flattens out until it is an abscess of color over the land. Rolling, checking itself, and curdling into the fog wheedling in from the ocean. And across the Irish Sea, he can't see anything. Not the boats, not the gray specter of coast in Galloway, not the lighthouses on the islands.

He closes his eyes . . .

It may have been a second.

It may have been a thousand years.

Oh no you don't, a voice says.

"What? Who? What game is this?"

A white form on the sand, ten yards from his upturned toes.

Death?

But Death isn't real. Death is the personification of an event.

White, glowing, unhuman.

Recognition comes. He knows what's going on. Oxygen starvation in the brain. He's hallucinating before he dies. His brain is losing coherence and the cortex is firing randomly. It's mere wish fulfillment—that somehow his consciousness can be preserved and that Death is going to take him off to some place of future reward or punishment.

Reward, more than likely, after teaching for thirty-five years in Harlem and the South Bronx.

"What am I going to see next, a tunnel with all my war buddies waiting at the end? How pathetic."

Yet the illusion persists and Thaddeus begins to have doubts. Surely if his brain is dying he'd be seeing all sorts of things, not just a creepy-looking dude in a Snoopy Halloween costume.

And, on the other hand, it looks pretty real. *They* look pretty real. For there are two more behind the first one.

Thaddeus shuts his eyes quickly.

Opens them.

They're not going away.

Damn it.

"Are you an angel?" he asks.

You don't believe in angels, do you? the First asks.

"No."

Very wise.

"So what are you saying? You're not an angel?" he asks.

No. Not an angel.

"What are you then?"

Why don't you come with us, come and see.

"No, no, not me, I ain't going anywhere. I don't even buy a MetroCard without reading the small print," he says.

We'll show you then, the First says.

And they show him.

A little piece of everything.

"Wow," he says. "But I—I still don't get it."

We know. But nevertheless.

Thaddeus sits up from his seaweed-covered deathbed.

"What do you want from me?" he asks.

We're friends of Jamie's.

Thaddeus nods. "Ahh, now it all makes sense. Kid always had weirdo pals. Now you're talking sense."

He told us about you, the First says.

"Yeah?"

We'd like you to come with us, the Second says.

"Why?"

We think you'll find it interesting, the First explains.

Of course, you'll have to leave that body behind, the Second says.

It will only get in the way, the Third adds.

"Where are we going?"

Far from here.

"And the alternative?"

Nature will take its course.

Thaddeus doesn't have to consider it too long.

"I'll be food for crabs? OK, I'm game," he says.

Good.

You've made the right choice.

"When do we—"

Immediately.

"Wait a minute."

Yes?

"Well, if you don't mind, I'd like to come back now and again, to check on the kid."

Certainly, the First says.

At least until 2012, the Second says.

Thaddeus frowns. "What happens in 2012?" he asks.

A comet strikes the Earth and wipes out everything.

"Really?"

Really.

"We might have to see about that," Thaddeus says.

Perhaps.

Now relax.

This won't hurt a bit . . .

"That tingles. Hey, gently does it . . . Hey, I can't feel my toes," he says, but before he can speak further he finds himself flying.

Up above the Antrim Coast, Ireland, Europe. Up and up. To the thin filament of the highest layers of the atmosphere. To the edges of water condensing in the tangled air.

To the slope and spirals of the raven stars and along the backbone of the sky.

There is sadness as well as wonder.

And above all a great, tremendous silence.

Silence.

Hushed are the sounds of Earth.

Quiet the universe talks.

And if this is death, it is a sweet thing. The cold, tenebrous night and the galaxy vast, austere, and beautiful.

He drifts in the embrace of the solar wind, farther and farther from the safe shore.

And in the dark he watches not the world of men.

There are other forms of life.

Strange at first, but, after a time, familiar.

He swims among wonders.

And no one has to tell Thaddeus how the narrative will end, for the end is always same. As the Chinese proverb says, happy are those whose names are unnoticed by the history books.

Jamie will live, marry, defy biology, have children, and grow old.

Jamie and Wishaway. Ramsay and some wild, redheaded Irish girl. Brian and Anna.

All of them, well and content, and yes, happy. Safe too. For although *they* may not intervene to save the Earth, no such injunction lies upon him. A breath. A push, and a big rock moves in a different trajectory . . .

And time will pass.

Weeks.

Months.

Years.

Good years.

And then one day, when Jamie has grown aged and tired and the decades are beginning to lie heavy. Perhaps out for an early-morning walk. Alone. When night hasn't quite gone and the moon's breath is vapor upon the Earth. Near a beach. In the shadow of an ancient round tower that was used briefly as a lighthouse . . . then will his friend come back, out of the mist, like a forgotten story, with the old songs, and the stray dogs, and all the lost.

ABOUT THE AUTHOR

ADRIAN McKINTY
was born and grew up in Carrickfergus,
Northern Ireland. He studied philosophy at
Oxford University and in 1993 emigrated to
the United States. He lived in Harlem, New
York, for eight years, working in bars, on
building sites, and in bookstores.
In 2001 Adrian moved to Denver,
Colorado, where he taught high school
English and began writing fiction. His first
full-length book, the adult crime novel *Dead I
Well May Be*, was shortlisted for the 2004 Ian
Fleming Award and was picked by *Booklist* as
one of the best debuts of the year. His books
have been called "unputdownable" (*Washington
Post*), "exceptional" (*San Francisco Chronicle*),
and "profoundly satisfying" (*Booklist*). He and
his wife have two daughters.

This book was designed
and art directed by
Chad W. Beckerman.
The text is set in 11½-point
Adobe Caslon, a font designed
by Carol Twombly and
based on William Caslon's
eighteenth-century typefaces.
The display type is set in Eremaeus.